Best Bedtime Stories

Best Bedtime Stories

Jane Carruth

Illustrated by
Francis Livens and Nina O'Connell

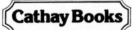

Cathay Books

First published 1982 by
Cathay Books
59 Grosvenor Street
London W1

Reprinted 1983, 1984

Copyright © 1982 Cathay Books

ISBN 0 86178 178 3

Printed in Portugal by Gris Impressores, S.A.R.L.

D.L. 3828/84

Contents

The Three Bears

There were once Three Bears who lived in a little house in the middle of a big green wood. They weren't all the same size, of course.

There was Huge Daddy Bear, who slept in a huge bed and sat in a huge chair and ate his porridge out of a huge bowl.

Then there was Middling-sized Mother Bear, who slept in a middling-sized bed and sat in a middling-sized chair and ate her porridge out of a middling-sized bowl.

And finally there was Tiny Baby Bear, who slept in a tiny bed and sat in a tiny chair and ate his porridge out of a tiny bowl.

Each morning Mother Bear came downstairs into the kitchen and made the porridge for the Three Bears' breakfast. One morning she made the porridge far too hot to eat straight away.

'Let's all go for a walk in the woods,' suggested Huge Daddy Bear.

'That's a good idea,' said Tiny Baby Bear.

'I'll come with you,' said Middling-sized Mother Bear.

So all Three Bears rose from the breakfast table and went out of their house and into the woods.

As the Three Bears were enjoying their walk a little girl called Goldilocks, with long golden curls, was also walking in the woods. She wasn't enjoying herself nearly as much as the Three Bears. She was lost and trying to find her way out of the woods.

Just when she was wondering what to do next she came upon the Three Bears' little house. When she saw the house she thought how nice it would be to have someone say, 'Come in, my dear. Sit down and have some breakfast.' But no one came to the door in answer to her gentle knock, so she ran round to the window and peeped through and saw that the room was empty.

She went back to the door, and when she pushed against it, it opened and she stepped inside.

'What a dear little house,' said Goldilocks, and she tiptoed into the kitchen.

Now the Three Bears ate all their meals in the kitchen, so the first thing that Goldilocks saw was the table with its three bowls of porridge.

The lovely creamy porridge made Goldilocks remember that she was very hungry. She skipped over to the table and sat down in front of the biggest bowl of porridge.

'I am going to enjoy this porridge,' Goldilocks told herself, as she took a big spoonful of the creamy porridge. But she didn't enjoy it one little bit. The porridge was so hot that it burnt her tongue.

'I'll try the next bowl,' Goldilocks decided, going round to the other side of the table. She sat down in front of the middling-sized bowl, but the porridge in the middling-sized bowl was not to her liking either.

'Why, this porridge is still too hot!' she cried.

And she dropped the spoon back into the porridge bowl with a splash. Now there was only one bowl of porridge left to try. Goldilocks sat down in front of it and dipped her spoon into the tiny bowl.

The porridge in the tiny bowl was lovely. It was just right! It wasn't too hot and it wasn't too cold, and Goldilocks ate up every bit of it.

'That *was* good,' Goldilocks said happily, when she had scraped the tiny bowl quite clean. 'That was very, very good!'

And not for one single moment did she feel sorry that she had eaten somebody else's breakfast!

Now, with so much porridge inside her, Goldilocks began to wish there was somewhere she could have a little rest. So she went into the sitting-room and sat down in the biggest chair which belonged to the Huge Daddy Bear.

But, oh dear, it was really much too hard to be comfortable.

Then she tried the middling-sized chair which belonged to the Middling-sized Mummy Bear.

But, oh dear, it was much too soft to be comfortable.

The only chair left to try was the one belonging to Tiny Baby Bear and when she sat down on that – something dreadful happened. The bottom fell out and one of its legs broke off.

Goldilocks landed on the floor with a crash. She wasn't hurt and she wasn't even sorry that she had broken the little chair. She was just cross that she hadn't found anywhere to have a rest!

So she went upstairs into the room where the Three Bears slept. There were three beds in the room. The first was a huge bed. The second was a middling-sized bed and the third was a tiny bed.

Goldilocks lay down on the huge bed. But it was so far from the ground that she began to feel dizzy, so she jumped down and went over to the middling-sized bed. But that felt lumpy in all the wrong places and, after a moment, she jumped down from it and went over to the tiny bed.

To her joy, the tiny bed was just right. It wasn't too high and it wasn't too lumpy!

With a contented sigh Goldilocks snuggled down under the blankets, closed her eyes and was soon fast asleep.

And while she slept the Three Bears were beginning to think that their porridge had had time to cool.

'We might as well go home,' said Huge Daddy Bear.

'I agree,' said Middling-sized Mummy Bear.

'Oh yes, let's go home to breakfast,' said Tiny Baby Bear, eagerly.

So the Three Bears set off through the woods at a fast pace, and were soon home. But when they went into the kitchen, the Huge Daddy Bear saw at once that somebody had been tasting his porridge. And he cried out in a deep, gruff voice, 'Who's been at my porridge?'

And the Middling-sized Mummy Bear saw that somebody had been tasting her porridge too, and she cried out in a high, shrill voice, 'Who's been at my porridge?'

Then the Tiny Baby Bear looked at his bowl and he couldn't see any porridge in it at all, and he cried in a small, squeaky voice, 'Who's been at my porridge? Who's been at my porridge and eaten it all up?'

The Three Bears looked at each other in dismay. Then they went into the sitting-room. And the Huge Daddy Bear saw at once that somebody had been bouncing up and down on his favourite chair.

'Who's been sitting on my chair?' he cried in a deep, gruff voice.

'And who's been sitting on my chair?' cried the Middling-sized Mummy Bear, when she saw her beautiful cushion on the floor.

Then the Tiny Baby Bear saw his chair, and he cried in a small, squeaky voice, 'Who's been sitting on my chair – and broken it all up?' And he rubbed his eyes to stop the tears coming.

Without saying another word to each other, the Three Bears left the room and pounded upstairs to the bedroom.

All three stopped in front of the Huge Daddy Bear's bed, and he cried in his deep, gruff voice, 'Who's been on my bed? Somebody's been on my bed and crushed the cover!'

And then the Middling-sized Mummy Bear went over to her bed, and she cried in her high, shrill voice, 'Who's been on my bed? Somebody's been on my bed and knocked the pillow on to the floor!'

Now it was the Tiny Baby Bear's turn to go to his bed. Its top cover wasn't crushed and the pillow was still in its place at the top of the bed. But there was a golden head on the pillow, and there was a pair of little feet sticking out from underneath the cover. 'Somebody's been sleeping in my bed – and she still IS!' cried the Tiny Baby Bear in his small, squeaky voice.

Now Goldilocks had been sleeping so soundly that she had not heard the Three Bears come into the bedroom. But now as the Three Bears gathered round the bed and stared down at her, she woke up.

What a fright she got when she saw them! She sat bolt upright. Then she scrambled out of bed and ran to the window. It was lucky for her that the window was open! She scrambled through it and jumped to the ground. It was quite a big jump but she wasn't hurt and so she picked herself up and ran away through the woods.

She ran and ran and even if the Three Bears had wanted to catch her,

they wouldn't have been able to because she ran so fast.

But the Three Bears were too sensible to go after the naughty little girl. They went down to the kitchen instead, and the Middling-sized Mummy Bear made some more porridge. And this time it wasn't too hot to eat right away! So while Goldilocks was running as fast as she could away from their house, the Three Bears were enjoying their porridge.

'She'd better not come back here again,' said the Huge Daddy Bear, as he finished his porridge.

'She'd better not,' said the Middling-sized Mummy Bear. 'We'll catch her if she does!'

'If she ever comes back,' said Tiny Baby Bear, 'I'll eat her up!'

But, of course, Goldilocks never did come back, and the Three Bears soon forgot all about her!

The Magic Pot

There was once a young girl called Florence who lived with her old widowed
mother. Their house was little better than a hut on the edge of the village,
for they were as poor as church mice.

Florence did all she could to make her mother's life comfortable and
whenever she could she tried to find nice things for the old lady to eat. Now
her mother was fond of stewed fruit and one day Florence went into the
woods to gather wild strawberries.

She took with her a slice of bread and the smallest imaginable piece of stale cheese, thinking that the bread and the cheese would serve for her dinner.

But Florence could not find many wild strawberries that day and she was feeling very sad as she sat on a log and unwrapped her food. She was just about to eat the bread when an old woman, dressed in black from head to foot, suddenly appeared before her.

The old woman was much, much older than her own mother and Florence's heart went out to her.

'Where did you spring from, old lady?' she asked gently. 'I did not see you come through the trees.'

'Never mind that now, child,' said the woman. 'I'm starving hungry and the sight of that bread and cheese makes me even hungrier. Will you share your meal with me?'

'I'll do more than that!' Florence cried. 'Take all the bread and the cheese. I have a mother at home and I know how hungry she gets!'

'You're a pleasant young maid, I must say,' replied the old woman, as she accepted the bread and cheese. 'There are not many left with such generous natures.'

'Oh, I don't know about that,' said Florence, with one of her shy, gentle smiles. 'I expect I shall find something to eat when I get home. At any rate I shall be able to eat some of these wild strawberries.'

'You are poor then?' asked the old woman.

'I'm afraid we are,' said Florence. 'I wouldn't mind being poor if only I could be sure that there would be enough food for my old mother.'

At this the black-robed woman nodded her head. She went on eating in silence until every morsel of the bread and the cheese was gone. Then she fetched out from the depths of her big cape a small black pot.

'Take it,' she said, holding the pot out to the girl. 'It's yours! You've earned it for your kindness to a stranger.'

'I wasn't kind because I expected a present from you!' Florence cried. 'But if you really wish me to have the pot I accept it gratefully.'

'It's a magic pot,' said the old woman unexpectedly. 'You and your mother will have all the sweet porridge you want if you put it on the table and say *Little pot, boil!*'

Florence was speechless at the very idea of being the owner of such a wonderful pot. Then she asked timidly, 'What words do I use to make it stop cooking?'

'Just say, *Little pot, stop!*' replied the old witch – for these were the words the little pot understood. 'All you have to do is to remember the words. . . .'

And before Florence could thank her again for such a magnificent present, she vanished.

All thought of searching for more wild strawberries went clean out of Florence's head. All she could think of was to run home with the magic pot and see if it really and truly was magic.

'Mother, mother!' she cried, when she reached the hut. 'Come and see what I have brought back!'

Then she put two bowls on the table and two spoons and when her mother came she sat her down on a chair.

'Watch,' said she. 'Watch what happens to this little black pot I have here. I'm going to put it on the table and tell it to give us lovely sweet porridge.

And she put it on the table and said, 'Little pot, boil!'

At once the little black pot began filling up with sweet porridge, and when the porridge was in danger of spilling over, Florence cried, 'Little pot, stop!' And the porridge stopped coming into the pot.

'Mercy me!' cried the old lady in amazement. 'Truly, this is the most marvellous pot in the world.'

And she began filling up her bowl with the sweet porridge. It tasted so delicious that she ate perhaps more than was good for her, but Florence was so happy to see the look of contentment on her mother's face that she did not try to stop her.

Well, Florence and her mother had now no cause to worry about food. But one day, about a week after the pot's arrival, Florence thought it would be nice to have some wild strawberries as a change from their porridge.

While she was in the woods searching for the fruit, the old widow-woman began to feel hungry. Often, as the hours passed, did she glance at the little black pot on the table. Then she began asking herself if the pot would obey her as it obeyed Florence.

'Perhaps I could ask it in a whisper,' she told herself. 'It's only the smallest bite of porridge that I need to keep me going until my daughter returns.'

In another minute she had made up her mind and she crossed to the table, and bending over the pot, whispered, 'Little pot, boil!'

To her delight the black pot began filling up with its delicious sweet porridge and the old woman ran to the sink to wash the bowl and spoon which she had used for breakfast.

But, oh dear me, when she came back the pot was boiling over, and the sweet porridge was spilling all over the table. Then it poured on to the chair and on to the floor.

'Stop, stop!' shrieked the old woman in sudden fright. 'Stop, will you?'

But these were not the words which the little black pot understood, and it continued to make porridge.

By now the sweet porridge was spreading. It spread all over the kitchen floor and over the step and into the garden, and the poor widow-woman was soon knee-deep in it.

'Porridge, stop!' she screamed. 'Boil no more!'

But these were not the words which the little black pot understood, and so it continued to make porridge.

The porridge spread all over the garden and poured out of the gate. And the old widow-woman lifted her skirts and scrambled on to the hen-house while it flowed all around her.

It reached the road and flowed like a river as far as the village hall, and all the people ran into their houses and shut and bolted their doors at the sight of it.

It rose so high against the village hall that the Lord Mayor, in his gold chain, had to eat great mouthfuls of it before he could get out of the hall and rescue his wife and two children who were waiting for him on the village green.

And just at that very moment – the very moment when the Mayor and his family were in danger of being swallowed up by the porridge – who should come along but Florence!

At the sight of the sea of porridge she guessed at once what had happened, and she shouted at the top of her voice, 'Little pot, stop!'

These were the words the little pot understood. It stopped making porridge immediately, and Florence and all the ladies of the village swept up the mess. But never again did Florence leave her mother alone with the magic pot. She locked it away in a tall cupboard and only brought it out when it was time for them to eat!

The Water of Life

There was once an old king who fell sick from a mysterious illness. The king was greatly loved and respected throughout his kingdom, and physicians came from the farthest corners of the vast land to examine him and suggest a remedy. But it was always to no avail.

At last the old king gave up all hope. He sent for his three sons and told them that he feared he had not long to live.

'I know that you love and honour me,' he said, 'and that you will carry out my wishes.'

'You're right, Father,' said the eldest son. 'After you are gone, we'll do whatever you ask of us.'

Now the eldest said this thinking that he would surely inherit his father's kingdom, for he was proud and ambitious and thought that he would make a very good and successful king.

To his surprise, the old king said, 'I love you all equally, so I do not wish that you, my eldest son, will inherit the whole kingdom on your own.'

This pleased the second son, who was almost as proud and ambitious as his older brother.

'Well spoken, my Father!' he cried. 'I will rule over one half of the kingdom and my brother the other half!'

The king shook his head, casting a glance at his youngest son, John, who had so far remained silent.

'No, that's not what I wish,' he said. 'I wish that my kingdom be shared equally between the three of you.'

The old king then dismissed his sons, and they went into the palace gardens to talk over his wishes.

The two oldest brothers, who had hoped so much that their father would leave them his kingdom, looked angrily at young John as they paced up and down.

'It's clear that our father is losing his senses,' said the oldest, at last.

As he spoke an old man, whom they thought at first must be one of the gardeners, approached them.

'I have heard,' said he, 'that the king is not long for this world.'

'That's true,' said John, 'and we are greatly saddened to see him age and grow so feeble.'

'Would you be prepared to face great dangers to find a cure for his sickness?' the stranger demanded.

'Of course we would!' exclaimed the brothers with one voice.

'Then one of you must set out on a long journey and search for the water of life,' continued the stranger, 'for that alone will save him.'

'I'll find it!' cried the oldest son. 'I'll find the water of life and bring it back to my father.'

'Very well,' returned the old man. 'But remember what I say: the road to the water of life is long and hard.'

When the brothers began eagerly to question the old man, he refused to speak further on the subject and walked away.

'My father will not refuse me the right to search for this water of life,' declared the oldest brother. 'I will go to him now and ask his permission to leave the palace.'

To his surprise the old king did not immediately agree to his request, for he feared greatly for his son's life.

The prince, however, was so confident that he could overcome every danger that he might face that at last the old king gave him his blessing.

'If I succeed, Father,' said the young man, 'will you leave me your kingdom when the time does come for you to die. Surely you can see now that I love you more than do my two brothers!'

'I shall owe you my life,' said the king. 'You will have earned the right to wear my crown.'

Well satisfied, the ambitious young prince began making preparations for his journey, but he said nothing to his younger brothers of what had passed between himself and the king.

'They will know soon enough what the true wishes of my father are,' he told himself smugly.

Early the next morning, the prince set out on his journey. He rode a fine horse and carried a purse stuffed with gold, for he had every intention of eating and sleeping at the most expensive inns.

Presently, as he rode along, a voice hailed him from the cliff-top, and, looking up, he saw an ugly little man with a long, sharply pointed nose and huge ears.

'Did you say something?' the prince inquired haughtily.

'I did,' answered the dwarf. 'I gave you "good-morrow".'

'I'm a king's son,' replied the young man in scornful tones, 'and not to be adressed in such a familiar manner.'

'Maybe not,' retorted the dwarf, with a merry laugh. 'But at least you can do me the favour of telling me why you ride out so early?'

'Miserable little monster!' exclaimed the prince. 'What impudence you have to question me!' And, spurring his horse, he galloped away.

The dwarf's eyes sparkled with anger at this insult, and as the prince rode off he put an evil spell on him.

Soon after meeting the dwarf the prince found himself in a narrow ravine. The road he was following took him between high mountains; these gradually closed in on him, and presently he found himself their prisoner – unable to either advance or retreat.

The king waited for the return of his eldest son for many weeks. When he did not appear, he began to mourn him and concluded that he must have been killed.

'I feel that my life is ebbing away fast,' he told his second son. Ah, if only my eldest son had been successful!'

'Father, you must send me to find the water of life,' cried the second son. 'I will not fail as my brother must have done! Let me go, I beg you. And if I succeed, then surely you will agree that I inherit the kingdom when the tragic time does come for you to die!'

The king shook his head. 'I have lost one precious son,' he said. 'How can I send another to his death?'

'I'll succeed, I know I will!' declared the prince, and he spoke so confidently that at last the old king gave him his blessing and sent him on his way.

The prince took the same road as his brother and as he rode along, he was presently saluted by the same ugly little dwarf as before.

'Where are you going and what is your business, young man?' asked the dwarf.

'It's no concern of yours where I'm going,' replied the prince rudely, 'and I've no intention of telling you my business.' Then he added for good measure, 'Ugly little monster!' before riding away.

As with his brother, the road he followed grew narrower and narrower. The mountains closed in on him until he found he could neither advance nor retreat, and he became their miserable prisoner.

When his second son failed to return the old king vowed that he would keep his youngest son at his side. But John, who truly loved his father and had no secret ambitions to be king, could not bear to see his old father so unhappy. And, at last, he persuaded his father to allow him to go in search of his two brothers and of the water of life.

John set out on foot and presently he, too, was hailed by the ugly little dwarf, who asked him where he was going and what he was seeking.

'My father is desperately ill,' John told him, 'and I go in search of the water of life. It may be that I can also find my two older brothers, who have so mysteriously vanished.'

'Do you know where to look for the water of life?' asked the dwarf.

'No,' said John. 'Do you know where it is to be found? If you do, I should be most grateful for your help.' He spoke so humbly that the dwarf's ugly face broke into a smile.

'You are not like your proud, scornful brothers,' he said, 'so I will help you. At the end of this road you will find an enchanted castle, and there, in the courtyard, is a fountain from which springs the water of life.'

As John began to thank the little man, he went on, 'But you cannot enter the castle without my help.' And he gave the prince a wand and two loaves of bread.

'What must I do with these?' John asked, puzzled.

'Strike the iron door of the castle three times with the wand,' the dwarf told him. 'When the door opens you will be faced with two lions with gaping jaws. Throw the bread to them and they will not attack you. Remember – do not draw the water of life until the clock actually strikes twelve.'

Once again John thanked the dwarf from the bottom of his heart before going on his way. When he came to the enchanted castle, he used the wand to gain admittance, and when the two lions with the gaping jaws prepared to spring at him, he tossed them the loaves of bread and they allowed him to pass.

Now he had safely gone through the great door which barred the way to the great castle itself.

'What a strange, silent place,' John thought as he entered the castle and found himself in a vast hall. This led into a second, smaller chamber where, to his astonishment, lay a number of young princes in an enchanted sleep.

John's wonder and amazement grew when, on entering a third room, he came upon a most beautiful girl, who welcomed him with the words, 'Brave prince, your presence here has freed me from a wicked enchantment. Return a year from now and I will be your bride. Will you give me your word that you will come?'

'I promise,' John gasped, scarcely able to believe his good fortune.

Then the princess gave him a sword and a loaf of bread, telling him to keep them safe until he had need of them. John accepted them gratefully, dazzled by the girl's beauty.

It was still some hours to midnight and John, mindful of the dwarf's words, determined to seek somewhere to rest before going to the magic spring. He passed from one great room to the next until he came upon a large and splendid bed and, throwing himself upon it, he was soon sleeping soundly.

He awoke with a start just as a clock, somewhere in the castle, was striking a quarter to twelve. In sudden fright that he would arrive too late at the spring, John got up in haste and rushed towards the courtyard. But there were many great halls and chambers through which he had to pass to reach the yard, and as he ran he wished with all his heart that he had not been tempted to sleep so long.

As the clock's hands moved to twelve he was in the courtyard at last and there, before him, was the magic spring. Thankfully, the prince knelt by the spring and filled the cup that was lying there with the water of life.

Full of thankfulness that he had succeeded in his task, he ran towards the huge iron door, and was going through it as the clock finished striking twelve. The door slammed shut with such violence that he was very nearly crushed as he squeezed through.

On the road John once again came upon the friendly dwarf.

'Well,' said he, 'did you obtain the water of life?'

'I did,' said John, 'and if there is anything in the world I can possibly do for you, then you have but to name it.'

The dwarf gave him a knowing smile. 'Your success is no more than you deserve,' said he, 'and what's more that loaf of bread, which you have there, and the sword will prove of great assistance to you in the future.'

'How so?' John demanded.

'The bread will never come to an end,' the dwarf told him. 'With it you can satisfy the hunger of whole cities. The sword will put whole armies to flight and make you the most powerful and warlike of all men.'

'What you say astonishes me,' John declared, 'and I will keep them safely, as I promised the princess. But I cannot return to my father without my two brothers, whom he loves. Will you help me to find them, or at least tell me where they are?'

'They are trapped by the mountains,' said the dwarf. 'I imprisoned them because of their haughty manners. If you're wise you will leave them there, for they have evil hearts and will do you harm if the chance comes their way.'

The prince, however, refused to listen to the dwarf's warning and continued to plead passionately for his brothers' release – and the dwarf said that he would set them free.

John rejoiced to see his brothers again, and they fell upon his neck and pretended to be equally glad to see him. But when he told them how he had found the water of life, and a beautiful princess who would wait for him for a year, they were madly jealous, and began to plot how they could destroy him.

On the way home, they asked John many questions about the enchanted castle and how to find it, and they waited and watched for an opportunity to take from him the cup that contained the vital water of life.

John suspected nothing, and was so full of joy at being able to save his father and restore to him his two sons that he laughed and talked and even began to plan his wedding.

'You'll both be there,' he promised his brothers. 'It will be a wedding to remember, I promise you.'

This only served to inflame the brothers' jealousy, and whenever they found an opportunity to talk privately they did so, considering one plot after another in their efforts to find a way to destroy the young hero without bringing suspicion on themselves. John must be killed, they decided at last, and the order for his death must come from none other than the king himself!

Now it chanced they must pass through a great city whose ruler was a friend of their father the king. The city had been under siege for many days, and the people were starving.

John used his magic sword to put the enemy to flight, and he gave the grateful ruler his bread and told him that there was no end to the loaf. 'Feed your starving people with it,' he insisted, 'and you will find that I speak truly.'

The ruler's gratitude knew no bounds when he found that the magic loaf was sufficient to satisfy the hunger of all his citizens, including his army.

'The time will come,' he promised, 'when I shall be able to repay you with rich gifts. I shall have them sent to the palace as soon as the first of my treasure ships sails into port.'

John thanked the ruler – and the brothers, who had taken no part in saving the city, could scarcely hide their envy.

'He will be richer than the king himself,' they told each other, as they continued their journey.

When they were less than three miles or so from home, the eldest saw John lay down the cup containing the precious water of life, leaving it unguarded while he went ahead to see if he could catch a glimpse of the palace.

The eldest took the container and emptied its contents into a flask of his own. Then he filled John's special cup with salted water.

As they approached the palace, they heard news that the old king was not expected to live much longer and John, full of hope and joy, rushed ahead.

'I've found it!' he cried, as he knelt at his father's bedside. 'Drink the water of life and you will be restored to health.'

The old king took the cup but no sooner did the bitter salt water touch his lips than he fell back in a coma and John, heartbroken at the sight of his father, dying it seemed before his eyes, dashed from the room.

Almost at once the two wicked sons entered, and the eldest bathed the king's face and lips with the water of life. Scarcely had he done so than the old man sat up, his eyes bright and his cheeks rosy.

'Father, we rejoice to see that the water of life has restored you,' said his eldest son. 'We faced many dangers to find it, and now we are happy that you are well again because of it.'

'John only pretended that he had the precious life-giving water,' said the second son. 'He offered you nothing but useless salted water – no doubt hoping to hurry your death so that he could be king.'

The old king, in great distress, looked from one son to the other, but so sincerely did they speak, and so much did they seem to know about their journey to the life-giving spring, that he believed them.

'You must have John killed before he tries again to kill you,' urged the eldest. 'Order one of your huntsman to take him into the forest and shoot him.'

The poor king, his heart turned to stone at the thought of John's treachery, sent for his most trusted huntsman and gave the order. But the huntsman had known the young prince since he was a child, and when the moment came to kill him, he could not perform the act. Instead, he exchanged clothes with the prince and begged him to hide away in the forest and never to return home.

Time passed and the two evil brothers, certain that they had now destroyed their rival, easily persuaded the king to promise to leave the kingdom to them. One day, however, something happened which disturbed the king and caused him to think deeply about his youngest son.

Messengers came from the rich ruler whose city John had saved from their enemy. They bore gifts for John, which were equal to a king's ransom, and they sang the praises of John, saying that their ruler honoured and respected him above all living men.

'Surely what they say must be true,' thought the old king as he listened to them. 'And if it's true then my youngest is no villain, as his brothers declared, but a hero!'

For many hours he questioned the messengers and at last his heart melted within him and he knew for certain that he had been unjust.

The old king wept bitter tears, thinking that he had caused the death of his youngest son so recently, but the huntsman, seeing his grief, told him that John was alive and perhaps in hiding in a nearby town or village.

'Then let it be known throughout my kingdom,' cried the monarch, 'that my youngest son, John, is to return home. I must speak with him.'

So in towns and villages and hamlets throughout the land, the king's messengers proclaimed that John was again welcome at the palace.

Alas, John heard nothing of the proclamation, for the messengers did not venture into the dark, deep forest where the prince had been hiding alone for so many months.

In the meantime, the beautiful princess of the enchanted castle had not forgotten John or her promise to marry him at the end of a year. When the period of waiting was nearly over, she summoned two members of her guard.

They came to her immediately and she ordered them to have a new roadway made up to the castle gates – a path laid with pure gold.

'This roadway,' she said, 'must be of bright gold and there must be no twists or curves anywhere in it. It must be absolutely straight.'

When the guards showed their amazement at such a strange command, she added, 'The man I intend to marry will come riding up this golden road. He will not ride to the left of it nor to the right.'

Far away in their own castle the two wicked brothers often talked of John, whom they now believed to be dead, and of his story about the lovely princess who had promised to marry him at the end of a year if he returned.

'The year has almost passed,' the eldest said one day. 'Let's try our luck with the beautiful princess.'

'We can't both marry her,' the second brother protested. 'Shall we toss for it?'

'No,' said his brother. 'I'm my father's first-born son. The right to go to her is naturally mine.'

'And if she refuses you?'

'Then it will be your turn,' replied the eldest. 'That's only fair. I shall set out at once.' And he called for his horse and rode away. When he reached the castle and saw the bright, golden roadway leading to its gates he could not bring himself to ride on such a magnificent road for fear of spoiling it. So he turned to the right and approached the castle by another entrance.

But the princess would not see him and told her guards to drive him away.

Later it was the turn of the second brother, and when he saw the splendid golden roadway leading to the castle he too could not bring himself to ride on it. So he turned to the left and rode into the castle by another entrance.

But the princess would not see him and her guards drove him away.

At the very end of the year John left his hiding-place in the forest and set out for the enchanted caste. The princess had been in his thoughts day and night ever since he had spoken to her, and when he came to the shining golden roadway he did not even notice its beauty, but galloped straight up the middle of it – and into the princess's welcoming arms!

After the wedding, John took his bride to meet his father, and he told him the true story concerning the water of life. The old king ordered his soldiers to arrest his two lying sons. But they escaped their father's wrath by boarding a fishing trawler which, according to rumour, was later lost in a storm-tossed sea. At any rate, they were never seen again.

The old king lived many long happy years and, when at last he died, he left his kingdom to John – the only one of his sons who truly deserved it.

Miss Mouse – Housekeeper

There was once a little gnome who very much wanted to find a housekeeper for his small, dark house under a big oak tree. To begin with he thought it would be quite easy to find a housekeeper.

He wrote out an advertisement in big bold handwriting which said,

'Wanted – a housekeeper. House under Oak Tree in Middle Wood. Wages One Silver Penny at the end of each month.'

The little gnome was pleased with his advertisement. He climbed out of his underground house and pinned it on the oak tree. He thought somebody would be sure to see it that same day, so he sat down near the tree to wait.

For some time nothing happened. The Middle Wood was unusually quiet. Even the birds, which usually annoyed him with their loud chirping, were silent.

'I wonder if a storm is coming?' the little gnome asked himself. 'I hope not. I do so want to get fixed up quickly.'

He was just beginning to think he should fetch his umbrella when along came a small, very dainty little lady mouse. He watched her stop before the notice and read it carefully.

'Are you interested?' he asked at length, giving a gruff little cough. 'The house is neat and tidy and I don't think you will find the work very hard.'

Miss Mouse gave a start and her long delicate whiskers trembled. She had not noticed the little gnome until he addressed her and she did not altogether like the look of him.

'No, no,' she said quickly. 'Not really – I – er – am out of a situation it is true, but I had no thought of becoming a housekeeper.'

The gnome took a silver penny from his pocket and held it up, twisting it this way and that before Miss Mouse's bright eyes. Just then the sun came out through the clouds, and the silver penny became shining and beautiful. Little Miss Mouse could not take her eyes off it.

After a moment's silence, she said, 'I – I left home this morning. There was a disagreement – a quarrel, you might say. I have been taking care of my brothers for five long years and well – they didn't seem to be very grateful.'

She gave a little sigh as she remembered how she had walked out of the only home she had ever known. She cried, 'You won't see me again! Find somebody else to do your cooking and your dusting and your mending!'

'That's excellent!' said the gnome. 'I mean it must have been unhappy for you – the quarrel. But now that you are on your own you must find a roof over your head at least for tonight.'

As he spoke, dark clouds hid the sun again and down came the rain. It splashed on Miss Mouse's dainty bonnet and she put up her hands to protect it.

'Come,' said the gnome, taking down the notice. 'Follow me down these steps. You may find my house a trifle dark to start with, but you will soon get used to it. . . .'

To his annoyance, Miss Mouse shook her head. 'No, no thank you,' she said, in quite a firm voice. 'I have a relative, an aunt on the far side of

Middle Wood, I thought I might pay her a long visit.'

The gnome hid his anger and disappointment. 'Oh, please yourself,' he said. And he began pinning his notice on to the oak tree again. 'I don't think she will be offering you a silver penny. . . .'

Miss Mouse gave him a timid smile before hurrying away and the gnome, seeing that the rain was not likely to stop for some time, ran down the winding stairway to fetch his umbrella. He was no sooner indoors than there was a loud clap of thunder and he decided to make himself a strong brew of dandelion tea before venturing out in the open again.

As he sat there drinking his tea and thinking how useful Miss Mouse would have been, he heard another loud threatening clap of thunder and quite suddenly the door of his kitchen burst open and there stood Miss Mouse, soaked to the skin and looking very frightened.

'I – I simply can't bear storms,' she whispered. 'There is a terrible one raging overhead. If you don't mind – I – I think I will be your housekeeper. I will stay for a month and earn that beautiful silver penny you showed me.'

'Delighted,' said the gnome. 'Sit down and have some tea with me. Then we can talk over your duties and I will show you where you will sleep.'

Miss Mouse took off her wet bonnet and cape and sat down at the table. She sipped the dandelion tea, which she found absolutely horrible, and listened while the gnome began explaining why he needed a housekeeper.

'I am a very neat, tidy person,' he said. 'You have only to look round my kitchen to see the truth of what I say. I cannot bear to see a speck of dust on the furniture or a crumb on the floor. It sends me quite mad with rage.'

'I understand,' said Miss Mouse. 'I like a tidy house myself.'

'You have not heard all the story,' said the gnome quite sharply. 'Until now I have done everything myself in the house. From tomorrow I will do nothing. . . .'

'Nothing!' echoed Miss Mouse, looking dazed. 'Nothing at all?'

'Nothing,' repeated the gnome firmly. 'Nothing at all. Tomorrow I start on my life's work. I will be busy, day and night, for one year and a day.'

'What – what is your life's work?' asked Miss Mouse.

'I have been asked by the Council of Aged Gnomes to write the history of our people,' replied the gnome with great seriousness. 'It is the highest honour they can pay me. I begin tomorrow. You, my dear Miss Mouse, must see to the cleaning, the cooking, the washing. I must not be disturbed. If I am disturbed or in any way put out there will be trouble. . . .'

Miss Mouse did not like the sound of this. She looked at her wet bonnet as if she longed to put it on and be off – as far away as possible from the fierce little gnome who sat with his sharp eyes fixed upon her face. But another tremendously loud clap of thunder told her that the storm was still raging outside and she knew she did not have the courage to leave the shelter of the gnome's house.

'I – I understand,' she said in a low voice. 'At the end of the first month you will pay me with the silver penny?'

'Yes, yes,' said the gnome impatiently. 'Now I will show you where you can sleep. It is in one of my bigger cupboards. Quite cosy and very clean.'

When Miss Mouse saw her new room she began to think longingly of the pink bedroom with its rosebud frilly curtains and its soft pink rug which she had so recently left. The cupboard was certainly clean but there was only a tiny bed in it and a box for her bonnet and cape.

'It is small,' she began, 'and – and dark. . . .'

'You won't be in it much,' replied the gnome airily. 'There will be plenty to do around the house all day, I can assure you.'

The very next day Miss Mouse, after a restless night, was awakened by her new master who told her crossly that he had been up and about for nearly an hour.

'Get the breakfast first,' he ordered. 'Then wash the kitchen floor. I will have all my meals served in the sitting-room, which is now my workroom. Move softly about for I cannot bear noise – and the work I am now engaged on is of the utmost importance.'

Miss Mouse put on the plain brown apron he gave her and went into the kitchen. The gnome went into his study with a bundle of clean white paper and two black writing pens.

'I'll give him what my brothers used to like best,' Miss Mouse thought, as she bustled about the kitchen. 'Some raisins sprinkled with brown sugar and a square of cheese.'

Alas, this kind of breakfast did not please the gnome. He flew into a rage at once when he saw what the plate contained. 'I'll have bran flakes, no sugar,' he shouted, 'and a cup of strong dandelion tea to help me to think.'

And he scowled so ferociously that Miss Mouse dropped the tray at his feet.

'Clumsy idiot!' he snarled. 'You know I can't stand a mess.'

Poor Miss Mouse – she made so many mistakes the first day that she was sure the gnome would send her packing – and she would have been glad to go had it not been for the sound of heavy rain falling outside, and the thought of the beautiful silver penny she would be given at the end of the month.

That night she was so weary that she dropped on to her hard little bed and fell fast asleep at once, and in the morning she managed to rise before the gnome was about. This gave her a chance to peep into his sitting-room and see the sheets of white paper covered with black spidery writing.

'He must be clever,' she thought, as she stared down at the writing, 'but I can see now that he does not want a housekeeper but a slave!'

Miss Mouse, however, had a very determined streak in her nature and she made up her mind to work as hard as she could and to try and please her master as well as she could. 'He might even give me two silver pennies,' she told herself, as she measured out the bran flakes. 'I will take them back to my brothers, and they will see how clever I am. Then I will put up new pink frilly curtains in my room, and buy a new carpet for the passageway – and perhaps, yes, perhaps, I will give my brothers a present each. They may not have been very grateful – but they always treated me kindly.'

She was so busy with her thoughts that she put sugar on the bran flakes by mistake and had only just time to throw them away and start again before the gnome came into the kitchen.

'Hurry, hurry,' he said grumpily. 'I want to start work as soon as I have eaten.'

'It won't be long,' replied Miss Mouse. 'The water is almost boiling. . . .'

The days were so long and hard for the new housekeeper that she almost lost count of them. But whenever she thought a whole week had passed she crept into the gnome's work-room early in the morning, before he was about, and looked at his calendar.

'I came on a Friday so I will get paid on a Friday,' she told herself as she counted the days. 'I have twenty-one left. Oh dear!'

But the thought of the silver penny always helped Miss Mouse to put up with the gnome's bad-temper and, as the days passed, she began to understand that he found her useful and that he had no intention of giving her the sack.

One morning she looked at the calendar and saw, to her delight, that she had only seven days left to the end of the month. She could scarcely believe it.

The next morning – there were only six – and then five and then four and then three and then two and then *ONE*!

On the day itself – the day when she was to get her silver penny – Miss

Mouse was so happy that she broke into a soft little song as she bustled about the kitchen. And she prepared the gnome's breakfast tray with the utmost care.

'I will tell him I am leaving today,' she thought. 'I will ask him for my silver penny and leave this dark horrible place as soon as I can.'

The gnome was already seated at his desk and writing busily as Miss Mouse came into the room with his breakfast. As usual he waved at her impatiently, grunting, 'Put it down, put it down!' Don't disturb me!'

'But I must disturb you,' said Miss Mouse firmly, as she put down the tray. 'The month is up. Give me my silver penny and I will be off.'

'What – what's that you say?' muttered the gnome, still writing, and not looking at her. 'What's this about the month being up and the silver penny? I told you my work would take a year and a day . . . you'll stay, if you please, and you'll get your silver pennies when I am ready to give them to you. . . .'

'But – but we had an agreement,' cried little Miss Mouse, holding back her tears. 'You said I would have that beautiful shining silver penny at the end of one month. . . .'

'That was a long time ago,' muttered the gnome, fixing her with his sharp, spiteful eyes. 'You'll stay because you're useful to me. Now don't stand there. You have plenty of work to do. . . .'

Miss Mouse left the room with bowed head. But once in the kitchen she blinked away her tears, made herself a cup of the disagreeable dandelion tea, which she looked upon as a pick-me-up, and sat down to think.

'I'll just take the silver penny,' she told herself, 'and creep away after he's gone to bed.'

Then she remembered how the gnome always locked the door and slept with the heavy key under his pillow. It would not be so easy to escape. And there was, too, the matter of the silver penny. Somewhere in his room he kept all his treasures. It would not be easy to make a search.

All that day and the next and the next Miss Mouse made plan after plan and still not one of these seemed likely to succeed. Then one morning, at the end of the most miserable week she could remember, the gnome told her that he had finished the first four chapters of his history. 'I must take it to the Chairman of the Council for Aged Gnomes for approval,' he said. 'I'll be gone for just three hours. Don't sit about when you find yourself on your own. There is plenty to keep you busy.'

'Three hours!' Miss Mouse thought to herself. 'Three hours will give me time to find the box with the silver pennies – surely it will!'

No sooner had the gnome left the house than she began her search. She looked under the pillows of her master's bed, and then under the bed itself. She looked in the sock drawer and the shoe cupboard and the big chest where he kept his paper and pens. And not a silver penny did she find. Then, with only one hour left, she looked in the wardrobe and there, hidden under some tunics, was a big brown box and inside were ten silver pennies.

Miss Mouse squeaked with joy. She took just one of the silver pennies and carried it to her small, dark room. Then she tied it up in her best blue handkerchief, put on her bonnet and cape, and ran to the door. Her heart went pit-pat uncomfortably fast. Had he remembered to lock the door? If he had and if he had taken the big key she would still be a prisoner.

But that morning the gnome had been too excited at the idea of showing his Chairman what he had written to think about locking up. The door was unlocked and Miss Mouse scampered up the winding stairway to freedom.

The sun was shining as she fled through the long grass and made her way home. She thought of all the beautiful, forgiving things she would say to her dear brothers and she thought of the new frilly curtains and the new carpet for the passageway. And she was so happy that she forgot all about the dreadful time the horrid gnome had given her.

And do you know – it was all just as Miss Mouse hoped it would be – there were her brothers watching out for her as they had done for a month or more. And there she was hugging and kissing them and showing them the splendid silver penny.

'I'll never, never leave home again,' Miss Mouse promised them, as they fussed around her – 'unless, of course, it's to go to market to buy the curtains and the carpet and a present for each of you with my new silver penny.'

And if you are wondering about the grumpy gnome and his great work – well, he never did manage to finish it because he never did find another housekeeper who would stay – even as long as Miss Mouse!

The Old Woman's Pig

Once upon a time an old woman was sweeping her house, and she found a crooked sixpence.

'What shall I do with this little crooked sixpence?' she asked herself. 'I know, I will go to market and buy a little pig with it.'

So the little old woman went to market and with her crooked sixpence she bought a little pig and set out for home. But the piggy wouldn't go over the stile.

She went on a little farther, and she met a dog.

'Dog! Dog!' said she. 'Bite the pig. Piggy won't go over the stile, and I shan't get home tonight.'

But the dog would not.

The old woman went a little farther, and she met a stick.

'Stick! Stick!' said she. 'Hit the dog. Dog won't bite pig. Piggy won't get over the stile, and I shan't get home tonight.'

But the stick would not.

She went a little farther, and she met a fire.

'Fire! Fire!' said she. 'Burn stick! Stick won't beat dog. Dog won't bite pig. Piggy won't get over the stile, and I shan't get home tonight.'

But the fire would not.

She went a little farther, and she met some water.

'Water! Water!' said she. 'Quench fire! Fire won't burn stick. Stick won't beat dog. Dog won't bite pig. Piggy won't get over the stile, and I shan't get home tonight.'

But the water would not.

She went a little farther, and she met an ox.

'Ox! Ox!' said she. 'Drink water! Water won't quench fire. Fire won't burn stick. Stick won't beat dog. Dog won't bite pig. Piggy won't get over the stile, and I shan't get home tonight.'

But the ox would not.

She went a little farther, and she met a butcher.

'Butcher! Butcher!' said she. 'Kill ox. Ox won't drink water. Water won't quench fire. Fire won't burn stick. Stick won't beat dog. Dog won't bite pig. Piggy won't get over the stile, and I shan't get home tonight.'

But the butcher would not.

She went a little farther, and she met a rope.

'Rope! Rope!' said she. 'Hang butcher. Butcher won't kill ox. Ox won't drink water. Water won't quench fire. Fire won't burn stick. Stick won't beat dog. Dog won't bite pig. Piggy won't get over the stile, and I shan't get home tonight.'

But the rope would not.

She went a little farther, and she met a rat.

'Rat! Rat!' said she. 'Gnaw rope! Rope won't hang butcher. Butcher won't kill ox. Ox won't drink water. Water won't quench fire. Fire won't burn stick. Stick won't beat dog. Dog won't bite pig. Piggy won't get over the stile, and I shan't get home tonight.'

But the rat would not.

She went a little farther, and she met a cat.

'Cat! Cat!' said she. 'Kill rat! Rat won't gnaw rope. Rope won't hang butcher. Butcher won't kill ox. Ox won't drink water. Water won't quench fire. Fire won't burn stick. Stick won't beat dog. Dog won't bite pig. Piggy won't get over the stile, and I shan't get home tonight.'

The cat said to her, 'If you will go to the cow and fetch me a saucer of milk I will kill the rat.'

So away went the old woman to the cow.

And the cow said to her, 'If you will go to the haystack, and fetch me a handful of hay I will give you the milk.'

So away went the old woman to the haystack, and she brought back the hay to the cow.

When the cow had eaten the hay, she gave the old woman some of her milk, and the old woman took it in the saucer to the cat.

As soon as the cat had lapped up the milk, it began to kill the rat. The rat began to gnaw the rope. The rope began to hang the butcher. The butcher began to kill the ox. The ox began to drink the water. The water began to quench the fire. The fire began to burn the stick. The stick began to beat the dog. The dog began to bite the pig. The piggy in a fright jumped over the stile, and so the old woman got home that night!

The Snow Queen

Once upon a time when there were a great many more goblins about than there are today, there lived a very wicked goblin indeed. He kept a school for goblins and, one day, to amuse his pupils he made a magic mirror.

Now this magic mirror delighted the young goblins who were learning to be as wicked as their master, for it had the power to make the most beautiful things in the world look hideously ugly.

One day four of them flew into the sky with the mirror to try it out on the angels. But the closer they flew to the angels, the more difficult it was to hold the mirror. At last it slipped out of their hands and shattered into a hundred million pieces as it fell to earth.

The goblins were sorry to lose their mirror but when their master told them the fragments would not be lost forever, they began to giggle.

'The fun will continue!' their master assured them, 'for when the splinters of glass enter a human heart they will turn it into ice.'

Now in the poorest quarters of a big town lived two children, a boy called Kay and a girl called Gerda. They had been the closest friends for as long as they could remember. If Gerda stepped out of her attic window and Kay stepped out of his, it was possible to meet on the balcony that connected their two houses. And here they had their happiest times together. Gerda's old grandmother had given them a rose tree and Kay had filled a box with earth and planted the tree and together they took care of it.

One winter's morning, Kay and Gerda were on the balcony. Gerda, as usual, had gone to the little rose tree while Kay stood staring out over the silent white town as he watched the snow fall. Suddenly, just as the church clock struck twelve, Kay cried, 'Gerda! Oh! Quick! Something is flying around; it has struck me, pricking my eye. Now, even my heart hurts!'

Gerda ran to her friend, peering into his eyes and holding him tightly. But he pushed her away roughly. 'Don't bother, Gerda! Whatever it was has gone.'

But, of course, it had not gone for it was one of the glass fragments from the mirror that had entered Kay's eyes and now, already, his heart was icy cold.

'Play by yourself!' he suddenly shouted. 'You're nothing but a stupid girl. I'm taking my sledge into the Square and I don't want you to come.'

The great Square in the middle of the town was a favourite place with the big, strong boys, for when the snow lay thick on the ground, the boldest tied their sledges to carts for a free ride.

Kay had never done this for he had always wanted to be close to Gerda and take care of her. Now, as he looked about him for a suitable cart, he saw a huge sledge come into the Square pulled by two prancing horses. The sleigh was painted white and in it sat somebody wrapped in white furs. Kay, as he watched it, made up his mind to tie his little sledge on behind. The magnificent sleigh stopped close to him and he quickly made his sledge secure and jumped on to it.

The sleigh raced round the Square once and then straight into the street. Soon it had passed through the town's gates.

On and on went the sleigh, travelling as fast as the wind and it seemed to Kay that they were really flying over hedges and ditches. Now the snow was falling so quickly that he could scarcely see as he clung to his own little sledge.

'Stop!' he shouted desperately. 'Please stop!' But the driver whipped up his horses and they went on faster than ever. The snowflakes were, by now, so big that Kay thought they looked like white hens, and suddenly he began to feel afraid.

All at once, the great sledge stopped and the driver stood up and turned round. The big fur cap and the fur cloak, that Kay had admired so much when he saw them first, changed to ice. And Kay, as he stared up at the tall figure saw that the driver was no man but a lady, tall and slender and very beautiful. It was the Snow Queen!

'Why do you tremble?' she asked the boy. 'Creep into my sledge.' And when he obeyed, the Snow Queen bent down and kissed him. For a moment, Kay felt as if he was going to die. But it was only for a moment; the very next, he was himself again but his heart, which was already cold and hard thanks to the splinter from the goblin's mirror, now changed completely into a lump of ice. He forgot his parents, he forgot Gerda. He forgot everything at home that he had once held dear. The Snow Queen had him in her power.

The sleigh sped away; over lakes and across seas it flew until at last it reached the Snow Queen's ice palace.

Meanwhile, Gerda waited all that day for Kay to come back from the Square. Then she went out to search for him herself.

'We saw him fasten his little sledge to a very big one,' one of the boys told her. 'It raced away through the town gates, but it never came back.'

'Perhaps it fell into the river,' another boy suggested. 'Perhaps your friend Kay is drowned,' he added cruelly.

That night Gerda cried herself to sleep. Early the next morning she rose, put on her new red shoes after she had dressed, and crept silently away.

'If I give my new red shoes, which I love so much, to the river,' she told herself, as she left the town and ran towards the river, 'perhaps it will tell me about Kay.'

When she reached the broad river, Kay took off the red shoes she loved so much and threw them into the water. 'There are my red shoes,' she called. 'Now tell me about Kay. Did he drown in your waters?'

But the little waves sent her red shoes floating towards the bank and

Gerda thought that perhaps she had not thrown them far enough into the water.

'This time I will make certain the river has my shoes,' she said aloud. And she climbed into a boat that was moored to a post and so was able to fling her shoes further into the water. Alas, the boat was not securely tied up, and it began to glide away from the bank.

Gerda sat quite still in the boat as it drifted away down-stream, her precious red shoes floating behind it.

At first she was so frightened that she cried a little; then she thought that the kind river might be taking her to Kay. So she dried her eyes and looked about her. The banks on each side were very pretty but she saw no houses until, after what seemed hours, a little house came into view.

Gerda noticed that it had wonderful red and blue windows and that two wooden soldiers stood on guard by the gate. An old woman leaning on a crutch was standing outside the pretty house. She was so close to the river that Gerda shouted, 'Help! Help!'

Just as the boat floated past, the old woman leant forward and seized the boat with her crutch and drew it on to the grass. Then she lifted Gerda out of the boat and took her into the strange little house.

Now the old woman was a witch but a very kind, lonely witch who had wanted a little girl of her own for a very long time. She put a bowl of lovely red cherries on the table and she told Gerda that she could eat as many as she wanted. And while Gerda enjoyed the sweet-tasting cherries, and told her story, the old woman began combing her hair with a golden comb. And Gerda soon forgot about her search for Kay. The comb, you see, was magic but not wicked magic like the goblins' mirror.

Then the old witch said, 'You are just the kind of pretty little girl I have always wanted. Stay with me and I will make you very happy.'

Now, the witch had no great powers of magic but there were certain things she could do; she could make people forget the past as she combed their hair and she could make flowers disappear with her crutch-stick. And that night she went out into her beautiful garden, which was full of flowers, and passed her crutch over the roses until they disappeared into the ground.

She was afraid that if Gerda saw the roses she would remember her own little rose tree and then that would help her to remember Kay.

The next day she took Gerda into the wonderful flower-garden and Gerda played happily there until it was time to think of bed. And the old witch watched her and was happy too for at last she had a child of her own.

Now the old lady loved flowers so much that she had embroidered them on the velvet cloak she always wore and she had painted them on her tall pointed hat. Such wonderful flowers they were – all the colours of the rainbow and among them, on her hat, some tiny pink rosebuds.

One day, Gerda found the hat outside one of the red and blue windows and began playing with it. Then she saw the rosebuds and something stirred in her memory. She could not find a single rose in the garden but whenever she looked at the pointed hat, she saw only the roses there! And the roses at last made her think of Kay. What a lot of time she had wasted! Now it was Autumn and the trees were turning yellow and still she was no nearer finding him.

Early the next morning, she crept out of the witch's house and set off down the road, but the hard road hurt her feet, and the grey sky was heavy with black clouds. Her heart was heavy too, and she felt very sad.

On and on she walked until her feet ached so much that she sat down on a stone to rest. And, presently, a big crow came out of the bushes, nodding its head at her.

'Good-day to you,' said the crow, who liked the look of the little girl with the golden hair. 'Good-day!'

'And to you,' said Gerda. 'Have you by any chance seen my friend, Kay? He has been lost for a long time, nearly a whole year, and I must find him.'

'It is possible, quite possible,' said the crow. 'Tell me the whole story.'

So Gerda told him the story and the crow, at the end of it, said, 'I saw a young fellow just like your Kay. Yes, yes, it's possible. He met the Princess you know, and she took him to live with her in her castle. She was lonely you see, but clever, oh yes, very clever.'

'Kay was clever too,' Gerda burst out. 'He could do mental arithmetic and add up so fast it took my breath away.'

'That's why the Princess would like him,' said the crow wisely, nodding his head once or twice. 'Yes, yes!'

'Will you take me to the castle?' Gerda asked. 'When Kay sees me he will want to return home, I'm sure.'

'Certainly I will,' said the crow. And Gerda was suddenly so happy that she bent down and kissed his head.

The crow took Gerda to the castle which was not, after all, very far away. Then he said, 'Go in by the servants' entrance. No doubt you will soon find Kay for they say the Princess keeps the boy by her side most of the day.'

With her heart beating so fast that she thought she would die, Gerda thanked the crow and entered the castle. She followed the servants as they ran up and down the narrow wooden stairs until she came to a vast hall, and there, on golden thrones sat the Princess and the boy.

The boy looked like Kay for his face was pale and his hair dark and curly, but it wasn't Kay. And Gerda, in her disappointment, let out a great sob as she stood there by the doorway.

Then the Princess rose from her throne and called the boy to her side. Together they went to Gerda, and she told them her story.

'Poor child,' said the Princess. 'You can stay with us if you like. You can wear my clothes and pretend you are my sister.'

But Gerda shook her head, 'All I want is a little carriage, with a horse to draw it,' she said, 'so that I may search more and more of the big wide world as fast as possible.'

'And so you shall,' said the Princess. And she ordered her ladies-in-waiting to dress Gerda in some of her own rich clothes. And when this was done and Gerda herself looked like a Princess, a coach drawn by two horses carried her off into the forest. 'Goodbye! Goodbye!' Gerda shouted, waving to the beautiful Princess as she stood, with the crow on her shoulder, at the top of the castle steps. 'And thank you!'

Now the coach was so splendid and the coachman so handsomely attired that, not surprisingly, a band of robbers began following it through the forest. And at the right moment, they seized the horses, and dragged little Gerda out of the carriage.

'How prettily she is dressed!' cried the robber chief's only daughter. 'I'll have her dress and muff and those warm fur boots.'

Gerda stared at the big strong girl with her brown skin and white flashing teeth and was very frightened. But the robber's child was not nearly as fierce as she looked. She stayed close to Gerda as the men returned to the old building with its crumbling walls, which was their headquarters. And that night, as they lay down to sleep on a pile of wolves' skins, she asked Gerda to tell her how she came to be riding like a Princess in a fine carriage.

So, once again, Gerda told her story. 'If I don't find Kay, I shall die,' she said to the robber girl. 'Won't you help me?'

'It's a sad story,' said the girl at last. 'I've not heard such a sad story in all my life. Yes, I will help you. In the morning ask the reindeer who is tied up outside. He knows most things for he is quite old.' Then she put her strong brown arms around little Gerda and fell fast asleep.

In the morning, the robber chief's daughter took Gerda to meet the reindeer. 'I heard the pigeons say something about the Snow Queen,' said the reindeer. 'It seemed that she passed through their forest last winter on her way to Lapland. She had a boy with her. I wish I were there. I would run, free as the wind, over the glittering white plains.'

And the reindeer heaved a great sigh at the very thought of being free and in Lapland.

'I will set you free,' said the robber's child, 'so that you can carry this little girl to Lapland. But you must promise to take good care of her.'

Then she gave Gerda back her warm fur boots and an old warm cloak, for she could not bring herself to part so soon with the pretty clothes she had taken from Gerda the previous night.

Gerda wept for joy as she climbed on to the reindeer's back, and she bent down and hugged the robber child.

The reindeer set off with a bound, running as fast as he could go – through the forest and over the hills, never stopping to rest, and running and running, faster and faster, day and night. He stopped, at last, in front of a little hut with a roof that sloped down to the ground.

'Now we are in Lapland,' the reindeer said, 'The woman inside this hut knew me when I was young. She will know about the Snow Queen for she is one who knows everything.'

The Lapland woman was old and bent and wrinkled. 'You have a long way to go yet, she told Gerda, after she had heard her story. 'The Snow Queen is staying in Finland, a hundred miles from here. I have no paper but I will write a few words on a dried cod to the Finnish woman, who will know where her palace is.'

Then she gave Gerda some of the fish she was cooking, and warmed her hands and feet at the oil stove, before setting her on the reindeer's back.

Away went the reindeer once again, moving as strongly as if he were young again, and when they reached Finland, he carried her without stopping to the hut where the Finnish woman lived. 'She is clever, that one,' he said. 'She has great powers – even over the winds.'

But Gerda could see nothing but a broad chimney sticking out of the ground, and the reindeer told her, 'In her wisdom she lives in a chimney. Take my word for it – it is so hot in there you will have no need of your fur boots.'

Then they went inside and the Finnish woman made them welcome. She pulled off Gerda's fur boots and put a block of ice on the reindeer's head before reading her friend's message on the piece of dried cod.

'You'll help the child,' said the reindeer, after a long silence. 'You know you have the powers. . . .'

'Her own gentle goodness is the only power she needs,' said the woman, after she had looked into Gerda's eyes. 'The Snow Queen's palace is only a mile or two from here. Take the child and put her down by the great bush bearing red berries that stands at the entrance to the gardens. Her friend, Kay, is in the palace and he is alone, for the Snow Queen is absent at this time on her travels.'

On hearing that she was close to Kay, Gerda ran out into the snow forgetting, in her excitement, to put on her warm fur boots. Her feet were blue with cold as she sprang on the reindeer's back and urged him forward. But when they reached the great bush with its red berries, her excitement faded and fear entered her heart. Now, she must go on alone.

The reindeer watched her for a moment as she began running through the gardens. Then he went back to the Finnish woman to wait. As Gerda ran towards the beautiful, shining ice palace, huge snowflakes came, not from the sky but from the ground. They were the Snow Queen's soldiers, and they took on ugly fearsome shapes as they pursued her. Brilliant white, some were like porcupines, others like dancing bears, but it was the giant loathsome wriggling worms that scared Gerda most. And, when she reached the palace itself, she clasped her hands together in prayer!

How empty and vast was this palace of snow and ice. Gerda went from one great hall to the next, calling for Kay. She found him at last in a huge room whose ceiling was held up by great pillars of ice.

'Kay! Kay!' she called as she ran towards him. 'I have found you!'

But the boy did not even raise his head at the sound of her voice, and Gerda ran to him, throwing her arms about him and kissing and hugging him.

How stiff and cold he was! How blue his face! Out of pity for her friend, Gerda began to weep and her warm, loving tears fell like gentle rain on his face. They entered his eyes, washing away the splinter of glass from the magic mirror which had been lodged there for so long. And they thawed the lump of ice which had been his heart.

Slowly, slowly, Kay raised his head. He looked at Gerda and, at last, he knew her. 'Gerda! Where have you been?' he whispered, rubbing his eyes. 'It's so cold here.'

Then he clung to her as if he would never let her go, as she told him of her search. 'Remember, you are still in the Snow Queen's power,' she warned him finally.

'I know,' Kay answered, 'but before she went away, she gave me a task to do. I had to form these letters you see here at our feet into a word. If I found the right word she promised that I would be my own master again.'

'Then let us find this word together,' Gerda said. And they began pushing the great letters, fashioned from ice, this way and that across the floor until at last the word was made: ETERNITY.

'Now she cannot come for you ever again!' Gerda cried happily. 'Let us leave her palace and go home.'

The faithful reindeer was waiting for them by the bush with its red berries and beside him stood another younger reindeer to carry Kay.

So began their journey homewards, across wide frozen lakes and over snow-clad mountains, until they came at last to the green forests.

'Here we must leave you,' said the old reindeer. And Gerda wept at the thought of saying goodbye to her faithful friend. But she knew he would find true happiness in running, free as the wind, across the glittering icy plains of Lapland.

Hand in hand, Gerda and Kay ran through the green forest and across the golden meadows, and though they covered many miles they never grew tired. Then, as the old church clock struck twelve, they passed through the town gates.

'We're home!' Gerda exclaimed joyfully. 'What a long, long time it has been!'

And Kay, his eyes shining with gratitude and love for the friend who had dared so much to save him, took her in his arms and kissed her.

The Little Fir Tree

The pretty little Fir Tree had a good place in the forest. There was plenty of sunshine and fresh air and there were lots of other trees around him – tall, stately trees which reached up to the sky.

The little Fir Tree should have been happy and content. But he was not. He wanted to be as tall and strong as his friends.

'Oh, how I long to be as great as they are!' he often sighed. 'I don't want to be so small. If I were big like them I could spread outwards and the birds would build their nests in my branches.'

The first winter the little Fir Tree was in the forest it snowed. It snowed so much that he began to think the snow would cover him completely. This made him feel sad and frightened – and, yes, I'm sorry to say, jealous of his tall friends.

'Why, the snow doesn't bother them at all,' he told himself. 'Oh, how I wish the years would pass quickly so that I could grow like them!'

The next winter some woodcutters came to the forest. They cut down a number of the young fir trees – those which were just a year or two older than the little Fir Tree. These trees were very handsome and the little Fir Tree wondered why they were put on waggons and dragged away.

'I wish I knew where they were going,' the little Fir Tree said aloud.

And the sparrows chirped, 'We know, we know! They are going to the town. They will be dressed in great glittering splendour. We have looked in at the windows and seen them. They stand in the middle of warm rooms and silver stars and sparkling bells hang from their branches. Sometimes they are lit by hundreds of candles.'

The little Fir Tree sighed with envy. Then he asked, 'What happens to them after that? Do they stay in the warm room?'

'We don't know what happens to them after that,' said the sparrows. 'We really don't know!'

'Perhaps one day I shall stand in a warm room and have silver stars and sparkling bells hanging from my branches,' said the little Fir Tree. 'Oh, how I long for that day to come!'

After the long, hard winter came the spring, and the little Fir Tree began growing fast.

'You are very beautiful,' the birds told him. 'You are so young and fresh and strong. How lucky you are to be here in this beautiful forest!'

'I am not happy here,' said the little Fir Tree. 'I want to see the world. Why am I left here? I want to travel.'

'Be content, be happy,' the birds told him.

But the little Fir Tree was not content and he was not happy though he went on growing and growing. The next winter more woodcutters came into the forest. They looked at the handsome dark green Fir Tree and they said, 'Well, there's a splendid one! We'll take him!'

When the little Fir Tree heard this he was wildly happy. Then he felt the pain of the axe striking him and he was all at once afraid. But there was no time to feel sorry for himself. With other young trees he was loaded on to the waggon and taken away out of the forest.

He was too faint and weak to take much notice of the town when the waggon rattled through the streets. And the busy market frightened him. But then, no sooner was he placed on the ground than two serving-men came along and the Fir Tree heard one of them say, 'Look, there is a capital tree. We will take that one!'

Presently he was loaded into a barrow and taken into a fine garden.

'How pretty this is,' the little Fir Tree thought. 'Now I am really seeing the world!'

But he was not left there. Soon he was carried into a large beautiful room. The walls were hung with wonderful pictures, there were vases with birds and trees painted on them, and sofas covered with velvet. There was also a rocking-horse and a great pile of toys and picture-books.

The room was warm and brightly lit and the little Tree sighed with satisfaction as he was placed in a great tub filled with sand. Children came into the room and shouted with delight at the sight of the lovely Christmas Tree. And servants came with silver stars and sparkling glass balls and tinsel and they decorated the Fir Tree's dark green branches.

Then the children hung some packages tied up with ribbon on the Fir Tree and one little boy put his drum at the foot of the tree, while the master of the house fastened a hundred little candles, red, white and blue on the boughs.

'Just wait until tonight,' said the master of the house to the children. 'The Christmas Tree will shine and shine. It will be the finest we have ever had.'

'Oh, how I long for the night to come,' thought the Fir Tree. 'How I long to shine! I wonder if the sparrows will come and look at me? If they do, they will see me in all my glory. I hope they go back to the forest and tell the other trees. How they will envy me!'

When darkness came at last, the mistress of the house fixed a great gold star on top of the Christmas Tree and then lit the candles. The Fir Tree trembled with pride at the thought of how beautiful he looked.

The children rushed into the room and joined hands, making a circle.

'Dance, dance! Let us dance around the Christmas Tree,' they shouted. And the Tree stood tall and straight in his tub of sand, as the children pranced round him.

Then the grown-ups came into the warm room with lots of presents for the children.

'Your presents are on the Tree,' the little boy cried, and he snatched the boxes and the parcels from the dark green branches. In his excitement he broke some of the Fir Tree's pretty twigs.

When all the presents had been handed round, the candles were put out, and no one paid any more attention to the Christmas Tree. There were so many more important things to look at.

The Fir Tree tried to stand up straight but he could not help feeling sadly lonely until at last one of the children, tiring of her presents, called out, 'Who will tell us a story, a story?'

And a big jolly fat man sat down beneath the Tree and gathered the children about him.

'If I sit here,' said the fat man with a jolly laugh, 'the Tree can hear my story too.'

'What is your story about?' demanded the boy.

'About a little round man who fell down the stairs,' said the storyteller. 'He rolled over and over and he made a beautiful Princess laugh and he ended up marrying her.'

The little Fir Tree listened thoughtfully. The birds in the forest had never told such a wonderful story as that. 'Perhaps I shall fall down the stairs too and marry a Princess,' he told himself, as the children and the storyteller were called away to eat dishes of white and pink ice cream.

And that night, when the grown-ups and the children had gone to bed the Fir Tree passed the hours dreaming of the happiness that was still to come to him.

But in the morning two servants came in and took off his decorations. They couldn't reach the star so they left it on. Then they dragged him out of the room. They took him upstairs to the attic and put him in a dark corner where there was no sunshine.

'What can this mean?' the Tree asked himself. 'What am I doing here? What is going to happen next?'

And he stood in his dark corner until he grew so faint that he fell against the wall. All through that long, black night he thought and wondered what would happen. And the next day he imagined the beautiful Princess was coming to find him and marry him. But it was the servants who came. They piled empty boxes in front of him so that he was completely hidden from sight.

As the weeks and months passed the little Fir Tree thought more and more about the beautiful forest he had so willingly left. 'It was not lonely and dark like it is here,' he told himself. And he almost wished he was back there again.

The only company he had now were two little mice. He did not talk to them for many weeks until one day they called him 'Old Fir Tree', and he could not help exclaiming, 'I am not old! I am young and very splendid!'

'You *are* old,' said one of the mice. 'You must have seen a lot of the world.'

'I have still a great deal of it to see,' said the Fir Tree. 'But what I remember best is the forest where I was born. It was so green and the sun was so friendly and warm – and then there were the birds. . . .'

'You must have been happy there,' said one of the mice. 'Tell us more about this wonderful forest.'

So the Fir Tree talked about the forest and the mice brought their friends to hear about it. And they told the Tree that they enjoyed listening to him.

After that the Fir Tree became the attic's storyteller and when he did not talk about his forest he told the mice about the most wonderful evening of his life.

'I was so beautiful,' he sighed. 'A golden star decorated my head, and silver stars and sparkling balls of coloured glass hung from my branches. The children loved me. I was the centre of attention. I can scarcely wait for that time to come again. . . .'

But when the time came for the Fir Tree to leave the attic he was not taken down to the warm room with its beautiful pictures and sofas covered with velvet.

Oh no! He was dragged down the stairs and out through the kitchen into the courtyard.

'Now I shall be happy again,' thought the Tree, and he spread out his branches in the sunshine. But, alas, his branches were all withered and yellow, and the servants threw the Tree into a corner among the nettles and weeds. Only the golden star on his head looked splendid for it had managed to keep some of its glitter.

Soon, two of the children from the big house came into the courtyard and were almost at once drawn towards the rubbish heap by the sparkling golden star. The boy went up to the little Fir Tree and tore off the star.

'We can save this!' he cried. 'But who wants that old Christmas Tree? Look how ugly it has grown!' And he began jumping on some of the Tree's slender branches. 'I know – let's ask if we can make a bonfire and burn it!'

A servant came with an axe and chopped the Fir Tree into small pieces, and the children laughed as they helped to make the bonfire.

'It is finished,' the Fir Tree thought sadly, as the last of him was thrown into the flames. And the boy who had snatched the golden star from him, pinned it on his jacket and shouted, 'I'll keep the star for ever – at least until next Christmas. Then we'll get another star and another beautiful Christmas Tree!'

The Gingerbread Man

Once upon a time there was a little old woman who lived with her little old husband in a little old house in a little old village, somewhere far away.

The little old woman and the little old man were very fond of children but they didn't have any. So one day the little old woman said to her little old man, 'I know what I can do. I can make us a boy out of gingerbread!'

And she got out her mixing bowl and the flour and the treacle and all the other things she needed to make a gingerbread boy. And she mixed everything up after she had added the ginger.

The little old woman worked swiftly and when she had finished rolling him out she gave him two blackcurrant eyes and fixed raisins on his jacket for buttons.

'He hasn't got a nose and he hasn't got a mouth,' said her little old man.

'He shall have a pink sugar nose,' said his wife, 'and a rose-red mouth of sugar-candy.'

Then she shaped his little feet and put him on a baking tray and popped him into the oven.

The little old woman and the little old man stayed in the kitchen until it was time to take their gingerbread boy out of the oven. But no sooner had they done this than their fine new child hopped off the tray and jumped down on to the floor.

'I'm not your little boy!' he cried. 'I'm the Gingerbread Man!' And he ran out of the kitchen and out of the house into the street.

The little old woman and the little old man ran after him as fast as they could but they could not catch him.

On and on ran the little Gingerbread Man. He was still running when he came to a cow by the side of the road.

'Stop, stop, little Gingerbread Man,' said the cow. 'I would like to eat you.'

But the Gingerbread Man only laughed and said,

'I have run away from a little old woman.

And a little old man. And I can run away from you.'

And he ran on. The cow ran after him and the Gingerbread Man called over his shoulder, 'Run, run as fast as you can. You can't catch me. I'm the Gingerbread Man!'

On and on ran the little Gingerbread Man until he came to a horse in a field.

'Stop, stop, little Gingerbread Man,' said the horse. 'I would like to eat you.'

But the little Gingerbread Man only laughed and said,

'I have run away from a little old woman.

And a little old man.

And a cow. And I can run away from you.'

And he ran on. The horse ran after him, and the Gingerbread Man called over his shoulder, 'Run, run as fast as you can. You can't catch me. I'm the Gingerbread Man!'

On and on ran the little Gingerbread Man until he came to a farmyard.

The poultry-maid saw him and tried to pick him up.

'Stop, stop, little Gingerbread Man,' said she. 'You look good enough to eat.'

But the Gingerbread Man only laughed and said,

'I have run away from a little old woman.

And a little old man.

And a cow and a horse. And I can run away from you.'

And he ran on. The poultry-maid ran after him and the Gingerbread Man called over his shoulder, 'Run, run as fast as you can. You can't catch me. I'm the Gingerbread Man!'

On and on ran the little Gingerbread Man until he came to an inn. The innkeeper saw him and tried to pick him up.

'Stop, stop, little Gingerbread Man,' said he. 'You are good enough to eat.'

But the Gingerbread Man only laughed and said,

'I have run away from a little old woman.

And a little old man.

And a cow and a horse and a poultry-maid.

And I can run away from you.'

And he ran on. The innkeeper ran after him and the Gingerbread Man called over his shoulder, 'Run, run as fast as you can. You won't catch me. I'm the Gingerbread Man!'

On and on ran the little Gingerbread Man until he came to a field. There was a fox in the field and when he saw the Gingerbread Man he began running towards him.

Now, by this time, the little Gingerbread Man was so pleased with himself that he was not afraid of ever being caught. So he called out to the fox, 'Run, run as fast as you can. . . .'

At this the fox ran harder than ever, and the little Gingerbread Man shouted,

'I have run away from a little old woman.

And a little old man.

And a cow and a horse.

And a poultry-maid and an innkeeper.

And I can run away from you.'

And he ran on. The fox ran faster than ever after him and the Gingerbread Man called over his shoulder, 'Run, run as fast as you can. You can't catch me. I'm the Gingerbread Man!'

But the fox did not stop running, so the Gingerbread Man did not stop running – that is until he came to a river. Now the little Gingerbread Man did not know how to swim so he could not cross the river. But, of course, he wanted to because he wanted to keep running away from the little old woman and the little old man and the cow and the horse and the poultry-maid and the innkeeper.

As he stood there by the river the fox ran up to him.

'If you jump on my tail I will carry you across the river,' said the fox.

The Gingerbread Man was sure that he could run away from the fox once he was on the other side of the river. So he said, 'I don't mind if I do.' And he jumped on the fox's tail, and the fox stepped into the water and began to swim.

When he was a little way from the bank, the fox looked over his shoulder at the Gingerbread Man, and said, 'I find you are too heavy for my tail. Please jump on my back.'

So the little Gingerbread Man did this.

After a little while, the fox looked over his shoulder again and said, 'The water is growing deep, Gingerbread Man. You will get wet if you stay on my back. Jump on my shoulder if you please.'

So the Gingerbread Man jumped on to the fox's shoulder.

When they were in the very deepest part of the river the fox stopped swimming and said, 'I am worried about your safety, little Gingerbread Man. If you jump on my nose I will be able to hold you out of the water.'

So the little Gingerbread Man did this. But, oh dear, as soon as the fox was on the bank, he lifted his head, and gave a sudden quick snap.

'What's happening?' cried the little Gingerbread Man. 'I've lost my feet!'

The greedy fox gave another quick snap and the little Gingerbread Man lost some more of himself. The fox's third quick snap put an end to the Gingerbread Man for ever! And the fox ran off into the woods, hoping that he might come across another foolish little Gingerbread Man who was running away from home.

The Two Magicians

Once upon a time there were two magicians. They lived a long, long time ago and their names were Taplow and Tiplow.

The two magicians were famous for their powers of magic and all the people treated them like kings. Taplow lived in a cave in the mountains, and Tiplow lived in a hut by the river and they met quite often. Sometimes Taplow paid Tiplow a visit and sometimes Tiplow paid Taplow a visit.

When the two friends met they usually spent the first hour telling each other how clever they were.

'I changed old Mother Rafferty into a hen,' Taplow would boast. 'But only for a minute or so – just long enough to show her my powers. She gave me some of her goat's milk afterwards.'

'Indeed!' Tiplow would exclaim. 'Well, I have had my fun too. I changed the Carey children into minnows – but only for a minute or so – and their mother gave me some of her smoked fish.'

One winter the snows came early and the two friends did not see each other for some months. Alone in his cave Taplow began to think up some fresh bit of magic which would surprise his friend.

At last he thought, 'Just as soon as the long winter is over I'll invite Tiplow to stay with me in the cave. I'll lay in food and wine and then, after the feasting, just for a joke, I'll turn him into some small creature for a short while.'

And in his hut by the river Tiplow was also making plans to entertain his friend, Taplow, as soon as the winter had come to an end.

The two friends waited impatiently for the snow to disappear and when it did Tiplow sent his pet raven to the mountain cave with an invitation to Taplow to come and dine with him.

When Taplow received the invitation he was sorry that he had not managed to get in first with his invitation. But he accepted it willingly.

'I'll give Tiplow the fright of his life,' he told himself as he took out his medicine-bag and filled it with the magic powder that would change his friend into a small forest creature. 'What a joke!'

Meantime, as Taplow was making his way down the mountainside, Tiplow was taking out his medicine-bag and filling it with a dark reddish powder.

'I'll play a joke on my old friend,' he thought. 'I'll change him into a large bullfrog – not for long – but just long enough to give him the fright of his life.'

The meeting between the two magicians was warm and friendly.

'Come in, come in,' cried Tiplow. 'It's been a long time!'

'It has indeed,' said Taplow, as he followed his friend into the hut. 'But we shall make up for it by telling each other all the news.'

'I see you have brought your medicine-bag with you,' said Tiplow. 'Just put it on that high shelf over there out of harm's way. That is where I keep mine.'

So Taplow placed his medicine-bag on the high shelf beside his friend's. But he kept a small grain of his magic powder between his fingers and when

he sat down to eat he managed to drop it on Tiplow's food.

Tiplow had been busy too – before he served the meat to his guest he had dropped a grain of his magic powder on to his plate.

Suddenly, as they sat opposite each other at the table enjoying the tender meat dish, Taplow cried, 'Why, my old friend, I do believe you're changing . . . !' And he began to laugh loudly.

'Is that so?' Tiplow exclaimed, looking somewhat bothered. 'Then I can say the same about you, old friend. You're changing!'

A second later Taplow had changed to a giant bullfrog, and Tiplow had changed to a prickly porcupine.

Now it was no laughing matter for either of the two magicians for they wished with all their hearts to change back to their own selves – and they could not! Their two medicine-bags lay far out of reach on the high shelf, and the bullfrog could not hop so high and the porcupine could not hop at all.

So that was the end of the two magicians. The bullfrog went down to the river, and the porcupine went into the forest, and they never saw each other again. And for all we know the two medicine-bags are still there on that high shelf in the hut!

The Three Axes

There was once a young woodcutter who was so honest that sometimes his friends laughed at him.

'You will never get rich,' they would say. 'You are too honest! If you found an old boot in the forest you would waste half a day looking for its owner!'

The young woodcutter did not mind being teased by his companions. He went on being kind and honest and truthful and though he did not grow rich, he was happy.

Now, on the edge of the forest there was a very deep, dark pool and the honest woodcutter sometimes went there after his day's work. One day, he went there on his way home. As he sat on the bank his trusted axe fell into the water.

The woodcutter jumped to his feet, despair written all over his kind face.

'What shall I do?' he cried aloud. 'Without my old axe I cannot work and I have no money to buy another!'

As he stared down into the dark water he almost made up his mind to plunge in and try to find his precious axe. But he knew the pool was dreadfully deep and that it would take an expert swimmer and diver to rescue the axe.

'I must not risk my life,' he decided. 'That would be wrong.' And he sat down again, his head in his hands.

Suddenly, as he sat there, out of the dark waters rose the most beautiful lady he had ever seen. She held in her hands an axe of gold, an axe of silver and his old iron axe.

The young woodcutter stared at her in astonishment.

'I am the Fairy of these waters,' she said. 'I have brought back your axe. Which of the three is yours? Is it the gold one or the silver one or this iron one?'

'Why, the iron one is mine!' exclaimed the woodcutter. 'It would be truly wonderful to have the gold or the silver one. But I must be honest.'

'And because you have been so honest,' the Fairy smiled, 'you shall have all three axes.'

The woodcutter was overjoyed to be given such wonderful presents, and he thanked the Fairy with all his heart before she vanished beneath the water.

That night, as he sat in the inn, his three axes on the table beside him, one of his friends sat down at the table, and the young woodcutter told him the story of the Water Fairy and the three axes.

'My, you're a lucky fellow!' said his friend. 'The gold and silver axes are worth a small fortune. I have never seen anything like them in my life.'

'I should have been grateful to the Water Fairy if she had only returned my faithful old iron axe,' said the woodcutter. 'I don't know why she treated me so generously.'

His friend continued to look enviously at the splendid axes and though he said nothing he was already making up his mind to try his luck with the Water Fairy.

Early the next morning he took his old axe and set out for the forest pool. Once there he threw his axe into the water. Almost at once the Fairy appeared, and, as before, she had three axes in her hands.

'Which of these is yours?' she asked.

The man fixed his eyes greedily on the gold axe.

'Why, the gold one!' he cried eagerly. 'Give me the gold one. It is mine!'

'You are neither honest nor truthful,' said the Fairy. 'You shall not even have your own axe returned to you.'

And with that she vanished under the water.

Sadly, the unhappy woodcutter returned home. And never again did he mock or tease his young friend whose honesty had won him a fortune.

The Little Red Hen

The little red hen lived in a neat little house at the foot of a hill. On the other side of the hill lived a crafty old fox. He lived with his mother who did the cooking.

Now the crafty old fox knew all about the little red hen, and he often talked about her to his mother.

'She would make a tasty supper,' he would say.

'She would indeed,' agreed his mother. 'Why don't you catch her, son, and bring her back here? I would have the big black pot boiling.'

'I have thought and thought how to catch her,' the old fox said. 'I have watched her little house these past four weeks but she is too smart for me. . . .'

'Don't be a fool,' his mother said sharply. 'You're a cunning, clever hunter. You're my son and I'm proud of you. You just make up your mind to catch that little red hen – and you will!'

But the old fox did not catch the little red hen. The little red hen was too clever for him. She knew all about the wicked fox and whenever she went to market she took great care to shut and lock her door with a big key which she always carried in her apron pocket.

'I know you are just longing to get inside my little house!' she would shout. 'And don't pretend that you are not hiding in the woods. I can't see you, fox, but I know you are there! Anyway you are wasting your time.'

The little red hen, after she had mocked and teased the hungry fox, would run back to her neat little house, shut and lock the door behind her and sit down to a refreshing drink of dandelion tea.

Sometimes she peeped out of her window and sometimes she saw the old fox skulking among the lavender bushes at the far end of her garden.

'You can't catch me!' she would cry before leaving the window. 'The only way you can catch me is to get inside my little house and that you will never do!'

The fox thought so much about catching the little red hen that he took to dreaming about her. But even in his dreams he did not manage to catch her and each morning when he opened his eyes he felt tired and discouraged.

Soon he lost some of his skill as a hunter and his old mother began to grumble. One morning she said to him, 'Son, you have not brought home anything tasty to eat for a week or more. There will be no supper for us tonight for there is nothing in the larder.'

The fox looked at his mother in dismay. 'Nothing to eat!' he said stupidly. 'Nothing at all in the larder?'

'You heard,' said his mother crossly. 'I could die of hunger for all you care!'

Now the fox, though he was mean and crafty, was very fond of his mother and when he saw how upset she was, he cried, 'Put the big black pot on the fire, mother dear. Let the water bubble and boil. Tonight I will bring you the little red hen for our supper.'

'That's more like it!' cried his mother, and she began filling the big black pot with water. 'Off you go and the best of luck to you.'

Meantime the little red hen had been peeping through her window to see if she could spy the old fox.

'He must be taking a day off,' she told herself, when she failed to catch a glimpse of him. 'Oh well, I'll get on with my housework. There's plenty of dusting to be done.'

So the little red hen put on her apron with the big wide pocket in it, which held her scissors, and began to dust and sweep and polish. She enjoyed herself so much that the fox went right out of her head. And when all the cleaning was done she decided to go into the garden and collect some twigs.

Now every other morning, when the little red hen left her house, she shut and locked the door and put the key in her apron pocket beside the scissors. But, oh dear me, this morning she forgot to do this. She ran out of the house, leaving the door wide open.

Alas, the little red hen was wrong in thinking the old fox had taken a day off. He was, in fact, much, much closer to her little house than he had ever managed to get on other visits. And, no sooner did he see the little red hen leave her house and go into the garden for firewood, than he slipped into the house through that open door!

The fox was so pleased with himself that he could scarcely stop himself from laughing. Then he hid behind the china cupboard and waited for the little red hen to appear.

She came into the room at last and went over to the stove to put the kettle on.

With a triumphant shout the fox showed himself and sprang towards her, a wicked grin on his ugly face.

The little red hen gave a frightened cluck and managed, just in the nick of time, to fly up on to the rafters.

'You can't stay up there for ever, little red hen,' snarled the fox. 'So you might as well come down and let me catch you!'

'Cluck-cluck!' cried the little red hen. 'I can stay up here for ever, so you might as well go home, you wicked creature!'

The fox thought for a moment. Then he said, 'We'll see about that!' And he began to whirl round, chasing his own tail, and going faster and faster, till he seemed to be spinning as fast as a great spinning top.

Watching him the little red hen felt her own head going round and round. Soon she was so dizzy that she toppled off her perch – straight into his paws.

'Got you!' chuckled the fox. And he popped her into the sack which his mother had given him. 'Now for home and supper!'

It was dark and horrible inside the sack and the little red hen was in despair as she was bumped along the road and then through the woods.

'If I don't escape from this sack quickly, this will be the end of me,' she told herself. 'What can I do?'

But though her life depended on quick thinking, the little red hen could think of nothing except the greedy fox and the supper she would soon make him.

Now it was quite a warm day, especially when the sun came out, and the little red hen, being plump and well-fed, was very heavy. Soon, as the fox ran along with the sack, he began to feel very tired. And, at last, he decided to take a short rest. He sat down, with his back to a tree, and put the sack on the ground beside him.

Well, the sun was very hot, and the old fox was tired and presently he closed his eyes and fell asleep. And while he slept the little red hen had a brilliant idea. She brought out the scissors she always kept in the pocket of her apron.

Snip-snip, snippety-snip – in no time at all she had cut a hole in the sack and crept through it. When she saw how soundly the fox was sleeping she took time to find a large heavy stone and this she managed to push into the sack.

'You'll enjoy *that* for your supper,' she thought, as she set off through the woods, 'I'd like to see your face when you open up that nasty sack!'

As soon as the little red hen was safely home she put the kettle on and made herself a cup of strong dandelion tea. Then, as a special treat, she ate two corn biscuits and some grain candy before going to bed for a rest.

And while the little red hen was lying snug and warm in bed, the old fox had taken up the sack and was carrying it through the woods and round the hill.

His mother was waiting for him at the door and she called out, 'Well, son, have you got her? By the looks of the sack she is plump and heavy.'

'I've got her, mother,' replied the fox, as he entered the kitchen and flung the sack into a corner. 'Is the big black pot boiling?'

'It's boiling,' said his mother. 'Now, open the sack, and grab hold of the little red hen. This is a supper we won't be forgetting in a hurry.'

The fox went over to the sack and as he bent over it he licked his lips with his long tongue.

'Fetch it to the pot,' ordered his mother. 'Drop the little red hen straight into the pot!' And she, too, licked her lips.

But when the old fox held the sack over the pot and shook it – no plump little red hen fell into the black pot – only a big heavy stone.

'Mercy upon us!' screamed the old mother fox, as the hot water splashed on her head. 'Is this another of your fool jokes!'

'No, mother, no!' cried the old fox.

But, his mother had taken up her broom, and at the sight of the angry old lady, the old fox lost all his courage and fled from the kitchen.

'Boiling is too good for that little red hen!' he shouted, as he ran into the night. 'I'll roast her when I catch her!'

But, of course, he never did!

The Emperor's New Suit

Many years ago there lived an Emperor who loved fancy clothes so much that he spent all his money on elegant suits and cloaks. He took no interest in his army or the theatre or in driving through the country, unless it was to show off his new clothes. He had different clothes for every hour of the day and, just as you might say of an important person that he was in council, so it was always said of the Emperor, 'He's in the wardrobe.'

One day two swindlers arrived in the city. They told everyone that they were weavers and could weave the very finest materials imaginable. Not only were the colours and designs unusually attractive, but the clothes made from these materials were so fine that they were invisible to anyone who wasn't terrifically smart and fit for his job.

'Well!' thought the Emperor. 'They must be wonderful clothes. If I wore them I could see which of my statesmen were unfit for their jobs and also be able to tell the clever ones from the stupid. Yes, I must get some of that stuff woven at once.' And he paid a large sum of money to the swindlers to make them start work.

The swindlers then made a great fuss about setting up their workshop; they put up looms and pretended to be weaving, but there was no thread on the looms. They demanded the richest silks and finest gold thread, which they promptly hid in their own bags, and then they went on working far into the night at the empty looms.

'I wonder how they're getting on?' the Emperor thought, and then he became rather nervous. He was a bit worried at the idea that a man who was stupid or unfit for his job would not be able to see what was woven. Not that he thought he was no good – oh, no – but all the same, he'd feel happier if someone else had a look at the stuff first.

'I'll send my honest old prime minister to the weavers,' he thought, 'He's the best one to see the stuff first, for he has plenty of good sense and nobody does his job better than he.'

So off went the honest old prime minister to the weavers' workshop, where they were sitting at their empty looms. 'Good gracious me!' thought the old man in dismay, 'Why, I can't see a thing!' But he was careful not to say so. 'Good lord!' he thought, 'Is it possible that I'm stupid? I never knew, and I mustn't let anyone else find out. Can it be that I'm unfit for my job? I must on no account admit that I can't see the material.'

'Well, what do you think of our work?' asked one of the weavers.

'Oh, it's charming! Exquisite!' said the old minister, peering through his spectacles. 'What a pattern and what colouring! I shall certainly praise it to the Emperor!'

The old minister listened carefully as the swindlers gave details of the colours and the design, and repeated it all to the Emperor.

The swindlers now demanded more money, more silk, and more gold thread, to continue the weaving. They stuffed it all into their own pockets and continued to pretend to weave on the empty frames.

By and by the Emperor sent another trusted official to see how the weaving was going on. The same thing happened to him as to the prime minister; he couldn't see anything but the empty looms. 'I know I'm not stupid,' thought the man, 'So it must be my fine job I'm not fit for. I mustn't let anyone know!' And so he praised the material that he couldn't see, and told the Emperor of its charming shades and beautiful design and weave.

Then the Emperor himself said he must see it, and invited all his court to come with him. When they arrived at the workshop they found the cunning swindlers weaving for all they were worth at the empty looms.

'Look! Isn't it magnificent!' all the officials said, feeling sure that the others could see it.

'What's this?' thought the Emperor, 'I can't see anything – this is dreadful! Am I stupid? Am I not fit to be Emperor? This is the most awful thing that could happen to me. . . . Oh, it's quite exquisite,' he said aloud, 'It has our gracious approval.' He nodded at the empty loom, for he wasn't going to say that he couldn't see anything. Then all the courtiers nodded and smiled at the empty loom and said, 'Yes, it's quite exquisite,' and advised him to have some robes made of it, to wear at the grand procession the next week.

'Magnificent!' 'Delightful!' 'Superb!' were the words of praise that filled the air; everyone was enormously pleased with the cloth. The Emperor bestowed a knighthood on each of the swindlers, with a badge to wear on his lapel, and gave them the title of Imperial Weavers.

On the eve of the grand procession the swindlers sat up all night, with twenty candles burning in their workshop. People watched them from outside, busily finishing off the Emperor's new clothes. They pretended to take the material off the loom, they snipped away at the air importantly with scissors, they stitched away with their needles without thread, and at last they announced, 'There! the Emperor's new clothes are finished!'

And when morning came, the Emperor ate his usual hearty breakfast, for he loved food almost as much as he did clothes, and then, attended by his most noble gentlemen-in-waiting, went in person to the weavers' workshop to be arrayed in his new finery as befitted the great occasion.

'Ah, your imperial majesty!' The two weavers bowed and scraped low in unison as the Emperor made his entrance. 'You do us honour!' And the one posed each thumb, each finger daintily aloft as if holding up a confection really too delicate for human handling. 'Here, your majesty, are the breeches!' he said almost in awe, while the other went through the same gesturing motions with a fulsome, 'And here is the robe! And now the mantle! You can feel they are as light as down; you can hardly tell you have anything on, your majesty – that's the beauty of them.'

'Yes, indeed,' chorused the gentlemen-in-waiting enthusiastically. But of course they were only fooling themselves and each other, for there was no more to be seen now than there had ever been.

'Will your imperial majesty now graciously take off your clothes?' said the swindlers. 'Then we can fit you with the new ones, in front of that big looking glass.'

So the gentlemen-in-waiting helped the Emperor out of the clothes he was wearing, upon which the swindlers set about their pretence of dressing him in the new raiment they were supposed to have made. They took their time about it, the Emperor twisting and turning this way and that the while, apparently admiring himself in the ample mirror, the swindlers consulting him and each other without cease as to the cut, set, appearance of each separate item.

'The breeches – not too tight, too loose about the waist? Ah no, I can tell, snug as kidskin,' approved the one, with an appraising pat at the Emperor's paunchy stomach. And, 'The ruffle, your majesty, a soupçon higher perhaps – so,' suggested the other, tweaking at the air about the Emperor's throat. 'Gentlemen,' the first one at last challenged the bemused courtiers, 'perfection, would you not say?'

'Goodness! How well they fit your majesty!' they all exclaimed. 'What a cut! What colours! How sumptuous!'

The master of ceremonies came in to announce, 'The canopy to be carried above your majesty's head is ready and the procession is waiting.'

'Tell them I am ready,' said the Emperor. Then he turned around once more in front of the glass, to make quite sure that everyone thought he was looking at his fine clothes.

The chamberlains who were to bear the train aloft groped on the floor as if they were picking it up; they walked solemnly and held out their hands, not daring to let it be thought that they couldn't see anything.

The Emperor marched off in the procession, under the grand canopy, and everyone in the streets and at their windows said, 'Good gracious! Look at the Emperor's new clothes! They are the finest he's ever had. What a sumptuous train! What a perfect fit!' No one would admit to anyone else that he couldn't see anything, because that would have meant that he wasn't fit for his job or that he was stupid. The Emperor's new clothes were praised by everyone.

'But he hasn't got anything on!' exclaimed a little child. 'Hush! what are you saying?' cried the father. The people around him had heard, however, and repeated the child's words in a whisper. Then someone said them a bit louder.

'He hasn't got anything on! There's a little child over there saying he hasn't got anything on!'

'That's right! HE HASN'T GOT ANYTHING ON!' the people all shouted at last. And the Emperor began to feel very uncomfortable and embarrassed, for it seemed to him that the people were right. But his royal upbringing prevented him from running away, and he thought to himself, 'I must go through with it now, procession and all.' And he drew himself up haughtily, while the chamberlains tripped after him, bearing the train that wasn't there.

The Golden Fish

There was once an old fisherman and his wife and they lived in a little wooden hut by the edge of the sea. The old fisherman went out in his boat every day, and sometimes at night, but he caught very little and he was always poor.

'You are not lucky like the other fishermen,' his wife would grumble. 'You never bring home any fish that are fine enough to fetch a good price.'

'I do my best,' the old man would answer. 'I do my best. But what can I do if the fish won't bite?'

One day his wife grumbled so much about the miserable way they had to live that her husband said, 'Hold your tongue, woman! I will take the boat out tonight. Who knows my luck might change!'

The night was dark and stormy when the old fisherman pushed his boat into the sea and then climbed into it. 'I had better stay close to the shore,' he told himself, as he began to row.

When he had gone as far as he dared the old man cast his line. Hours seemed to pass before he felt a feeble tug and when he brought in his line he saw that he had indeed caught a fish.

It was only a little fish but it was the strangest fish he had ever seen. It was golden! The fisherman stared down at the golden fish in astonishment, and the little fish cried, 'Let me go, let me go! I am too small to be of any use to you!'

The old man stared into the bright shining eyes of the little fish for a moment. Then he said, 'Oh, very well, you may go.' And he threw it back into the sea.

As the golden fish swam away to freedom, the fisherman heard it call, 'You have a kind heart, old man. If you want anything badly enough, come to this spot and call me. I will help you to get it.'

The fisherman rowed away from the spot where he had caught the golden fish and once again cast his line but though he fished until dawn he caught nothing.

His wife was in bed and asleep when he got back home but the sound of his steps in their tiny hut awakened her.

'Well,' she shouted, 'did you have any luck? Have you brought back some fish we can sell in the market?'

'I had no luck,' replied her husband. 'But I did catch a golden fish.'

'A golden fish!' exclaimed his wife, jumping out of bed. 'Where is it? What did you do with it?'

'I threw it back into the sea,' said her husband.

'Fool, idiot, donkey!' his wife raged. 'The fish might have been small but it was golden. It would have fetched a good price in the market.'

'There was something strange about that fish,' her husband said thoughtfully. 'It spoke to me. It told me it would help me to get what I wanted.'

'Then go out this very night in your boat and find it again,' his wife snapped. 'I'll tell you what we want – after today there will not be a bite to eat in the house. And we have no money left to buy more food.'

That day the old fisherman had only a slice of stale bread for his dinner for there was nothing else to eat. But he scarcely noticed how hungry he was – he was thinking so much about the little golden fish!

As soon as it was dark he went down to the sea and got into his boat and rowed out to the spot where he had caught it.

'Little fish, little golden fish!' he called softly. 'Will you come to me? I need your help!'

Almost at once the golden fish appeared.

'What is it, old man? What do you want?'

'We have nothing left to eat at home,' said the fisherman. 'I do not like to ask you for such a big favour, but perhaps you could tell me how to get money enough to buy food for my wife and myself.'

'Go home, old man,' said the golden fish. 'You will find all the food you can eat in the cupboard. It is there already.'

The fisherman thanked the golden fish and rowed as fast as he could back to land. He was not sure if he believed the golden fish or not, but oh, how wonderful it would be if there really was something to eat!

As he rushed into the hut he saw by the pleased look on his wife's face that the golden fish had kept its promise. And then he saw the table and all the bread and plates of cold meat and roast chicken, and he said a silent 'thank you' to the fish, as his smiling wife pushed him into a chair.

'Well, I must say,' his wife began, after they had eaten the most splendid meal in their whole lives, 'that golden fish of yours has some powerful magic.'

'I am very grateful to it,' said her husband. 'If I ever see it again I shall tell it so.'

'Oh, you'll see it again,' exclaimed his wife, folding her arms. 'You'll see it tonight. Of course I am very grateful for all this food, but there is something else. . . .'

'Something else?' her husband asked, looking upset. 'Surely not!'

'I want a new washtub,' replied his wife. 'My old one is too small and no longer holds water. I must have one. That golden fish of yours won't mind getting me one, I am sure.'

Now the old fisherman had long been afraid of his large, bullying wife and he dared not go against her wishes. So that night he got into his boat and rowed again to the spot where he had first seen the golden fish.

'Little fish, little golden fish!' he called softly. 'Will you come to me? I need your help!'

Almost at once the golden fish appeared.

'What is it, old man? What do you want?'

'My wife wants a new washtub,' said the fisherman. Then he added, 'I am sorry to put you to so much trouble after your great kindness in giving us all that lovely food.'

'Go home, old man,' said the golden fish. 'You will find the new washtub in the kitchen.'

When the fisherman got home he found his wife in the kitchen and there in front of her was a splendid new washtub.

'This is the best one I have ever seen!' she cried, when she saw him. And she smiled and offered to make her husband a hot drink before he went to bed.

For a few days the fisherman led a happy, peaceful life. There was always food in the cupboard and his wife did not scold him as much as she usually did. But then one day, towards the end of the week, she told him that she wanted something else from the golden fish.

'What more can we want?' her husband asked. 'We have plenty to eat and you have your new washtub.'

'I've been thinking,' said his wife. 'I have been thinking how nice it would be to have a new house. This hut is such a miserable place. That's what I want. I want a big new house!'

The fisherman looked worried and anxious when he heard this. But his wife raged at him until at last she drove him out of the hut, shouting. 'Go and ask the golden fish for a new house. Go now!'

The old man put on a hat with a feather in it, got into his boat and put out to sea. When he reached the spot where the golden fish was, he called softly, 'Little fish, little golden fish, will you come to me? I need your help?'

This time the golden fish did not appear at once and the fisherman began to be afraid that it would not come at all. But it came at last.

'What is it, old man? What do you want?'

'My wife wants a big new house,' said the fisherman, and he sounded very ashamed. 'Is it too much to ask?'

'Go home, old man,' said the fish. 'Your wife is already in her big new house.'

After thanking the fish with all his heart the old man rowed back to the shore and ran as fast as his legs would carry him back to his hut. But the hut had vanished. In its place stood a fine new house with many windows which looked out on to the sea.

He found his wife seated in a fine armchair, covered with velvet, and she smiled at him.

'Your little fish is quite clever,' she said. 'We must see to it that we keep it busy. Tomorrow night you can ask it for a carriage and horses and a whole new set of clothes for me.'

'I will not ask the golden fish for a single thing more!' the fisherman cried. 'I am ashamed that I have asked it for so much already.'

'You will, you will!' his wife screamed at him. 'I will not allow you to stay in my new house unless you do.'

Well, the fisherman did ask the golden fish for a carriage and horses and for a whole new set of clothes for his greedy wife. And the little fish said as usual, 'Go home, old man. Your wife has already got her carriage and horses and new clothes.'

But now – though the fisherman's wife had everything in the world to make her happy – she was not happy. She wore her fine clothes and rode out in her splendid carriage but neither the clothes nor the carriage made her content. It seemed to her poor husband that she grew more and more bad-tempered and disagreeable with every passing day.

At last she said to him, 'I dreamt last night that I was a queen. That is what I want to be – I want to be a queen.'

'But that is impossible!' her husband gasped. 'You cannot be a queen.'

'Oh yes I can,' shouted his wife. 'I can be Queen of the Sea – and that is what I want most of all. When I am Queen of the Sea I shall be able to command that little golden fish of yours to do anything I want.'

'Surely you do not expect me to ask the golden fish to make you Queen of the Sea!' cried her husband, turning pale. 'Oh no!'

'Oh yes!' screeched the woman. 'I do! I do!'

The fisherman was so afraid of his wife that he put out to sea that very night, and in fear and trembling he called to the golden fish, 'Little fish, little golden fish, will you come to me? I need your help.'

This time the golden fish did not come for a long time and the fisherman was certain in his own mind that it would not come at all. But at last he saw a gleam of gold and then he heard it say, 'What is it, old man? What do you want now?'

'My wife wants to be Queen of the Sea,' the old man whispered, in a voice full of shame.

'That she will never be!' cried the fish. 'Never, never, never! She is not fit to be a queen! Go home, old man. You will not see me again!'

When the old man returned home he found that there was no big house to enter. It had vanished. In its place stood his old hut. And there at the door stood his wife. She was not dressed in satins and velvet but in her old striped apron and worn-out dress which he knew so well.

'It's all gone, husband,' she said. 'There is nothing – not even my beautiful washtub!'

The fisherman nodded. He was not surprised and he was not sorry.

'The hut suits me better than the fine house,' he said quietly, 'and I like you best in your old dress and apron.' And he reached out and took his wife's hand and stroked it gently.

'Come in and rest your feet,' said his wife, in a voice so friendly that it quite astonished the old man. 'We'll manage very well, I am sure.'

And from that time onwards the fisherman's wife was much nicer and much, much easier to live with. The fisherman's luck changed in other ways. He found that now when he fished he always caught enough to keep them in food. Sometimes, of course, he searched the water for his friend, the golden fish, not to ask it for anything, but just to tell it that all was well. But no matter how patiently he waited or how softly and gently he called to it, the golden fish did not come, and he was never to see it again.

The Clever Rabbit

A very long time ago it chanced that a whale and an elephant had a conversation. It went like this.

'You are the biggest, the very biggest animal on land, Brother Elephant,' said the whale, as she watched him standing on the seashore.

'That's true,' said the elephant proudly. 'I am the biggest animal on land. But then you, Sister Whale, are the biggest animal in the sea.'

'That's true,' said the whale. 'The sea is my kingdom and I am the biggest and most powerful in it.'

The two huge creatures looked at each other in silence for a long time. And they, in their turn, were watched by a little rabbit who was playing with his drum behind a coconut tree.

'Now what can these two great stupid creatures want with each other?' the little rabbit asked himself. And he stopped beating his drum and began to listen.

The whale was the first to break the silence. 'Supposing we came to an agreement,' said she. 'If we became partners we would be able to rule over all the animals on land and in the sea. We would be the two most powerful rulers on earth. Everyone would have to obey us.'

The elephant raised his head at this. A cunning look came into his small eyes. 'I like that idea,' said he at last. 'Yes, I like it a lot. It is an excellent idea. Let us make a treaty.'

'Oh no you don't,' thought the little rabbit, when he heard this. 'I am not going to be told what to do by a whale and an elephant.'

The little rabbit remained behind his coconut tree until he saw the elephant wander away along the sand. Then he ran home and got two long, very strong pieces of rope. He carried them down to the sea and called out to the whale who was basking in the sunshine, 'Madam Whale, Madam Whale!'

'Yes, yes, what is it?' asked the whale. 'What do you want?'

'You are so big and strong and powerful,' said the little rabbit, 'I know you can help me. My cow is stuck in the mud some distance from here and only someone of your great size and strength can help me to pull it out.'

'I'll help you,' said the whale, who was very proud of her strength. 'Allow me to fasten one end of my rope to you,' said the rabbit. 'Then I will fasten the other end to my poor cow. When I have done this I will beat my drum and you, Madam Whale, must start to pull.'

'I understand,' said the whale, and she allowed the little rabbit to wade into the sea and fix one end of his rope to her powerful tail.

When this was done the little rabbit waded back to the shore and ran as fast as he could in the direction the elephant had taken.

'Lord Elephant, Lord Elephant,' he panted, as he drew near to him. 'There is no doubt you are the strongest, biggest animal on land. Will you please do me a favour?'

'What is it?' asked the elephant, pleased that the rabbit had spoken to him in such a respectful way.

'My cow has got stuck in the mud some way from here,' said the little rabbit. 'You are the only one who has the strength to pull it out. Will you

allow me to tie the end of this rope to your trunk? I will then go to my cow and tie the other end to it. When you hear me beat my drum you must start to pull.'

'I understand,' said the elephant, and he allowed the little rabbit to fasten the rope to his trunk. The rabbit then tied the ropes together.

Delighted that his plan was going so well, the little rabbit ran off and hid in some bushes which were about half way between the whale and the elephant. Then he began beating his drum and shouting, 'Pull, pull – pull your hardest!'

At the sound of the little rabbit's drum, the mighty whale began to pull. How she pulled! And the more she tugged and strained the more the little rabbit beat his drum and shouted encouragement.

The elephant pulled too. And how *he* pulled! He tugged at the rope as if his whole life depended on it and yet, for all his great strength, he found himself slowly being drawn towards the sea.

'That cow of little rabbit's must be well and truly stuck in the mud,' the elephant thought, as he began to slither forward.

And just about the same time as the elephant found himself losing his foothold the whale was finding herself being drawn slowly towards the beach.

'What a heavyweight that cow of little rabbit's must be,' she puffed. 'I am pulling as hard as I can and here I am being drawn towards the shore!'

She became so annoyed at this that she gave a mighty flick of her tail and this resulted in the poor elephant tumbling and crashing on to the sand.

The two great creatures saw each other almost in the same moment.

'I'll teach you to make a fool out of me!' trumpeted the elephant.

'I'll show you who is the stronger!' snorted the whale.

And they began pulling against each other until the rope snapped. The elephant fell back on the sand and the whale fell back into the sea.

'I'll thank you not to speak to me ever again,' said the whale, with all the dignity she could muster.

'And I'll thank you not to speak to me again,' said the elephant, as he got to his feet.

Behind his coconut tree the little rabbit smiled to himself. He had broken up a beautiful friendship. It was not likely now that the two most powerful creatures in the world would want to be partners and tell him what to do.

And of course he was right. From that day on the whale and the elephant would have nothing to do with each other!

Rosekin

Once upon a time a poor woodcutter and his wife had a pretty little girl called Roseken. Roseken's only friend from the village was a boy called Martin and the two often met and played together.

The woodcutter's cottage was on the edge of a wood where an ancient oak tree had once grown. Now, sadly, it was dead and the villagers believed that the little folk, the fairies and elves, had come to live around the old oak tree.

'You mustn't play near the old tree,' the woodcutter often said to his daughter. 'I do not believe in the little folk myself but you never know!'

When Roseken told Martin what her father had said, the boy laughed. 'I don't believe in the little folk either!' he cried. 'And anyway, just supposing they have come to live in the wood – what of it? All the people in our village are doing well. The grass is greener than I ever remember it. And the sun shines all day long – so the little folk have not brought us bad luck.'

'Well, I won't disobey my father,' said Roseken. 'So we had better play down by the river. You can see the old oak tree from there.'

The next day the two children met after school. 'There's time to have a game of hide-and-seek,' said Martin. 'You shut your eyes, Roseken, and I'll hide.'

Roseken shut her eyes and counted up to twenty. But when she opened them and looked round for Martin, he seemed to have disappeared. She ran to all his old hiding places but still she could not find him.

'Perhaps he has run all the way up to the oak tree,' she thought. 'I'll go and see.'

Roseken did not mean to go close to the tree but as she drew near to it she saw a dear little black and white dog come out of the bushes. It jumped about her and wagged its tail and was so friendly and playful that she longed to stroke it. But when she tried to catch it, it ran away from her.

Soon she had followed the dog round the old dead tree and into the woods and when she next looked about her, she found she was in a beautiful meadow where flowers of every kind grew. Brightly coloured butterflies flew about and pretty birds sang sweetly to her from the trees. And strangest of all – there were children in the meadow – tiny, weeny children, some making long daisy chains, others dancing in circles on the soft green grass.

Roseken rubbed her eyes, thinking that she must be dreaming. Then, when she looked about her again, she saw the most beautiful, dazzling palace at the far end of the meadow and she knew that she was in the land of the little folk.

'The Queen of the Fairies must surely live there,' she told herself, as she gazed at the glittering palace.

Just as she was wondering what to do next, Roseken saw one of the pretty little dancers break from the circle and come towards her.

'So you have come to us at last,' the fairy said. 'We have often watched you at play, Roseken, and wished you were with us.' And she plucked some of the fruit that grew near and offered it to Roseken.

No sooner had she tasted the delicious fruit than the girl forgot her home and her friends. She could not remember anything of her old life. Now all she wanted was to stay with the little folk for ever. She looked down and saw that her old dress had disappeared and that she was wearing a lovely long blue gown. She touched her hair and felt flowers in it.

Roseken danced with the fairies all through the night and then they carried her to the Queen's palace where the richest, most wonderful food imaginable was spread out before them.

After the feasting one of the fairies, whose name was Gossamer, whispered to Roseken that she would be her dearest friend and show her all the wonders of fairyland.

The next day Roseken and Gossamer visited the dwarfs, who were digging for gold by a silver stream. Then she watched the elves throwing seeds on the ground and saw how little trees sprang up almost at once.

There seemed to be no end to the wonders of fairyland and no end to the exciting things Roseken saw and did in the company of Gossamer.

'Everybody is so happy here,' Roseken said to her fairy friend one day, as they watched the elves sowing some of their seeds. 'Is the Queen happy too? Why have I never seen her? Why does she not come among us?'

'Hush!' said Gossamer. 'You cannot see her or know her. She is away at present. That is why we could take you to the palace. When she returns no one may visit her there unless they have a royal invitation.'

'I should like to meet her,' said Roseken.

'That is not possible!' the fairy exclaimed. 'When she returns to us it will be time for you to leave our land.'

'How shall I know when she is back?' Roseken asked.

'The meadow will look even prettier than it does now,' the fairy told her. 'The streams will be more sparkling and the sun brighter.'

Soon after this, Roseken began to think that the meadow did look more beautiful than usual, and the streams more sparkling and the sun brighter. And then Gossamer came to her and said softly, 'The Queen has returned. It is time for you to go!'

And she led Roseken to the old oak tree and gave her a ring as a token of their friendship.

'Goodbye, little friend,' Gossamer whispered softly. 'Think of us sometimes but do not try to find us. If you do, we shall leave this place for ever and joy will go out of the village. Do not tell anyone what you have seen.'

'Goodbye,' said Roseken sadly. 'I will never forget you.'

As she walked slowly through the woods she looked back, but there was

no sign of her fairy friend and she began to think about her home and what her father and mother would say. Would they be angry that she had stayed away for a whole night?

When she drew near to her cottage she scarcely knew it. And then she saw her father at the gate and he seemed much older. There were grey streaks in his hair and he was more bent.

'Father, father!' she cried, running towards him.

'Who are you?' the woodcutter asked, a look of surprise on his face. 'I do not know you. We had a little girl once but she disappeared seven years ago and we have had no word from her.'

'It is me – Roseken!' Roseken cried. 'I have come back.'

The woodcutter's surprise changed to joy when he heard her words and he took her in his arms.

'Whoever found you has taken good care of you!' he cried happily. 'Your mother will be overcome when she sees you.'

Soon Roseken began to feel at home in the cottage. Her mother fussed over her and petted her, telling her she had grown into an attractive young woman, and when her old playmate, Martin, came to visit her, he soon made it clear that he wished to marry her.

As the months passed Roseken began to think that her memories of fairyland were all part of a childhood dream. She became Martin's bride and the next year a dear little baby girl was born to them. Roseken called her new baby Elfie. She was so tiny and so sweet that she reminded her of a fairy child.

One day, when Roseken was dressing her child, she found a piece of gold hanging round her neck by a silken thread and she knew that it was the same kind of gold she had seen in fairyland. And she remembered how busily the dwarfs had worked in the gold mines by the river.

'Elfie, Elfie,' she whispered, hugging her little daughter. 'The fairies are your friends too! Perhaps Gossamer will visit you one day!'

As Elfie grew older, her mother was surprised at the long hours she spent in the garden. One day she followed the little girl into a shady corner and there she saw Gossamer sitting by Elfie's side and talking to her.

'I must tell Martin all about the little folk,' she decided, as she stole away. 'It is right that he should know. I cannot keep my secret any longer from him.'

But when Martin heard the story of her time in the land of the little folk he laughed loudly.

'What nonsense!' he exclaimed. 'Why, I have never in all my life heard such nonsense!'

'I tell you it is true,' Roseken protested, almost in tears. 'And if you don't believe me I will take you to the spot in our garden where Elfie meets my fairy friend of long ago.'

So, the very next afternoon, Roseken took Martin into the garden, and there were Elfie and the fairy talking quietly together. But no sooner did Gossamer know that Martin was there than she changed herself into a raven and flew away.

Elfie burst into sobs and so too did Roseken for she knew that Gossamer would never again visit them. But Martin was angry. He was so angry that he made up his mind to go to the old oak tree and find out for himself if the land of the little folk lay beyond it.

That night, as darkness fell, he set out. No sooner had he reached the ancient oak than the wind began to whistle fiercely through the trees. Then thunder rumbled and rolled and lightning flashed in the sky. The sudden violent storm frightened Martin, and he hurried home and went to bed without telling his wife where he had been.

In the morning when he went into the garden he saw that all his pretty flowers were dead, his precious apple tree was withered, and everywhere the grass was scorched and burnt. And when he went into the village, he soon learnt that the villagers had suffered in much the same way.

'What can have happened?' they asked Martin, fearfully. 'It looks as if our good luck has gone from us!'

Martin knew the answer but he said nothing, for now he was very ashamed of himself.

Roseken too knew the reason for the sudden misfortune which had struck the village.

'See how dull the grass is in the fields,' she said to her husband when he returned. 'And how grey and sad the sky looks. The little folk have gone and they will never come back!'

Roseken spoke truly. The little folk had gone! And from that day onwards nothing went right for the village. Some say the little folk used the old ferryman's boat to cross the wide river with all their treasures. This may be true for the ferryman now has a piece of glittering gold about which he will not speak. So what else can it be but fairy gold?

The Wolf and the Jackal

Once upon a time there was a little old Mother Goat who had seven kids. Old Mother Goat loved her children and took the greatest care of them. Whenever she had to leave them to go shopping in the market she worried all the way there and back – just as any other mother might who loved her children as much as old Mother Goat did!

Now Mother Goat and the kids lived in a small, cosy house on the edge of a deep forest and in this forest lived a cunning, wicked wolf who was nearly always hungry. For a long time he had kept watch on the goats' cottage, hoping that one day his chance would come to enter and eat up the seven little goats.

Of course Mother Goat knew all about the cunning, wicked wolf and so she never left her cottage for long. But then there came a day when Mother Goat knew she would have to leave her kids for one whole morning.

'Gather round, children,' she said to them, as she fixed her bonnet on her head and pulled on her long white knitted gloves. 'Gather round and listen carefully to what I have to say to you.'

The kids came to her eagerly. 'What is it, Mother?' asked the eldest. 'Are you going to take us out on a picnic?'

'Indeed not!' said Mother Goat. 'I am going to leave you here in the cottage for the rest of the morning. I must go to the next village to order a fresh supply of carrots and apples and that will take time.'

'Can we play outside while you are away?' asked the youngest.

'Certainly not,' said their mother, with an anxious frown. 'When I am gone you must shut and bolt the door and on no account open it until you hear my voice outside. Promise me, children!'

'We promise,' said the seven little kids.

'You all know about the wicked wolf in the forest,' Mother Goat went on. 'I am very much afraid that when he learns I am going on such a long journey he will try to get into our cottage. If he does he will gobble you up very quickly.'

'How shall we know if it is the wicked wolf who comes to our door?' asked the eldest.

'You will know him by his rough voice and his black feet,' said Mother Goat. 'Do not allow yourselves to be tricked by him. He will try everything to persuade you to open the door.'

'We will be on our guard,' the eldest said. 'We will not allow the bad wolf to trick us. Don't worry, Mother. We shall be quite safe. Will you bring us something nice from the shops?'

'Of course I will,' Mother Goat promised, and she looked happier as she picked up her shopping bag and made for the door. 'Goodbye, children. Play nicely together until I get back, and bolt the door the moment I am gone.'

The seven little kids bolted the door as soon as their mother was on the other side of it, and then they settled down to play guessing games.

They had not been playing for long when suddenly they heard someone knocking at the door.

'Who can it be?' asked the eldest.

'It can't be our dear mother come back so soon,' said the youngest. And he called out in a high, trembling kind of voice. 'Who is it?'

'It's me, your mother,' came the answer. 'I forgot my purse. Open the door, dear children, and let me in.'

'You do not speak with our mother's voice,' cried the kids altogether. 'Your voice is rough like the bad wolf's voice.'

'You *are* the wolf!' exclaimed the eldest kid, after a pause. 'Go away and leave us alone.'

When the wicked wolf heard this he gave up trying to persuade the little kids to open the door and ran off into the forest. 'Old Mother Goat has warned them against me,' he said to himself. 'She has told them I have a rough, growly kind of voice. Now if only I could make my voice soft and gentle like hers – ah, then they would not know the difference!'

And he hurried off to the nearest village and scared the shopkeeper, who sold schoolbooks and slates and chalk, and made him give him a great lump of chalk.

The wolf then crunched the chalk knowing that it would make his voice soft and gentle, and when he had eaten it all he went back to the goats' cottage, and knocked on the door.

'Who is it?' asked the kids.

'It's me, your mother,' came the answer. 'I forgot my shopping list.'

'That sounds like our dear mother's voice,' said the youngest. 'It is soft and gentle.'

'Let's open the door then,' said the fifth little kid who was wondering about the present his mother had promised to bring.

'No, no, look up at the window!' cried the eldest in great alarm. 'I can see something black – it's the black paw that belongs to the wolf!'

In his eagerness to lay eyes on the tender little goats the wolf had gone round to the window – and the eldest kid had spotted his black paw on the window ledge.

'Go away, wolf! We know it is you!' cried the eldest kid. 'Our mother has white feet. You have black feet.'

'That's right,' called out all the other little kids. 'You *are* the wolf, and we won't open the door!'

The wolf gave an angry snarl. He was furious that he had not managed to trick the seven kids but there was still a long time to go before their mother would be back.

'My black paws let me down,' thought the bad wolf. 'All I have to do is to make them white.' And he ran off to the nearest baker and scared him into rubbing dough all over his paws. And to make sure the kids would not recognise him, he made the baker give him his red trousers which the wolf put on.

So, for the third time he returned to the cottage and knocked on the door.

'It's me, your mother,' he called out. 'I forgot my umbrella. Open the door, dear children, and let me in.'

'Have you brought us a present?' asked the fifth little kid.

'Yes, yes, I have presents for you all,' replied the wolf.

'We can't let you in until you have shown us your paws,' said the eldest. 'If they are white we shall know you really are our own dear mother.'

At this the wolf went to the window and put two white paws on the window ledge and the kids looked up and saw them.

'It is our mother come back to us!' they cried happily, and the eldest ran to the door and drew back the heavy bolts.

Oh dear me! What a terrible fright the seven little kids got when, instead of their own dear mother, they saw the wicked wolf standing there! With squeaks and squeals of dismay they ran all about the kitchen looking for places to hide.

One dived into the cupboard. Another crept under the table. Two jumped into the sink, which was no hiding-place at all – and two jumped into Mother Goat's bed which she slept in during the winter. Only the youngest found a really clever hiding-place. He hid himself away in the big, tall grandfather clock.

Well, the wolf took his time in finding the little kids. But that was because he knew exactly where they were hiding. He strolled over to the cupboard and found the first little kid. And he gobbled him up with one swallow. Then he looked under the table and found the second kid and he gobbled him up with one swallow. The two little goats in the sink met the same fate as their brothers. And then it was the turn of the two in old Mother Goat's bed.

By now the wolf's hunger was satisfied and he looked about him for the seventh little kid without much interest. For the life of him he could not remember where he had seen him hide.

'I'll let that one go,' he decided at last. 'All I want now is a good sleep.' So he left the cottage and slowly made his way into the forest. He stopped at the well to draw some water as he was very thirsty.

Once in the forest, he settled down under a tree which stood close to a

stream and was soon fast asleep.

As he slept old Mother Goat returned home. When she saw the door of her cottage swinging open, her heart went pitter-patter with fear. Then she saw the topsy-turvy room, and she sat down on the only chair that was in an upright position and buried her face in her paws.

'My poor dear children,' she sobbed. 'The wolf has got them at last!'

As she sat there, sunk in despair, the thought came to her that perhaps, after all, her kids had been clever enough to escape the wolf's attention by hiding from him. And she got up and began calling softly, putting the room to rights as she did so. Alas, there was no answer to her calls until suddenly she heard a little squeak from the grandfather clock and, as she went to it, the door creaked open and out came her youngest.

'The wolf has eaten all the others,' the little kid told her, and he began to cry. 'We – we let him in because his paws were white like yours, Mother. We didn't know. . . .'

The poor mother comforted her youngest as well as she could and to cheer him up she said they would put some food in a basket and take it into the forest.

'I don't think we can possibly eat our dinner in the kitchen today,' she told the little kid. 'We shall both feel better outside.'

When the basket was packed with apples and carrots and fruit cake the two set off and, of course, no sooner did they come to the edge of the forest than they saw the wolf. There he was – fast asleep under the tree – and as Mother Goat stared at him with great bitterness she could not help but notice the size of his stomach.

'Goodness me!' she whispered to her kid, 'I do believe my six dear children are alive and well inside that monster's huge tummy. See how they are kicking and struggling to get out! Run home and fetch me my scissors and a needle and cotton.'

The little kid was gone in a flash and when he returned he had the scissors and the needle and cotton.

'That was quick!' said old Mother Goat, as she took the scissors and went up to the sleeping wolf. 'Now then – we shall see what we shall see!'

And she bent over the wicked wolf and made four or five very careful snips in the creature's stomach. And – would you believe it – out came the first of the little kids! Soon he was joined by his five brothers, all looking as good as new!

Mother Goat could hardly speak for joy as her children crowded about her skirts. Then, gathering her wits about her, she bade them run down to the stream and bring back as many big stones from there as they could carry.

When this was done she filled the wolf's tummy with the stones and neatly stitched it up again. It was quite surprising that the wolf slept on but then he had had a very busy morning!

As soon as Mother Goat was satisfied that she had done a neat job she set off for home, her kids frolicking about her feet. She was so happy that she could have burst into song. But long before they had reached their own cottage something very unpleasant was happening to that wicked, greedy wolf.

Almost before Mother Goat and her kids were clear of the forest he opened his eyes. His tummy felt very uncomfortable and heavy and his throat was dry. He struggled to his feet, thinking that he would make his way to the well and enjoy a drink of cool sparkling water. But the stones inside him shifted about as he walked and when he reached the deep well, he overbalanced and toppled over. Down, down, down he fell – and was soon drowned.

So that was the end of the cunning, wicked wolf and when Mother Goat learnt of his death she made apple pie for dinner and gave each of her children a paper hat to wear for the rest of the day.

The Proud Prince

There was once upon a time a prince who had a proud and haughty nature. He was also a poet, and he spent most of his time writing poetry which no one understood except himself.

Now this prince, whose name was Oscar, was the only son of a wise old king and a gentle, loving queen, and as the royal pair grew older and older they began to worry more and more about their son.

'He will be king after I am gone,' said the king, one day.

'He needs a wife,' said the queen.

'His foolish head is stuffed with poetry,' said the king.

'He does not think that any girl is good enough for him,' said the queen. 'He is so dreadfully proud.'

'It is my wish that he marries before the year is out,' said the king, after a very long silence.

'Then we must invite suitable girls, princesses from far and wide, to come to the palace,' said the queen. 'He must choose one of the princesses who come.'

That same day, invitations were sent out to a hundred princesses. They were invited to come to the palace and they were told that Prince Oscar would make one of them his wife.

The very next week some of the girls began to arrive. Many of them came in glittering gold coaches. Some arrived on horseback with their attendants. Others, whose fathers were rather poor kings, came in plain black carriages.

The queen was delighted when she saw them all standing there in the banqueting hall. They were as pretty and attractive a bunch of girls as you could imagine. She hurried off, after her inspection, to tell the king that Prince Oscar would most likely find a suitable bride within a day or two. Then she rushed off to find her son.

Prince Oscar was seated by the window in his room writing poetry. He was tall and dark and very handsome and, when he saw his mother, he smiled in a pleased fashion.

'I have just composed a long sonnet,' said he, 'to the girl of my dreams. Oh, I admit that I shall never meet her in real life, but I am content to put her in my poetry.'

'Do not be so sure that you will not meet her,' said the queen quickly. 'Your father and I are quite determined that you shall marry. We have invited some of the most beautiful girls we could find to come to the palace. You shall see them for yourself tonight at the banquet we are giving in their honour.'

When he heard this the smile vanished from the prince's handsome face. He scowled and managed to look most disagreeable.

'I refuse to meet them,' he said, in a proud and haughty voice. 'I will not attend the banquet. I do not want to marry any of your princesses.'

'Oh, but you will,' said the queen firmly. 'You will do as you are told or your father will banish you from the kingdom! What would you do then? You are quite useless at earning your own living.'

'I could write poetry,' said the prince.

'And who would buy it?' retorted his mother. 'It is rubbish, and besides you can't look after yourself. You have servants to do the smallest things for you. No, no, you need a wife, a sensible girl who will make *you* sensible and in time teach you to be a good king.'

Now the prince loved his life at the palace. He liked having servants to look after him. It suited his proud nature to be able to order them about. And he loved having all the time in the world to write his poetry. So, after a moment's thought, he said, 'Oh very well, I see you must have your way. I will attend the banquet and look at the girls.'

That night the prince did attend the banquet. To please his mother he had combed out his black curly hair and put on his richest brocade jacket and dark red velvet breeches. He looked so handsome that all the princesses fell in love with him on sight and all longed to find favour in his eyes.

The old king and queen were delighted at the way their son was behaving and, after the feasting and the merrymaking, they announced that their son, Prince Oscar, would retire to the throne room and interview the princesses, one by one.

There was a flutter of excitement among the girls, and then the royal couple withdrew, taking Prince Oscar with them. The Master of Ceremonies lined up the girls outside the great bronze doors of the throne room and, one by one, they were ushered inside to meet the prince.

'She is too tall,' said Prince Oscar, when the first of the princesses curtsied before him. 'No, no, take her away.'

'Your nose is not quite straight,' said the prince, when the second stood before him. 'I could never grow used to it.'

'Too short and round!' exclaimed he, when the third girl stood before him. 'My wife must be tall and slender like a willow.'

'What a tragedy your eyes are grey and not blue,' he cried, at the sight of the fourth princess. 'My dream girl has blue eyes – and besides I do believe your ears are too large for real beauty.'

The poor princess retired in tears, and the king and queen grew more and more upset and angry as their son continued to find fault with each of the pretty girls who appeared before him.

'You are quite impossibly rude and disagreeable,' the queen whispered, and the king frowned and tried to hide the anger which was rising in his heart.

At last, when the proud prince had seen and criticised nearly all the girls, one of the last to be interviewed came into the throne room. She was tall and graceful, with honey-coloured hair, and blue eyes the colour of cornflowers.

'Beautiful, beautiful,' murmured the queen, and she looked at her son hopefully.

The princess did not curtsy; she simply bowed her head slightly and stared at the young prince with questioning eyes.

'Yes, not bad at all,' said Oscar at last. 'I can't deny your eyes are blue or that you are tall and slender. But there is something about your mouth which does not appeal to me. Do you know I fear it is too wide for your face! Yes, yes, that's it! And you could not expect a prince and a poet to take to himself a wife whose mouth is too wide. . . .'

At this the old king exploded with rage.

'Oh, that a son of mine should have such a proud and foolish nature!' he cried. 'You are as vain as a peacock and as useless as all that poetry you write! You have insulted and criticised and found fault with girls who are a hundred times more gifted than you are. . . .'

'And now you dare to insult Princess Cherry!' cried the queen. 'One of the most beautiful and charming and intelligent girls in the world. I happen to know her aunt. . . .'

'I can't help it . . .' said the prince sulkily.

'Oh, but you can!' thundered the king. 'I declare I will put an end to all this foolishness. The princesses shall return to their kingdoms and you, my son, will marry the first beggar-maid who calls at the palace. . . .'

A look of distress and horror spread over the prince's face at these words but he saw, too late, that he had angered his father too much even for forgiveness. And as Princess Cherry swept from the room, her head held high, he did not dare ask for a second chance.

'Go to your room,' his mother whispered. 'Your father means what he says. You have brought this punishment upon yourself. . . .'

For the next few days Prince Oscar stayed in his room writing poetry. But he found, to his annoyance, that the words he sought would not come, and he wasted a great deal of parchment – which meant that his servants were constantly having to tidy up his room, and fetch him more.

At the end of the week, one of the king's attendants came to tell him that he was wanted in the throne room.

'They can't have found a beggar-maid so quickly,' Oscar told himself, as he made his way down the great marble stairs. 'Surely not!'

But when he entered the throne room he saw, to his horror, that the king and queen had indeed found a beggar girl. She was talking to the queen when he arrived, and she turned quickly as he advanced into the room and smiled at him.

The prince almost ran from the room at the sight of her uncombed hair, her dirty face and blackened teeth.

'No, no,' he cried. 'Not her! She's – she's positively dirty. Look at her dress – it's rags! And when did she last comb her hair?'

'She is the first of the beggars to come round to the kitchen to beg for food,' said the king sternly. 'The cook had orders to bring her into my presence. You are fortunate that she is at least young. It would have made no difference if she had been twice your age – you will marry her today. . . .'

'Never!' cried Prince Oscar.

But as he spoke the room was filling up with the lords and ladies of the court, and then came the chaplain.

'I – I will not marry her!' screamed the unhappy prince.

'You must,' said his father. 'You must! The penalty for disobeying the royal sovereign is death!'

Now the prince, when he heard this, knew that he was much too young and handsome to lose his head. He knew also that his royal father meant every word he said.

'I'll do it,' he told himself at last. 'I'll marry this dreadful fright of a girl and then send her away. . . .'

'Very well, father,' he said aloud. 'Let the wedding ceremony begin.'

But when the prince had finally married the beggar-maid he found that he could not send her away.

'She is your wife,' said his father sternly. 'Either she stays here or you go with her.'

'Go with her!' exclaimed Oscar.

'Oh, but you must,' said his new wife, who spoke in a shrill, whining kind of voice. 'I will not stay here in this palace so you *must* come and live with me!'

'You must go where your wife goes,' chorused the lords and ladies of the court, who did not approve of Prince Oscar. 'You cannot stay here!' And with so many against him, Oscar saw that he had no chance to plead his case.

'And don't come dressed like a peacock,' said his new wife. 'Borrow some clothes from the stableboy for where we are going your satins and velvets will be quite out of place.'

The proud prince bowed his head in defeat. He went to the stables and borrowed an old tunic and breeches from one of the stableboys. Then with nothing of his own – not even a poetry book – he left the palace in the company of his new wife.

'Where are we going?' he asked, after they had walked some miles. 'My feet are tired and I am hot and thirsty.'

'So am I,' snapped his wife, 'but that doesn't mean we can stop for a rest – not unless you want to spend the night in the forest.'

'Do – do you mean you have a house of your own?' asked the prince, casting a curious glance at his wife's dirty face.

'It's home –' said the girl, 'though you will find it a poor place, I daresay.'

After that they walked in silence until the girl left the road and the prince followed her into some thick woods. There, in a clearing, stood a miserable little hut whose roof had holes in it.

'Home at last!' she exclaimed, taking the prince's hand and dragging him after her into the hut. 'Now we can boil ourself some water and make some soup.'

'What!' exclaimed Oscar. 'Is this our home?' He looked round at the bare wooden floor, and the thick dust and litter of sticks and leaves which covered it. 'It's a filthy place and so untidy. Surely you don't expect me to live here?'

'It's *our* home,' said the girl softly, 'and you might as well get used to it as quickly as possible. You can call me Kirsty if you like – it's more friendly.'

'I'll not call you anything,' retorted the prince sulkily. 'And I won't stay here!'

'Oh yes you will,' said Kirsty. 'You have nowhere else to go. And if you want to sleep outside in the woods – watch out for the wolves. . . .'

At that, Oscar shuddered and when Kirsty told him to sweep the floor and then fill the pot with water and make the fire he found himself trying to carry out all those tasks as well as he could. But he was so slow and clumsy that presently she pushed him into a corner and told him that he was quite useless.

'I am a prince,' Oscar managed to say, with something of his old proud manner. 'You can't expect a prince to know about sweeping floors and making soup.'

'You're not a prince now!' Kirsty said mockingly. 'You have angered your father so much that he won't have you in the palace. And besides, you were just as useless there as you are here.'

And with that, she began tidying up the hut. The flying dust made Oscar sneeze and he longed to rush outside into the woods and leave the dreadful girl for ever. But he was afraid of the wolves which she had told him lived there and so he stayed in his corner.

Presently she made soup and offered him some in an old cracked bowl and the prince shook his head. But soon he was so hungry that he smothered his pride and asked her for some.

To his surprise the soup was so tasty that he could not stop himself from enquiring how it was made.

'It has got roots in it and a bit of rabbit,' she said. 'Tomorrow you'll have to learn how to dig up the roots we can eat and maybe catch a rabbit.'

'I would never eat rabbit!' declared the prince in a shocked voice. 'I believe some of our kitchen-maids do, but then they don't have refined tastes.'

'If you want to starve,' said Kirsty, 'you are welcome to. But there won't be anything else to eat except rabbit so you'll have to decide.'

The days and weeks that followed were so awful and so full of horror to the prince that he often wondered if he should go back to the palace and risk losing his head.

He tried to snare rabbits and failed. He dug up all the wrong, poisonous kind of roots, and he upset the pot of boiling water over his feet. It was lucky for him that Kirsty proved herself a good nurse and was able to rub some strange ointment on them which helped to heal them quickly.

At the end of a month he was as dirty and unkempt as his wife and he had forgotten every sonnet he had ever written. But the odd thing was that with every passing day Kirsty treated him more kindly. She smiled at him more often and stopped teasing him about being so useless. And Oscar grew to watch for her smile, and even began to smile back.

One night, as they sat by their fire, he said, 'You know, I think my father and mother were right. I was a pretty useless prince. I can see that now. I spent all my days writing poetry that nobody read instead of learning how to govern the kingdom.' Then he sighed and added, 'I wish I had another chance. . . .'

'When I came to the palace, begging for food,' said Kirsty, 'the scullery-maid told me that you could have married any one of a hundred beautiful princesses.'

'That is true,' replied the prince. And he sighed deeply. 'There was one I remember more clearly than the others. She had honey-coloured hair and eyes as blue as cornflowers. . . .'

'You should have married her,' said Kirsty softly. 'She would have made you a good wife. What was her name?'

'I can't remember,' said the prince. 'But what does it matter?' And he sighed again. 'In some strange way you make me think of her. But your hair is so tangled and your face always so dirty that I often wonder why. . . .'

Kirsty drew her ragged shawl more closely about her thin shoulders as she crouched over the fire. Then she rubbed her face with a grimy hand and the smear of dirt on her cheeks that was left behind almost made the young prince laugh.

'What do you really look like?' he asked. 'It is impossible for me to guess.'

The next night, as they sat by the fire, the prince brought out a dainty silver comb, decorated with precious stones.

'My mother must have slipped this into my pocket,' he said. 'I had forgotten I had it. Will you accept it as a gift?'

Kirsty took the comb and, hiding the pleasure his gift had given her, said sharply. 'If you sit watching the fire – it will go out. Put some more sticks on it quickly.'

On the following night, the prince brought out a tiny tablet of perfumed soap, prettily wrapped.

'My mother must have slipped this into my pocket with the comb,' he said. 'I had forgotten I had it. Will you accept it as a gift?'

Kirsty took the soap and then said quickly, 'Fill the pot with water – it will boil dry if you sit there looking at it.'

On the third night, the prince brought out a small silver mirror.

'This too my mother must have put in one of my pockets,' he said. 'I had forgotten I had it. Will you accept it as a gift?'

'Of what use is a mirror to me?' said Kirsty. 'You have told me many times what a sight I look!'

'Then you must forgive me for my rudeness,' said the prince, with a look full of shame. 'We should have starved here long ago if it had not been for your wits and hard work.'

At these words, Kirsty took the mirror and put it beside the silver comb and the scented soap.

That night when the prince lay down on his rough bed of straw he fell asleep almost at once and, while he slept, Kirsty combed out her tangled hair with the silver comb, and then washed it in the little stream that ran past the hut. Then she washed her face and hands with the scented soap until every particle of dust and grime had disappeared.

By the light of the round silvery moon she could see herself in the silver mirror and what she saw must have pleased her for she smiled and then laughed aloud, as she stared into it.

In the morning, when the prince awoke, he looked around for Kirsty. But he saw only a tall maid, as slender as a willow, and dressed in a gown the fresh green colour of the grass. Her long shining hair was the colour of honey, and her face was so delicately pretty that the poet in him came instantly to life.

Then, as she curtsied before him and raised her eyes to his, he saw that they were the glorious blue of cornflowers.

'Don't tell me,' he whispered, when he had recovered from his surprise. 'You are the last of the princesses I would not marry. You are Princess Cherry.'

The princess smiled and nodded and Prince Oscar, still bemused, but quite captivated by her beauty, held out his arms, and enfolded her in an embrace.

'I am both Kirsty and Princess Cherry,' said the girl at last. 'You are my true husband. There was no other way to teach a proud prince how to mend his ways.'

Well, in no time at all, the happy pair had left the hut and made their way back to the palace where they were warmly greeted by the king and queen. And if the queen was part of Princess Cherry's plot to teach the proud prince a lesson she never admitted to it!

It is enough to say that soon after the return of Prince Oscar and his beautiful princess, the old king handed his crown over to his son and, with his wife's help and advice, Oscar became a wise and thoughtful ruler and, strange to say, a much better poet!

Country Mouse in Town

There was once a little fieldmouse who had nothing much to eat except barley and grain. He had the same seeds for breakfast, dinner and high tea and he was happy that it should be so.

One day he had a visit from a Town Mouse who lived in a big town which was some distance away from his field.

'You may not know this,' said the Town Mouse, when the Country Mouse had invited him to eat with him. 'But we are related. I believe you are a cousin of sorts and when I heard you were living out here I thought it was my duty to come and see how you are getting on.'

'I am getting on very well, thank you,' said the Country Mouse, giving his guest a sideways look out of his keen little eyes. 'You can see for yourself – I lack for nothing.'

And he offered the Town Mouse a small dish of barley.

The Town Mouse did not trouble to hide his disgust at the sight of the barley.

'Do you mean to say that you eat this stuff for dinner? Have you nothing – er – more appetising to offer me? I have come a long way to meet you?'

'This is all I have,' said the Country Mouse, surprised and upset at his cousin's unkind remark. 'I have dried seeds for breakfast, dinner and high tea and I must confess that I have never grown weary of them.'

'You astonish me,' cried the Town Mouse, looking down his nose at his country cousin. 'You really do! Do you know what I have to eat?'

The fieldmouse shook his head.

'I'll tell you. Dried apricots or prunes for breakfast. Then for lunch a tasty morsel of the choicest cheese and raisins. For tea I might have a nibble or two of sweet brown sugar and perhaps a biscuit or a tiny piece of plum cake . . .' he paused, and then went on, 'In town – nobody has high tea – dinner is the meal for those living in high society. . . .'

'Well, then, what do you have for dinner?' gasped the Country Mouse, his eyes all misty at the very thought of the wonderful food which his cousin had described.

'Oh – that depends,' said the Town Mouse in a lofty voice. 'It might be a portion of German sausage or a piece of Stilton cheese – washed down by a sip of sweet red wine. . . .'

'Don't tell me more,' cried the Country Mouse, putting his dish on one side. 'I can't bear it – and now I have quite lost my appetite for seeds.'

'I tell you what!' exclaimed his cousin. 'Why don't you come and live with me? I can promise you the time of your life.'

The little fieldmouse did not take long to make up his mind. 'I'll come,' he said. 'Just give me a minute to gather up my precious bits.'

'Just bring a clean handkerchief and a brush for your whiskers,' said the Town Mouse impatiently. 'You won't need anything else.'

'Oh, very well,' said the Country Mouse. 'But I'd like to wear my hat if you don't mind.' And he put on a battered straw hat, which caused his cousin to smile in a superior fashion.

On the way to the town the little Country Mouse asked many questions about his new home, but his cousin told him sharply to hold his tongue. 'You'll soon find out for yourself how delightful it is,' he said. 'Just keep your mind on the business in hand. Watch out for the buses and the carriages when we reach the town and follow me closely.'

The little Country Mouse did his best to obey as they entered the town. But the roaring noise of the buses and the crowded streets quite terrified him and he was shaking with fright when at last they came to a tall grey house.

'Well, here we are!' cried the Town Mouse. 'It's a splendid house, isn't it? We'll go in by the back entrance and, with any luck, we can have our tea straight away.'

The fieldmouse could scarcely believe his eyes when he saw the fine home his cousin had made for himself. And when the Town Mouse took him into the kitchen cupboard and showed him where the brown sugar was kept he gave a great big gasp of pleasure.

'Help yourself,' said the Town Mouse. 'The brown sugar is on the lowest shelf and the white sugar – which I believe is not so good for one – is just above it.'

The Country Mouse ate so much of the delicious brown sugar that he thought it would come out of his ears.

'What do you fancy now?' asked his cousin after a while. 'Some juicy prunes or a nibble of apricot?'

'I – I don't really know,' began the fieldmouse. 'I think I would . . .' he stopped, as somewhere in the great house a door banged and a loud angry voice shouted, 'Here Tibs – into the kitchen with you. Drat these mice! I'm sure I heard them scratching around. . . .'

At the sound of the loud miaow which followed this remark the Town Mouse grabbed hold of his cousin. 'It's the cat!' he whispered. 'No time to waste. Follow me – I have an escape route into the cellar.' And he scurried away.   The fieldmouse scampered after him. The very idea of a cat being so close made his whiskers curl. But when they reached the cellar he saw, to his amazement, that his cousin was not in the least terrified.

'Oh, yes,' said he, 'the cat is my deadly enemy. He's a big black monster and he's been trying for months to get the better of me. Come, let's make the best of the cellar and try some of the cheeses they keep down here. . . .'

But the little Country Mouse had lost his appetite. He was still all of a-tremble and he was just beginning to tell his cousin how he felt when down the cellar steps came the monster-cat.

'L-Look out–' he squeaked, and the Town Mouse had just enough time to hide behind the wine barrel thanks to his cousin's warning.

As for the Country Mouse he was too scared to move and it was fortunate for him that the cat changed his mind about going further into the cellar when his mistress called, 'Tibs – fish, Tibs! Come and get your dinner.'

'Phew! that was a close one!' the Town mouse whispered, when they were once again on their own. 'Now for the cheese. . . .'

'No, no thank you, cousin,' said the Country Mouse. 'I have had enough scares to last me for the rest of my life. You can keep your prunes and apricots and brown sugar. I'm going back to my barley. At least I shall have peace in my field.'

'You don't mean to tell me . . .' began the Town Mouse.

'I do,' said his cousin, scampering to the door. 'I'd rather eat barley for breakfast, dinner and high tea for the rest of my life than be frightened to death every time I had a nibble of brown sugar. . . .'

'Poof!' exclaimed the Town Mouse scornfully.

'Goodbye,' called his cousin, disappearing round the door. 'You're welcome to come to high tea any time you choose!'

And do you know – when the Country Mouse was safely home he had a nibble of barley and thought that it was the best thing he had ever tasted.

Aladdin

Long ago, in one of the big cities of China, there once lived a tailor whose
name was Mustapha. He was so poor that he found it hard to earn enough
money to feed his wife and his son, Aladdin.

Now you might think that Aladdin as he grew older would try to help his
father. But this was not so. He was a lazy, careless boy who spent nearly all
his time playing in the streets.

When Aladdin was fifteen his poor father died and though he was sad that
now he and his mother were alone, he did not change his ways. More and

more of his time was spent playing about with his friends.

One day, in the middle of a noisy game, a stranger came up to him in the street. The stranger was an African magician, and he had been watching Aladdin for some minutes. Already he knew Aladdin's name and where he lived and how desperately poor his widowed mother had now become.

'Tell me boy,' said the magician, 'was your father's name Mustapha? And was he a tailor by trade?'

'The answer is "yes" to both these questions,' said Aladdin, not in the least shy. 'Why do you ask?'

For answer the African magician threw his arms around Aladdin's neck, and kissed him several times. Then he cried, 'I am your uncle! Your dear father was my own brother. I knew you at once because you are so like him.'

Then he pressed some money into the boy's hand and told him to let his mother know that he would be visiting her the very next day.

Delighted at the gift of money, Aladdin ran home at once.

'Mother, mother,' he cried, bursting into the small kitchen where she was ironing. 'What do you think? Our father's brother has come to the city to find us. And he has given us some money. He must be very rich.'

'Your father had no brother,' said the widow, shaking her head. 'This can't be a true story you're telling me, Aladdin.'

'I tell you it is true,' Aladdin protested. 'And he is coming to see us tomorrow.'

'If this stranger is going to be our guest,' said the widow, 'we had better spend the gold he gave you on food. I will go out and buy what I can, and make him welcome.'

For the rest of that day and a greater part of the next, the widow prepared for their visitor, and when night came the supper was ready and the house swept and polished.

'Perhaps the stranger won't be able to find our poor house,' said Aladdin's mother, as it began to grow late. 'Go and see if you can meet him.'

But as Aladdin was leaving, the magician himself appeared, carrying gifts of wine and fruit. He greeted the widow with great affection, as she made him welcome to her humble home.

'Do not be surprised that your husband did not mention me,' he said, as they sat down to supper. 'I have been out of this country for some forty years, and have travelled widely. My home is in Africa now but I wished to see my dear brother before I grew too old to travel.'

At the mention of her husband, the widow began to cry, and the magician said in a much more cheerful voice, 'Tell me, what trade does Aladdin follow?'

'He spends most of his time playing in the streets,' said the widow bitterly. 'I am ashamed of him.'

Aladdin hung his head at his mother's words, and his new uncle said, 'I do no like to hear this. You must let me help. I have an idea. What do you say to a shop – perhaps one that sells silks and linens?'

'There is nothing I should like better,' Aladdin cried, thinking that a shop would mean he had to work very little. 'Thank you, uncle!'

The widow dried her eyes and began to smile. Now she was ready to believe that the stranger was all he said he was, and she urged him to eat and drink and enjoy himself while he was their guest.

At the end of the meal the stranger promised to come again the next day.

'You will need some new clothes,' he told Aladdin. 'And your mother must have a new dress.'

'You have brought joy into our lives,' the widow told him gratefully, as she went with him to the door. 'Aladdin will be ready to go with you to the shops in the morning.'

That night Aladdin could scarcely sleep for excitement and for once he rose early and was waiting for his uncle when he appeared. They went to many different shops and soon Aladdin's head was in a whirl as he found himself the owner of a number of fine outfits.

He was so excited that for a time he did not notice that his uncle was leading him towards the city gates. When they had passed through and were some way into the countryside, the magician told him that he wished to visit a certain valley which was not far from where they were.

'Certainly,' Aladdin agreed. 'I expect it is a place you knew when you were a boy.'

When they reached the valley, the magician told Aladdin to gather some sticks.

'I mean to light a fire here,' he said, his eyes glinting strangely. 'So be quick about it.'

Aladdin did not question his uncle's words. He gathered the sticks and soon had a fire blazing.

'Do not be astonished or frightened at what I am about to reveal to you,' said the magician, as he approached the fire. 'Obey me in everything I tell you, and you will be well rewarded.'

Then he threw some sweet-smelling powder into the flames and muttered some magical words which Aladdin did not understand.

Almost at once the earth opened and Aladdin saw a large flat stone with a brass ring fixed in it. He was so frightened that he would have run away, but his uncle caught hold of him and held him firmly.

'Under this stone,' said he, 'is a hidden treasure which will make you richer than the sultan himself. 'You are the only one who is allowed to lift the stone, or enter the cave. Do what I command if you wish for riches beyond your dreams!'

'What do you want me to do?' Aladdin asked, suddenly ashamed of being so frightened.

'Just take hold of the ring and lift the stone,' said his uncle eagerly.

'I doubt if I am strong enough,' Aladdin objected, looking down at the great heavy stone.

'Do what I tell you,' ordered his uncle impatiently. 'Only *you* may touch the ring.'

Aladdin took hold of the ring and, to his astonishment, he found he could raise the heavy stone without any difficulty. He looked down and saw that there was a flight of steps which led to a door.

'Go down the steps,' the magician urged, 'and open the door. It will take you into a glorious palace, which is divided into three great halls. In the halls you will find chests full of gold and silver, but do not stop to help yourself to the treasure. Instead pass to the end of the third hall where you will find a door opening into a garden. . . .'

'Is there more treasure in the garden?' Aladdin interrupted breathlessly.

'There are trees loaded with fruit in the garden,' answered his uncle impatiently. 'Touch nothing. Go straight to a niche in the wall where you will see a lighted lamp. Take the lamp, put out the flame and throw away the oil. Then bring it to me.'

'Is that all!' Aladdin cried, in a disappointed voice.

'The mission is dangerous enough,' said the magician. 'If you touch any of the treasures you will die. But take this ring of mine,' he continued, pulling a broad gold ring off his finger and handing it to Aladdin, 'it will protect you from all evil.'

Aladdin took the ring and descended into the cave. As the magician had foretold, he found the three halls. And these he went through quickly. In the garden he soon spied the lighted lamp in a niche in the wall, and he put out the light and threw away the oil. Then he placed the lamp in his sash for safe-keeping.

As he passed through the garden he helped himself to some of the strange fruits which hung from the trees.

'I wish they were figs,' he told himself, as he plucked them. 'What strange brilliant colours they are!' Then he thought his mother might know what to do with them – not realising that what he took for fruits were really magnificient jewels; the most beautiful rubies, diamonds and pearls, of the finest quality.

Now Aladdin was loaded up and he was tired and hungry when he climbed the steps and arrived at the mouth of the cave.

'Lend me a hand, uncle,' he called. 'Help me to climb out!'

'Hand me the lamp first,' his uncle replied. 'Give me the lamp!'

'I can't do that easily,' Aladdin replied. 'It is caught up in my sash. But you shall have it the moment I am on firm ground. . . .'

'Wicked, disobedient boy!' shouted the magician in a sudden rage. 'Give me the lamp. I must have the lamp!'

'And so you shall when I am standing beside you,' said Aladdin obstinately. 'And not before!'

At this the magician flew into a passion. He put some of his powder on to the fire, muttered two magical words, and the stone moved over the mouth of the cave, closing it up.

Finding himself in darkness, Aladdin began to plead with his uncle to forgive him. But the magician was out of hearing. For years he had planned to get the lamp for himself. But in all the books of magic which had disclosed its presence there was always the warning that only a total stranger could take it from the garden and hand it to him. If the boy had only done what he was told the magician would have become the most powerful magician in the whole world!

Aladdin, of course, had no idea what wonderful powers the dusty old lamp possessed. But as he sat there in the dark cave the thought came to him that the stranger who had come to their house was not, after all, his uncle. He was some evil magician who, for reasons of his own, had wanted to lay hands on the old lamp in the garden.

He was now so frightened and tired that he began to cry, clasping and unclasping his hands. Without realizing it, he rubbed the ring the magician had given him. Almost immediately, a genie of terrifying appearance appeared before him.

'What would you have me do, oh Master of the Ring?' said the genie. 'I am ready to obey you, for I must serve the one who wears the ring.'

123

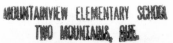

Now, only a moment before, Aladdin had made up his mind that he would almost certainly starve to death in the dark cave, and so the genie did not scare him as much as he would have done if he had met the towering creature in the woods.

'If you are as powerful as you look,' said Aladdin. 'Take me back to my mother's house.'

No sooner had he spoken than he found himself in his own street and standing outside his own door. He was so tired and weak that he could scarcely speak as he stumbled into the kitchen.

'What is it, son?' his mother cried anxiously. 'Where have you been? And where is your uncle?'

'He is no uncle of mine!' Aladdin said, finding his tongue at last. 'He is nothing but a wicked magician who tried to use me for his own ends.'

Then he told his mother the whole story, and the poor woman wept and then kissed him, so glad was she to have her son safely back home.

'Did you bring nothing out of that dreadful place?' she asked, when she was calm again.

'Only this dirty old lamp,' said Aladdin, and he gave it to his mother. 'And some strange fruits which, though they grew on trees, may be of some value.'

'You poor boy!' exclaimed the widow, examining the lamp. 'And to think I have nothing better in the house to offer you than a slice of bread!'

'What about the lamp?' Aladdin asked. 'Couldn't we clean it up and sell it?'

'I'll do just that,' said his mother. 'It will look better after I have rubbed it clean.'

And she took some fine sand and water to clean the old lamp. But no sooner did she begin to rub it than a dreadful genie of gigantic size appeared before them.

In a voice so loud that it could have been heard all down the street he cried, 'What do you want? I am your slave, and the slave of those who have that lamp.'

Terrified out of her wits, the poor woman fainted away, and Aladdin snatched the lamp out of his mother's hand, and cried, 'I am hungry, bring me something to eat.'

The genie vanished and, in a flash, had returned with a great silver tray which held silver dishes containing food which Aladdin imagined the sultan himself would have been glad to eat.

When his mother had recovered her senses, Aladdin told her to sit down at the table and enjoy the feast and, as she ate, he warned her that she must never again think of selling the old lamp.

'Well, if we can't sell the lamp,' said his mother. 'We can sell these magnificent silver dishes. The money they will fetch will keep us in food and clothes for many a long day.'

So, for the next few months, the widow had no need to worry about providing for herself and her son. Aladdin sold the tray and the dishes and the gold he received for them seemed like a fortune.

There came a day, however, when the last of the gold was spent and once again Aladdin took down the old lamp from its place on the top shelf of the kitchen cupboard. He rubbed it boldly, and the genie appeared at once.

'What is your wish?' the genie asked in a voice of thunder.

'We want something to eat,' said Aladdin. 'And see to it that the food is set out on silver dishes.'

No longer so frightened at the idea of entertaining a hideous genie in her kitchen, Aladdin's mother rejoiced when he reappeared with a silver tray on which were set a dozen silver dishes filled with the most delicious food imaginable.

'Now we can sell the silver again,' his mother whispered, as Aladdin dismissed the genie. 'Our troubles are over!'

Soon after this Aladdin was walking through the town when he heard an order commanding the people to shut themselves in their houses and shops while the sultan's daughter passed along the streets.

Now Aladdin had heard stories of the princess's marvellous beauty. No man, he knew, was permitted to gaze upon her face. But his desire to see her was so great that he hid behind one of the shop doors. As she entered one of the buildings, attended by her slaves, Aladdin had a glimpse of her and was so dazzled and enchanted by her beauty that he fell instantly in love with her.

He rushed home in a daze and was unable to eat the meal his mother had prepared for him.

'I have fallen in love with the sultan's daughter,' he told his mother. 'I am determined to marry her.'

'You must be mad!' his mother cried in dismay. 'What are you saying? How can you imagine that the sultan will give you his only daughter in marriage?'

'I assure you I am not mad,' replied Aladdin. 'And remember I have the

slaves of the lamp and of the ring to help me.'

'What will you do to win the sultan's approval?' his mother asked, shaking her head. 'He will expect rich gifts.'

'I still have those strange fruits I brought back from the cave,' Aladdin reminded her. 'I know now they are not fruits but jewels of great value. All the precious stones in the world are not to be compared to them. Put them in your big porcelain dish and take them to the palace.'

At first his mother refused to do as her son requested. But Aladdin begged her with tears in his eyes to obey him. So the poor woman found herself agreeing to show the jewels to the sultan.

'Tell him these jewels are a gift from one who wishes to marry his daughter,' said Aladdin.

In fear and trembling the widow woman begged for admittance to the throne room when she went to the palace the next day. And when this was granted and the sultan had asked her to state her business, she stammered out the reason for her visit.

Then she took the china dish, which she had covered with a linen cloth, and set it down at the feet of the mighty sultan. His amazement and surprise, as she removed the cloth and he saw the glittering jewels, was so great that for a moment he could not find words to express his admiration for them.

'You say the jewels are a gift from your son,' he said at last. 'Never have I seen more beautiful stones! I am willing that he should marry the princess but only on one condition. He must send me forty trays made of gold, and filled with the same kind of jewels I see here. And these trays must be carried by black and white slaves, all magnificently dressed. Now go, woman, and give my answer to your son.'

The widow hurried from the palace and almost ran all the way home.

'Your idea of marrying the sultan's daughter has come to nothing,' she cried, as she burst into the kitchen where Aladdin was waiting for her. 'He has made an impossible request. How could you produce forty gold trays filled with jewels! – to say nothing of the black and white slaves!'

'Why if that is all he wants,' said Aladdin quietly, 'I see no problem in granting his request.'

And he went up to his room with the lamp and summoned the genie.

'I wish you to prepare forty gold trays, filled with priceless jewels, he commanded. And carried by black and white slaves, all splendidly robed.'

The genie bowed and disappeared and within a very short time, a train of slaves, both black and white, and bearing forty gold trays filled with jewels, pearls, diamonds, rubies and emeralds, appeared outside the house.

As soon as the wonderful procession, with Aladdin's old mother at its head, had begun to march to the palace, the streets became filled with people, anxious to catch a glimpse of it. And messengers ran on ahead to warn the sultan that he might expect it.

The great sultan was struck dumb with amazement when the slaves bearing their precious burdens entered the throne room, and before the widow woman had time to repeat her request, he was nodding and smiling.

At last he said, 'Yes, yes, go and tell your son I agree to give him my daughter in marriage.'

Full of joy, Aladdin's mother returned home with the good news, and Aladdin summoned his genie and asked him for robes which a prince would wear. He also commanded that a palace be built of the finest marble, with gold and silver walls.

Well, as you might imagine, such requests did not give the powerful genie any problems. After the marriage the beautiful princess went to live in Aladdin's palace, which lay within sight of the sultan's, and which was a thousand times grander than the one she had grown up in!

Now Aladdin was happy beyond his wildest dreams, and having no further need of the old lamp, he placed it on a high shelf in the cupboard of his own private room in the palace.

Some years passed and the fame of Aladdin and his palace spread to many parts of the world. News of the grand way Aladdin was now living came at last to the wicked magician who had returned to Africa. And when he heard the story of a poor boy's rise to fame and fortune, he guessed at once that Aladdin had escaped from the cave and made use of the lamp.

Filled with rage and envy the magician set off for China and on reaching the capital city he immediately bought a few dozen brand new copper lamps. Then, in the disguise of a street trader, he hurried off to the palace, knowing that Aladdin had left the day before on a hunting trip.

'New lamps for old!' he cried, as he stood outside the palace gates. 'Who will change their old lamps for new ones?'

It was not long before one of the princess's slaves heard the cry, and ran to her mistress, her eyes dancing with merriment.

'Just think, Madam,' she began. 'There is some fool out there wanting to give away splendid new lamps in exchange for old ones! The poor man must be out of his mind!'

'It is a chance too good to miss,' said another of the slaves. 'Prince Aladdin has a dirty old lamp in his room. I have often seen it. May we give the foolish trader the old lamp and surprise the prince with a beautiful new shiny copper one!'

'Why not!' exclaimed the princess. 'Take the old lamp and give it to the madman.'

So the deed was done and the princess, who had no idea of the true value of the old lamp, was delighted with her bargain.

The magician was delighted too. As soon as he had the lamp he threw away all his remaining copper lamps and hurried back to his lodgings. Then he rubbed it and summoned the genie.

'I am your slave,' said the genie. 'What would you have me do, master?'

'I command you to take the palace which you have built and all the people in it to Africa,' said the magician. 'I too must be taken there.'

Early the next morning when the sultan looked out of the window to admire his son-in-law's glittering palace, he saw nothing there. It had disappeared.

'This must be some wicked trick Aladdin has played on me,' he cried, thinking about his daughter and fearful for her safety.

And he sent his guards into the forest where Aladdin was hunting with orders that they should arrest him and bring him to the palace.

When Aladdin understood the reason for his arrest, he guessed almost at once that somehow the African magician had returned to the city and by some trick obtained the wonderful lamp.

But he said nothing of his thoughts to the heartbroken sultan.

'Give me forty days to restore your beloved daughter to you,' he begged. 'If I have not found her by then you may have my head on a silver plate.'

'Very well,' said the sultan. 'Forty days!'

As Aladdin left the palace on foot he remembered that he still had the ring and when he had reached a quiet place outside the city walls, he rubbed it, and the genie of the ring appeared before him.

'Show me where the palace I caused to be built now stands,' he said, as the genie bowed before him. 'And take me to it.'

The genie of the ring was not as powerful as the genie of the lamp, but Aladdin's wish was not too hard to obey. And in next to no time, Aladdin found himself in Africa and outside his own palace.

To his relief and joy, his lovely young wife was walking in the garden and he was able to make himself known to her. She was so happy to see her husband again that she wept, and then asked how she could help Aladdin to outwit the evil magician.

'I know, too late,' she added mournfully, 'the true value of the old lamp. He keeps it always about his person.'

'And I must find a way to get it back,' Aladdin whispered, lowering his voice as one of the magician's slaves passed close by. 'I know of a certain poison which I can obtain in the nearest town. Tonight I will give it to you, and when the magician asks you to dine with him you must accept his invitation graciously. He will be enchanted by your charming manners. Drop the poison into his wine secretly.'

The princess promised to try and be gracious to the magician, a man she feared and hated. Aladdin left her and hurried to the nearest town where he was able to purchase a quantity of powder drugs. These he then mixed together and as night fell hurried back to the palace garden where his young wife awaited him.

Shortly afterwards the magician returned home and was surprised and flattered to find the princess in a gracious, smiling mood, very different from the one he had been accustomed to.

'You must drink a goblet of wine with me,' she said at last.

And the magician vowed he would drink not only one but two goblets of wine with such a charming lady. While his attention was taken up with eating, the princess skilfully drugged the wine and handed him the fatal goblet. On drinking it, the evil magician collapsed and fell to the ground, dying in an instant.

Aladdin, as he heard his wife's cry, rushed into the room, and after making certain his enemy was dead, took the lamp from a hidden pocket in his robes, and rubbed it. The genie immediately appeared.

'Genie, I command you to take this palace and all in it, except this evil African magician, to the place where it stood before.'

The genie bowed and vanished, and the palace was once again transported to China.

Imagine the sultan's joy when, on looking out of his window, he saw that the magnificent marble palace had returned. Without waiting to change his robes he ran – in his nightgown and most gaudy bedroom slippers – out into the garden and across the square to the glittering palace, and was soon embracing his beloved daughter.

Then turning to Aladdin, he said, 'My son, forgive me for treating you harshly. It was only love for my daughter which put me in such a bitter mood. I declare now that when I am too old to reign – you shall be sultan in my place.'

So all ended happily for Aladdin and his lovely young princess. But though this story is as ancient as the hills, and has been told many thousands of times through the ages – not one of the story tellers has been able to say what happened to that wonderful lamp!

The Elf Hill

The Elf Hill was not very steep and not very high, but it was as old as the world itself! Some big lizards lived near the Elf Hill and they were always curious about what went on inside it.

'Something is going on in there', one of the big lizards announced with an air of importance, as his friends gathered round him early one morning. 'I couldn't sleep all night for the noise.'

'You may be right,' said another of the lizards. 'The earthworm says the elf girls have been learning new dances.'

132

'Their dancing and prancing most likely kept me awake,' said the first lizard. 'If they are learning new dances there must be a reason for putting themselves out in this way. I wonder if the Elf King is going to entertain strangers?'

Before any of his friends could make a reply, the Elf Hill opened and out tripped one of the old elf maids. She was housekeeper to the Elf King and knew all his business. The lizards hoped that she would stop and talk to them and tell them what was going on, but the old elf maid did not spare the lizards a glance. Instead she went straight to the tree where the raven sat, and the lizards followed her at a safe distance.

'You are invited to the Elf Hill for this evening,' said the King's housekeeper. 'There is going to be a great ball. The Elf King wants you to take the invitations to the guests he has chosen to invite. Go to the Merman and his daughters first.'

'Croak,' said the raven, which meant that he was pleased to oblige. And he flew off.

'So that's it!' exclaimed the largest of the lizards. 'There *is* going to be a great ball inside the hill. I expect the magicians will be there and lots of other important people.'

'We must watch out for the gnomes,' put in another lizard. 'I've heard tell of their powers, and the Elf King is sure to invite them.'

Now although the lizards would have given a year of their lives to be invited to the great ball – they were not. And so they had to content themselves with a view of who went in and out of the Elf Hill.

Inside the Hill itself the elf girls practised their dances, dancing with shawls woven of mist and moonshine, and looking very pretty. And in the underground kitchen all kinds of delicacies like frogs' legs and boiled seaweed and steamed mushrooms were being prepared.

In the ballroom itself, where the elf girls were practising their steps, the old Elf King sat on his throne polishing his seven crowns. He was attended by his daughters.

'Father,' said the youngest, 'isn't it time you told us who is coming to our great ball?'

'I suppose it is,' said the King. 'The guest of honour is my old friend, the Gnome of Norway. I have invited him to come and bring with him his two sons. The lads are on the look-out for suitable wives. It is my hope that they will find two among my daughters.'

'Will they really come – all the way from Norway?' asked the second daughter, who longed to be married. 'Are they rich?'

'The Gnome owns gold mines and rock castles and is very rich,' her father told her.

'Who else is coming?' asked the third daughter.

'Well, some of the local magicians and most likely the moor witch and anybody of importance in these parts,' said the old King. 'My housekeeper has seen to the invitations. I forget now . . .' and he yawned. 'Polishing all these crowns of mine is very tiring.'

As darkness fell the Gnome of Norway and his two sons arrived at Elf Hill and were at once admitted. The Elf King put on his best crown and bade them welcome, and his daughters smothered their gasps of surprise at the sight of the strangers, and the strange clothes they wore.

Being sea-folk, they were dressed in bear-skins and tall stout boots, and the young sons of the Gnome were tall and strong with rough manners. The Elf princesses were not certain in their own minds about the two young strangers but their father, the old merry Gnome of Norway, was quite different. He smiled at them and kissed their hands and began telling them marvellous stories of foaming waterfalls, and leaping salmon and vast forests.

At the end of his stories the elf dancers entertained all the guests with their graceful dancing. And when the display was over, the youngest of the Elf King's daughters was presented to the Gnome and his sons. She was so light and airy and so delicate that all the guests clapped their hands at the sight of her. But the Gnome of Norway shook his head.

'She will not make a good wife,' he whispered to the Elf King. 'No, no, she is not for us.'

The Elf King's second daughter appeared next. She told the old Gnome that she had been trained by the moor witch to cook and brew and was an excellent cook, and would make a very good housewife.

But the old Gnome winked an eye at his two sons and shook his head for he knew they could marry better housewives in Norway.

The Elf King's third daughter brought with her her golden harp. When she played upon it all who heard it must do what she told them to do. And this frightened the old Gnome's two strong young sons so much that they rushed out of the ballroom and out of the Elf Hill.

The lizards saw them leave the Hill and they told each other that something must be wrong for the two important guests to leave so early. But of course they did not know exactly what was wrong.

Now the Elf King had seven daughters in all – and the old Gnome interviewed them all in turn, but none met with his approval although they were all gifted in their own way.

At last came the seventh – she was not the youngest but the oldest and not nearly so pretty as her sisters.

'What can you do, my dear?' asked the Gnome.

And she took hold of one of his rough, lined hands and said, 'I can tell you a story – as many stories as you have fingers. . . .'

This made the old Gnome chuckle.

'Here are my fingers,' he cried, 'tell me a story for each.'

And the Elf King's daughter held him fast by the wrist and began telling him wonderful stories, one after the other, scarcely drawing breath between each. When she took hold of the finger on which he wore his wedding ring, he exclaimed, 'Stop, stop, I will have you as *my* wife! You are too good for either of my sons!'

At this the Elf King and the great company present in the ballroom clapped their hands loudly for they knew that the Gnome had lost his first wife twenty years before and that he was free to marry again.

Then the Gnome of Norway and the seventh daughter of the Elf King danced together, and the Gnome informed his future bride that she could tell him all her other stories after he had taken her back to Norway.

'We will spend the long, dark winters exchanging stories,' he whispered, as he led her round the ballroom.

Just then the two young men stamped into the ballroom, in their great tall boots, and asked what was going on.

'I have found you a new mother,' said the ancient Gnome with a merry twinkle in his eye. 'Now it is up to you to find yourselves suitable wives. . . .'

But the young men soon showed they had no love for any of the six remaining Elf princesses. They took off their coats and lay down on the table and were soon fast asleep.

'Never mind, old friend,' said the Gnome to the Elf King. 'I have taken one daughter off your hands.'

Just then the cock began to crow, and the elf housekeeper cried, 'Hark to the cock! It is time to bring the merrymaking to an end.'

The old Gnome shook his sons awake. The rest of the company fetched their cloaks and their sticks and the noble Elf King took off his best crown, which was very heavy to wear. He kissed his seventh daughter goodbye, and her sisters wept into handerkchiefs made out of moonshine.

Then the whole company of them trooped out of the Elf Hill which closed behind them.

All but one of the lizards had gone to sleep so they missed the wonderful procession that made its way into the forest and down to the sea. But the lizard who had stayed awake and saw the guests leave was delighted. Now he had a story to tell which would make him the centre of attraction for weeks to come.

The Magic Fishbone

There was once a king – and he was really a very handsome king – and a queen – and she was really a very lovely queen – and they had fifteen children, and were always having more.

Alicia was the eldest and she took care of all the children, who mostly did what they were told, even the baby, who was only seven months old.

To keep his large family in food and clothes the king went out every day to the office. His office was somewhere in the Government buildings, and he was quite important there.

One day the king was on his way to the office when he stopped at the fishmonger's to buy a pound and a half of salmon which the queen had asked him to send home.

'I'll see to that right away, sir,' said Mr Pickles, the fishmonger. 'Is there any other article I can send?'

But the king shook his head. He was feeling low in spirits that morning for it was some time before he could expect his wages and the children were growing so fast that they would soon all need new clothes.

As he walked along, his head bowed, an old lady came trotting up. She was dressed in shot-silk of the richest quality, and she smelt of dried lavender.

'King Watkins the First, I believe?' the old lady said.

'Watkins is my name,' replied the king.

'You are the father of the beautiful Princess Alicia, are you not?' asked the old lady.

The king nodded, and then said somewhat sadly, 'Yes, yes, and of fourteen other little darlings.'

'You are on your way to the office!' stated the old lady.

And the king suddenly realised that he must be talking to a fairy, for only a fairy would know where he was going.

'Yes,' said the old lady, who had read his thoughts. 'I am a fairy, a good one, in fact – the fairy Grandmarina. Now pay attention. When you eat your dinner tonight – see to it that the Princess Alicia shares some of the salmon you have just ordered.'

'I hadn't thought of doing that,' said the king. 'Alicia is only seventeen and has never eaten salmon – it might disagree with her.'

'Nonsense!' exclaimed the old lady. 'Just invite her to share your dinner, that's all. And after she has eaten the salmon I think you will find that she will leave a fishbone on her plate. Tell her to dry it, and rub it, and polish it until it shines like mother-of-pearl.'

'Why, why?' demanded the king, looking puzzled.

'The fishbone is a present from me,' said the old lady. 'Tell the beautiful Princess Alicia that the fishbone is a magic present which can only be used once. It will bring her, just once, whatever she wishes for. But she must make her wish at the right time. That is very important. Now don't forget to repeat my words when you get home.'

'I would like to know the reason' the king began, and got no further for the old lady flew into quite a passion of rage.

She stamped her foot on the ground and cried, 'Hoity, toity me! I am sick of grown-ups always wanting reasons for everything.'

At this the poor king apologised and the old lady quietened down and told him to be good and do as he was told. Then she vanished, and the king went on to the office. He stayed there all day until it was time to go home, and when he was back in the palace, he asked the Princess Alicia if she would sit down to dinner with the queen and himself.

Alicia was pleased to do this. She enjoyed the salmon very much, and when she had eaten her share, the king saw that she had left the fishbone on her plate.

'You must take care to dry the bone,' said he, 'and rub it, and polish it until it shines like mother-of-pearl. It is a magic present from a fairy called Grandmarina.'

'What a lovely present!' said Alicia. 'I'll do as you say, Papa.'

'It is very important that you use the magic fishbone for only one wish,' went on the king. 'And you must make your wish at the right time. That's all.'

Alicia dried the bone, and rubbed it, and polished it until it shone like mother-of-pearl. Then she put it in the pocket of her dress. But the next morning, the lovely queen was taken ill, and Alicia was kept very busy, taking care of her and the fourteen children, and so she did not have much time to think about her magic fishbone.

When the queen was feeling better and the Princess Alicia found she had an hour or so to herself, she hurried upstairs to tell her most particular best friend, who was a duchess, all about the magic fishbone.

Now most grown-ups would have said the duchess was no more than a doll, but Alicia knew better. And as Alicia knelt by her bed, where she lay fully dressed, the duchess winked an eye and put on a very serious expression, just as if she knew she was about to hear a very precious secret.

The princess told her all about the wonderful fishbone, and a few other things besides before hurrying downstairs again to take care of the queen, and her brothers and sisters.

At the end of the busiest day in her young life, Alicia went to say goodnight to her papa.

'Alicia,' said he, 'what has become of the magic fishbone?'

'It is in my pocket, Papa,' said Alicia.

'I thought you had lost it!'

'Oh, no, certainly not!'

'Or forgotten all about it!'

'I couldn't do that, Papa.'

The next day was even busier for the princess for the queen was still not well enough to come downstairs. It began with one of the young princes being bitten by a nasty, snapping little pug-dog. He rushed home in a terrible state, and the Princess Alicia bathed his wound and comforted him, and managed to stop the thirteen other princes and princesses screeching and yelling at the sight of the blood.

Then she dipped into the royal rag-bag, and with much snipping and cutting and making do, made a beautiful bandage out of some cotton and bound up the wound.

And when this was done, she saw the king looking at her as he stood by the door of the nursery.

'Alicia!'

'Yes, Papa.'

'What have you been doing?'

'Snipping, stitching, cutting and making do, Papa.'

'Where is the magic fishbone?'

'In my pocket, Papa.'

'I thought you had lost it!'

'Oh, no, Papa.'

'Or forgotten it!'

'No, indeed, Papa.'

After that, the princess ran to the duchess and told her all the difficult things that had happened that day, and then she told her about the magic fishbone all over again, and the duchess nodded her golden head and smiled all over her pink and white face.

The next day was even more difficult than the one before. The baby fell under the grate, and this gave him a swollen face and a black eye. This could never have happened on an ordinary day, but that very morning the cook had run off with a soldier, and Alicia was now in the kitchen with the baby and his thirteen brothers and sisters, peeling the vegetables for the broth which would help to make her mother strong again.

The baby set up a great roaring and weeping and so too did the others and Alicia felt like weeping herself. Instead she comforted the baby and, when the rest of the children were quieter, she set them on to making chefs' caps out of newspaper.

'Now you are all my cooks!' she told them. 'Who will take care of the

turnips? And who will take care of the potatoes?'

Soon there was peace in the old kitchen, and at the end of the morning, the broth was smelling beautiful, and the princes and princesses were all hungry and ready to eat it.

When the king came home and heard about the broth, he said,

'And what have you been doing, Alicia?'

'Cooking and making do, Papa.'

'What else have you been doing, Alicia?'

'Keeping the children happy, Papa.'

'Where is the magic fishbone, Alicia?'

'In my pocket, Papa.'

'I thought you had forgotten it!'

'Oh no, no indeed, Papa.'

Then the king sighed. He sighed so heavily that Alicia thought he might begin to weep. Instead he came right into the kitchen and sat down at the table.

'What is the matter?' she asked.

'I am dreadfully, dreadfully poor,' said he.

'Have you no money at all, Papa?'

'None, none at all,' replied King Watkins the First, with another heavy sigh.

'Is there no way you can get some?'

'There is no way,' said the king. 'I have tried and tried. My wages won't be paid for two months yet. I don't know what we can do.'

When the princess heard this, she put her hand into her pocket and brought out the magic fishbone.

'When we have tried very hard and in every way to put things right and they are still not going right, we have done our very, very best. Surely then we can ask for help!' said she, nodding her pretty head.

The Princess Alicia had discovered the secret of the magic fishbone all by herself! She knew, without any doubt at all, that this was the right moment to make her wish.

And she raised the magic fishbone, that had been dried and rubbed and polished until it shone like mother-of-pearl, to her lips and gave it a little kiss, and wished it was time for the king to receive his wages. Immediately, the king's salary came rattling down the chimney, and all the silver and gold coins bounced on to the floor.

But this was not all that happened – no, not by a long way. Immediately afterwards, the good fairy Grandmarina came riding in – in a carriage drawn by four peacocks with the fishmonger's young lad riding up behind. And he was splendidly dressed in silver and gold, with a cocked hat, and powdered hair. Down he jumped with his cocked hat in his hand and, with a great show of splendid manners, handed Grandmarina out, and there she stood in her rich shot-silk, and smelling of dried lavender.

As she fanned herself with a sparkling fan, she said, 'Alicia my dear, how do you do? I see you are pretty well. Come, give me a kiss.'

The Princess Alicia kissed the good fairy, and then Grandmarina turned to the king and asked him in quite a different voice, 'What about you? Are you being good?'

The king nodded and made her a shy bow.

'I suppose you know the reason why my god-daughter did not use the fishbone sooner?' she went on. 'She had to wait for the right time.'

Then the fairy Grandmarina waved her fan and the queen came in, quite cured of her illness, and all the princes and princesses came in, except the baby, fitted out from top to toe in new clothes.

After that, the fairy tapped Alicia with her fan, and the coarse apron and worn old dress she had worn all day, flew away and she appeared beautifully dressed, like a little bride, with a wreath of orange-flowers and a silver veil.

All at once the old kitchen dresser changed itself into a wardrobe, made of some very fine wood and decorated with gold leaf, and inside were rows and rows of dresses, all for Alicia, and all exactly her size.

Then the fairy asked to be introduced to the duchess, and Alicia brought her downstairs, and the two had a long private conversation, at the end of which, Grandmarina said, 'We are going in search of Prince Certainpersonio. The pleasure of your company is requested at church in half an hour precisely.'

So she and the Princess Alicia got into the carriage, and the fishmonger's boy handed in the duchess who sat by herself on the opposite seat, and then the boy put up the steps and got up behind, and the peacocks flew away with their tails spread.

Prince Certainpersonio was perhaps not all that Alicia would have looked for in a prince. But the fairy tapped him with her fan. And his face took on a fresh, newly-washed appearance, and his grubby suit changed to peach-bloom velvet. Then he was very handsome indeed?

The church was crowded with relatives and friends and the wedding ceremony was beautiful beyond words. The Princess Alicia's only bridesmaid, by request, was the duchess who remained in the pulpit supported by a cushion.

Afterwards there was a magnificent wedding feast at which the bride and the bridegroom cut the wedding-cake, which was decorated with white satin ribbons, and silver and white lilies.

Then the good fairy announced that in future the king would be paid every month instead of every four months which brought a smile to King Watkins' lips.

'As for you,' she said, turning to Alicia and Certainpersonio, 'you will have twenty children, and they will all be good and beautiful. They will all have curly hair, and they will never have the measles. . . .'

Then she asked Alicia to give her the fishbone.

'I must now make an end of it,' said she.

And, do you know, scarcely had she spoken than it flew off, and was almost at once swallowed by the little snapping pug-dog next door, who found it so unpleasant that he choked on it!

Mr Vinegar

Have you ever heard of Mr and Mrs Vinegar? They lived in a vinegar bottle, if you must know, and Mrs Vinegar kept it very neat and tidy because she was a very good housewife.

One day, when Mr Vinegar was away from home, Mrs Vinegar thought it would be a very good idea to spring clean. She was busily sweeping the walls when an unlucky thump of her broom brought down the whole house.

Down it came with a bang and a clatter and she was so upset that she rushed out to meet her husband.

146

When she came upon him, she cried, 'Mr Vinegar! Mr Vinegar! Something dreadful has happened. I have knocked the house down, and it is all in pieces!'

'It can't be helped, my dear,' said Mr Vinegar. 'The house is in ruins but I see we still have the door. Let us take that with us when we go out into the world to seek our fortune.'

So Mr Vinegar hoisted the door on to his back and when this was done, husband and wife set out to seek their fortune.

They walked all day and were very tired when night fell.

'We can't walk another step,' Mr Vinegar declared, looking around him. 'There is a deep forest over there to the left of us. Let us shelter there for the night.'

So they entered the deep forest and Mr Vinegar climbed one of the trees, dragging the door after him.

'We can sleep on our door,' he called down to Mrs Vinegar. 'Climb up, my dear. I have fixed the door among the branches.'

Soon Mr and Mrs Vinegar were stretched out on the door and fast asleep. But, some time, in the middle of the night, Mr Vinegar was wakened out of his sleep by the sound of voices beneath him.

They were rough, harsh voices and Mr Vinegar began to tremble as he listened.

One voice said, 'We'll share out the loot now. Here Lofty – here's five of the best for you. And Ginger – ten of the best for you. . . .'

As the thieves continued to share out their stolen money Mr Vinegar continued to tremble and shake. He shook so much that poor Mrs Vinegar was knocked sideways and had to support herself on a branch of the tree.

The door fell down and all but missed flattening the robbers. With yells of astonishment they got to their feet and fled in fright into the forest, whilst poor Mr Vinegar clung to the same branch that was supporting his wife.

You can just imagine how uncomfortable they were but neither of them dared move until it was broad daylight.

'They haven't come back!' Mr Vinegar ventured to whisper to Mrs Vinegar, as he peered downwards through the leafy branches. 'I'll risk going to see. . . .'

And he climbed down the tree. At the foot, lay his door and, when he lifted it up, there, to his surprise and delight, was a heap of golden guineas.

'Mrs Vinegar, come down, come down at once!' he cried. 'Our fortune is made. Come down at once, I tell you!'

Mrs Vinegar scrambled down the tree as fast as her long skirts would allow and, when she saw the money, she jumped high in the air with excitement.

'Now, my dear,' she said, 'do not rush madly into the next town and spend our newly found fortune on rubbish.'

'What do you have in mind, Mrs Vinegar?' asked Mr Vinegar.

'I know exactly what you must do,' said she. 'Take the forty guineas and go into the next town. . . .'

'Just what I had in mind,' put in Mr Vinegar.

'Yes, yes, but not to waste the money,' said Mrs Vinegar. 'You must go to the fair and buy a cow. The cow will give us milk and from its milk I can make butter and cheese.'

'We shall be better off than we have ever been!' cried Mr Vinegar, scooping up the golden guineas and putting them in his pockets. 'I'll set out for the fair at once.'

When Mr Vinegar arrived at the fair, he walked up and down until he spied a beautiful red cow.

'That's the cow for me,' he thought, and he went up to the man who was selling it, and asked if he could make an offer.

'You couldn't do better,' said the man. 'She's a fine milker and in every way a beautiful cow.'

'Just what I was thinking myself,' said Mr Vinegar. 'I'll give you forty guineas for her.'

The man seemed to hestitate, but this was only because he didn't want Mr Vinegar to think he was paying too much – which he was, of course!

'Well,' said he, at last. 'Seeing as how I feel I know you already, I'll take what you offer. The cow is yours!'

Highly delighted with his bargain, Mr Vinegar drove his cow up and down the market-place to show it off, and presently he saw a man playing the bagpipes.

A crowd of young people and children were listening to the player and, whenever he stopped, they filled his cap with coins and begged for more of his stirring music.

'The man is making a fortune,' thought Mr Vinegar, as he watched. 'Goodness – if I had those beautiful bagpipes I would be the happiest man alive, and the richest. . . .'

And he went up to the player and said, 'You are taking a great deal of money today. Is it the same every day?'

'Of course it is,' said the man.

'I'm not surprised to hear that,' said Mr Vinegar. 'You are playing a beautiful instrument. Would you care to take this red cow in exchange for your bagpipes?'

The man seemed to hesitate, but this was only because he didn't want Mr Vinegar to think he was offering too much – which he was, of course.

'Well,' said he, at last. 'Seeing as how I feel I know you already, I'll take the red cow. The bagpipes are yours!'

So Mr Vinegar took the bagpipes and the man took the beautiful red cow and drove it away out of the market-place.

'Now to make my fortune,' thought Mr Vinegar. And he began walking up and down and trying to play a tune on his beautiful bagpipes. But all he could get out of the bagpipes was a miserable wail. The crowd began to jeer and laugh, and the little boys pelted him with stones. Poor Mr Vinegar was forced to leave the market-place in a hurry.

When he got to the edge of the town his hands were so cold that he thought his fingers would fall off with frostbite. He couldn't put them in his pockets because he was carrying the bagpipes and so he didn't know what to do to get his hands warm.

Then he saw a man coming towards him wearing the most beautiful, warm gloves he had ever set eyes on.

'Oh, if only I had those gloves,' thought Mr Vinegar. 'I should be the happiest man alive.'

And he went up to the man and said, 'You have a fine pair of warm gloves on your hands.'

'They do keep my hands warm and cosy,' said the man. 'They're the best gloves I have.'

'I'm sure they are,' said Mr Vinegar. 'Would you give them to me?'

'I would,' said the man, and he didn't hesitate at all, 'if you would give me your bagpipes.'

'Done!' cried Mr Vinegar, and he gave the man his bagpipes, and put on the warm, cosy gloves.

He felt so much at peace with the world that he whistled a tune as he set off down the long road that led to the forest. But, oh dear, how long that road was. Presently Mr Vinegar's pace grew slower and slower. He grew so weary that he began to wonder if he would ever reach the forest and see Mrs Vinegar again.

As he dragged his feet along the hard, dusty road he saw, coming towards

him, a man with a good stout stick in his hand.

'Oh,' thought Mr Vinegar, 'if only I had that stick in my hand I would be the happiest man alive!'

When the man came up to him, Mr Vinegar cried, 'That's a splendid stick you are using to help you along the road!'

'It is indeed,' said the man. 'I never go for a walk without it.'

'I wish I had a stick like that,' said Mr Vinegar.

'It's yours for that pair of warm gloves you are wearing,' said the man quickly. 'What do you say?'

'Done!' cried Mr Vinegar. And he gave the man his warm gloves and took the stick in exchange.

With the help of the stick he could now walk much faster and so it wasn't long before the forest came in sight. But when he entered it and began walking through the trees, he heard his name being called. And, looking up, he saw a parrot perched on one of the branches.

'Mr Vinegar! Mr Vinegar!' squawked the parrot loudly. 'Foolish Mr Vinegar! What an idiot you are! You went to the fair and spent all your money on a cow. Then you changed the cow for bagpipes which you couldn't play. And no sooner did you have the bagpipes than you gave them away for a cheap pair of gloves. And when you had the gloves you changed them for a miserable stick. And now you have nothing to show for your forty guineas – nothing at all, except a stick which you could have cut for yourself in any hedge!'

The mocking voice of the parrot ended in harsh laughter. It laughed and laughed and laughed and Mr Vinegar, in a terrible rage, threw the stick at its head. The stick missed the parrot but was caught up in the branches of the tree and, seeing that he could not hope to shake it free, Mr Vinegar went on through the forest to where his wife was waiting for him.

When Mrs Vinegar heard his story and saw that he had come back to her without money, cow, bagpipes, gloves or stick, she shook him until his teeth rattled and his head nearly fell off which is, perhaps, no more than he deserved!

Komo's Sparrow

Long, long ago, maybe a thousand years ago, there lived a kindly old man called Komo. You might think Komo a strange name for an old man. But this old man lived in Japan, and so Komo was most likely a Japanese name.

Komo was poor and he lived in a tiny house in the mountains. But he had no wish for great wealth. He was content so long as he could count among his friends the birds in his garden. One bird he loved above all the others. This was his pet sparrow. The sparrow was so tame that it lived in his kitchen and fed out of his hand.

Now besides his pet sparrow, Komo had a wife. She was a fierce, bad-tempered old woman who seemed to be in a rage all day long, and she scolded Komo from morning to night.

It is true that she washed his clothes and cooked his rice and kept the house clean. But it is also true that she managed to make life very unhappy for the gentle old man.

Komo tried to keep out of her way as much as possible. But it wasn't easy to do this, and he never had enough money to go away for a holiday on his own or visit his friends on the other side of the mountain.

His greatest joy and comfort was his pet sparrow, and he would talk to the little brown bird for hours at a time, telling it how much he loved it. This made his wife furiously jealous, and she longed to be rid of her husband's pet.

Well, one day Komo left early in the morning to go into the mountains to search for firewood. He was glad to escape from the house, for his wife was in one of her bad tempers.

'Out of my way, you stupid bird,' the woman shouted at the sparrow, as soon as her husband was out of hearing. 'If I had my way I would drown you in one of my cooking pots.'

The sparrow flew on to the rim of her red rice bowl and looked at her with bright, knowing eyes. Then it put its head on one side as if daring her to catch it.

Komo's wife gave a cry of rage and attacked the bird with her twig broom. She managed to knock it off its perch, and the bird fell to the ground, quite badly hurt. Then the cruel woman picked it up, and hurled it out of the window.

'And don't come back,' she yelled after it, as it fluttered away with a feeble beating of its wings. 'I never want to see you again!'

Later that morning Komo came back with his bundles of firewood. He looked round the kitchen for his pet sparrow but could not see it.

'Where is the sparrow, wife?' he asked. 'It doesn't usually hide from me.'

'You'll never see it again,' said his wife, 'and a good thing too. I'm fed up listening to you talk to that bird. Anybody would think it was human!'

'You mean the sparrow is gone!' cried the old man, tears springing to his eyes. 'I can't believe it! What happened?'

'I chased it out of the house,' said his wife. 'Most likely it will be dead by now.'

The old man bowed his head in grief. He was too much afraid of his wife to shout angry words at her. But he knew that without his dear little pet his life would be miserable.

Weeks and months went by. Komo searched the garden each morning, hoping to see something of his little friend, but the sparrow did not appear and he made up his mind at last that the little bird must have died. Then, one morning, when he went up into the mountain to gather sticks he heard a familiar *chirp-chirp*. And looking up towards some bushes he spied his pet.

The old man was so delighted to see his sparrow again that he could not help going up to the bushes and bowing low – which was a very polite thing to do. And to his surprise the sparrow spoke to him.

'I am pleased to see you again, master,' said the sparrow.

'And I am pleased to see you again,' replied Komo.

'Would you honour our humble home with a visit?' went on the sparrow. 'My wife and family live not far from here.'

'You do me an honour when you invite me,' said Komo, with another low bow. 'Pray lead the way.'

The sparrow led the old man to a small clump of trees and there in one of the tallest was a simple but very pretty bamboo house.

'If you care to climb up,' the sparrow suggested, 'by means of the rope ladder you see hanging there, I will go on ahead and warn my wife that you are coming.'

So the old man clambered up the rope ladder and was presently seated in the pretty bamboo house, and enjoying a conversation with the sparrow's lady wife. Then his old friend brought him a tiny cup of green tea and introduced him to his young family of four.

'I hope you will stay with us for a few days,' said the sparrow at last, 'for I know my lady wife would treat you as an honoured guest.'

'Indeed I would,' said the sparrow's wife quickly. 'You were kind to my husband when he was a batchelor and had no one in the whole wide world to love – except yourself!' And she looked at Komo with great affection.

Komo hesitated but not for long. 'I will stay,' he cried. 'Only for a few days of course. But stay I will!'

The next few days passed so quickly that Komo could scarcely believe he had already spent a week with the sparrow family. It had been the happiest week of his life.

For one thing he had learnt all the secrets of the birds from his former pet, and for another he had been fed on the most surprising but delicious kinds of foods. He felt years younger when he said goodbye to the sparrow children

154

and then told them to go in search of their mother and father so that he could thank them again for all their kindness to him.

To his surprise, the lady sparrow, when she appeared, had too small wicker baskets with her.

'One of these is a parting gift to you,' she said, with an air of shyness. 'Please do not offend us by trying to refuse our gift. But you must say which one you want.' And she held out the baskets.

Now Komo was not a greedy man. He was just the opposite. And when he held the baskets in his hands he soon realised that one basket was much, much heavier than the other. So he decided at once to take the basket which felt the lightest.

'I will take the basket which is the least heavy,' he said quickly. 'You have given me so much pleasure just having me here as your guest that I would not care to choose the basket which must have a great many gifts in it.'

'Very well,' said the lady sparrow. 'You have made your choice. Keep the basket with the least in it and may your journey home be a safe one.'

Then the old man said his goodbyes all over again and his old friend accompanied him some of the way down the mountain.

'I wonder what my wife will say to me for having been away so long?' Komo asked himself, as he drew near to his house.

Well, his wife had plenty to say to him. She raged at him for the rest of that day and it was only when night fell and they sat down together to eat their bowls of rice that he was able to persuade her to listen to him.

'If only you will hold your tongue, wife,' he began, 'and listen to me I will tell of my strange adventure, and show you the present I was given by the sparrow family.'

At the mention of the word 'sparrow', the old woman was ready to explode all over again. But Komo, speaking quickly, gave her no chance. He told her of his meeting with his former pet and of his stay with the sparrows in their bamboo house.

'And what do you think?' he cried triumphantly. 'What do you think? After all their kindness to me they even gave me a present to bring back. The lady sparrow showed me two wicker baskets – one was heavy and one was light – and asked me to choose. . . .'

'I hope you chose the heavy one,' interrupted his wife.

'I chose the light one, of course,' said her husband. 'It would have been greedy to choose the heavy one.'

'Well, where is it? We might as well look inside and see what it holds,'

snapped the old woman. 'Twigs and stones – I expect.'

But when Komo fetched the basket and undid the clasp which held down the lid – there inside was a purse filled with gold and silver pieces, and some rubies and pearls – not many, but then each one of them would have kept the old man and his wife in food and clothes for a hundred years.

Komo stared down at the fortune in astonishment. Then grateful tears came into his eyes as he thought of how much he owed his little friend. But there were no tears of gratitude in his wife's eyes. She was beginning to frown angrily. And presently she shouted, 'Now do you see what a fool you were to choose the basket which weighed the least! Just think what you would have found in the heavy basket. Four times as many jewels I reckon. And maybe two purses filled with gold and silver!'

Komo blinked at his wife. Then he bowed his head sorrowfully. There was nothing he could ever do which would please her.

'Let us be grateful for our good fortune,' he said gently. 'We are rich now. We can do much good with our new wealth.'

'We could have been richer,' his wife screamed. 'I know what I'm going to do! I'm going up into the mountains to find that little sparrow. And if it asks me home I'll know how to behave!'

Well, the old man did his best to persuade his greedy wife to stay quietly at home. But she refused to listen to him and she managed to make life so hard for him that at last he agreed to tell her the exact spot where he had come upon the sparrow.

The very next day Komo's wife told him that she was going up the mountain to find the sparrow.

'I beg you to be content with the riches we already have,' Komo said.

But his wife simply shook her head and, as she set off, she called out over her shoulder that all the presents the sparrow gave her would belong to her.

'You are more than welcome to them, my dear,' the old man muttered to himself, as he watched her begin her climb up the mountain. 'I would gladly give away the gold and silver, the rubies and the pearls for just one year of peace.'

Meanwhile, the old woman was climbing up the mountainside as fast as she could and she did not allow herself a minute's rest until she came to the spot where Komo had come upon the sparrow.

To her delight the sparrow was there – perched on a low bush and chirping merrily.

'I must remember to treat him politely,' the woman told herself.

And she gave the sparrow a stiff little bow before saying, 'Komo has told me all about his meeting with you. I am anxious to meet your wife and family. Take me to your house, please.'

The sparrow did not look very happy when he heard this, and the woman thought that he was going to refuse her request. But, presently, he put his head on one side and told her to follow where he led.

'I know just where your bamboo house is,' said Komo's wife, 'so no tricks, if you please. Take me straight there.'

The sparrow flew off then and the woman followed and soon she saw the tall tree and the rope ladder which she knew she must climb if she were to enter the house.

Now the idea of climbing the ladder was not very appealing, and suddenly she saw a way of getting her present without even going to the bother of climbing the ladder.

'Tell your lady wife to come down here,' she said to the sparrow. 'We can talk just as easily at the foot of the tree and it will save me the long climb upwards.'

The sparrow nodded and flew up into his house. But when he came out of it again he was alone.

'Well, where is she?' demanded Komo's wife in a haughty way. 'Why doesn't she come out and greet me?'

'She is busy today,' said the sparrow. 'Perhaps another day. . . .'

'What manners!' exclaimed the old woman rudely. 'And I certainly don't mean to come back here another day. Just tell her to give me my present and I'll be off.'

The bird went back into the house and presently appeared with two wicker baskets. They were exactly the same as the one Komo had been given and the old woman's eyes glinted greedily.

'You must choose one,' said the sparrow. 'There is a heavy one and a light one. . . .'

'Let me have them in my hands!' cried Komo's wife. 'Let me see for myself which of the baskets is the heavier. I won't be cheated.'

And she took the baskets from the sparrow. There was no doubt about it – one was much heavier than the other.

'I'll take this one,' she said, scarcely hesitating. 'This is the heavy one!' And she thought to herself that the basket she now held would be packed with gold and silver and precious stones.

'Very well,' said the sparrow. 'May the basket bring you what you deserve!' And he flew up into his little bamboo house and shut the door.

The old woman was so pleased with the way she had obtained the basket that she ran down the steep mountain. When she arrived home she shouted to her husband to come at once and see how clever she had been.

Komo came quietly into the kitchen and watched as his wife, with trembling fingers, undid the clasp, and pushed back the lid of the basket.

Alas, there were no precious stones in the basket, no rubies or pearls, no purse filled with gold and silver pieces. A swarm of stinging bees flew out of the basket and flew at the greedy old woman, and a hissing snake rose out of the basket and coiled round her wrist.

Shrieking with fright and dismay Komo's wife rushed out of the house and into the mountains. Some say she escaped from the angry bees and the hissing snake and is now living somewhere in the valley, but no one really knows the truth of what happened to the disagreeable old woman. And it cannot truthfully be said that Komo missed her. He spent the sparrow's gifts on orphan children and led a happy and peaceful life for the rest of his days.

Are you wondering if he ever again met up with his former pet? Well, he never did come across the sparrow in the mountains, but his garden was always full of birds, and in time they came into his kitchen to keep him company – so it is no wonder he was happy, is it?

Percy's Tail

Everybody knows that little pigs have curly tails. Well, Percy didn't have a curly tail. He had a straight tail. When his mother saw that all her beautiful pink babies had curly tails except Percy, she was greatly upset.

'You're different from the others,' she said sadly. 'Your tail is straight and it should be curly. I don't know what to do with you. You'll be the laughing stock of the farmyard.'

'I don't mind being different,' Percy said boldly. 'I like being different. It means I'm not just a common, ordinary kind of pig. *They* might give me to a circus – then I would be famous.'

'*They* will do no such thing,' said his mother sharply. 'When *they* notice you have a straight tail, *they* are more likely to turn you into slices of bacon. Don't on any account let *them* see you, my son. . . .'

Now the idea of becoming bacon slices scared Percy so much that he made up his mind to put a curl in his tail as quickly as possible.

At first he thought wishing might do it. So that night, before he settled down to sleep, he crossed his legs and wished and wished and wished for a curly tail. But when morning came his tail was not curly; it didn't even have a tiny kink in it.

'Wishing is not going to work,' Percy told his eldest brother, who was the kindest to him. 'What do you think I should try next?'

'If I were you,' said his brother, 'I'd try sitting in the hot sun. There is nothing like heat to make things curl.'

So Percy waited until the afternoon when the sun was at its hottest. All the other animals were lying in the shade, but Percy went and stood beside the south wall of the old farmhouse. It was so hot there that he could scarcely breathe, and he longed for a drink of cool water. But he didn't move. He stood there for a whole hour without moving – and he felt his tail growing hotter and hotter. Soon it was so hot it was nearly scorching.

'It must be curly by now,' Percy told himself, at the end of the second hour. 'I expect it's full of curls and kinks!'

But when he ran off to the duck pond to look at himself in the water he saw that his tail was just as straight as it had ever been!

'The sun didn't make my tail curly,' Percy told his brother that night. 'What else do you think I can do?'

His brother thought for a while. Then he said, 'If I were you I would twist it round a stick!'

'I can't do that!' Percy cried. 'It would hurt – and besides, I can't do that all by myself.'

'I'll help you,' said his brother kindly. 'If you want a curly tail you must be ready to suffer.'

'I did suffer,' said Percy in a sad voice. 'I stood in the baking sun for two hours. I scorched my tail and it didn't curl – not even a tiny bit.'

'The stick is sure to work,' replied his brother confidently. 'As soon as it is dark, come to me in the old barn and I'll have the right kind of stick waiting for you.'

So that night Percy went to the old barn and his brother was waiting for

him with a piece of stick and some lengths of straw.

'Now stand still!' said he. 'Don't fidget while I wind your tail around the stick and then use this straw to keep it in position.'

'But I won't be able to sleep!' Percy cried. 'I'll have to stay awake all night!'

'Most likely you will,' said his brother. 'You are sure to suffer. But you will have to be ready to suffer if you want a curly tail.'

Percy stood very still as his brother wound his tail around the stick and then kept it in position with the straw.

'Ooh – that did hurt!' cried Percy, when the tail was fastened to the stick. 'Are you sure it will be curly in the morning?'

'Of course I am,' said his brother. 'Don't let mother see you. You'd better stay in the barn for the rest of the night.'

'But I can't lie down properly!' Percy squeaked. 'The stick is prodding me. . . .'

'You'll just have to keep standing,' said his brother. 'I'll go back to the others and you stay here.'

As soon as his brother had gone Percy tried to settle down for the night. But he could not find a way of sitting or lying that was comfortable, and he spent the long cold night standing up and feeling very miserable. But in the morning he felt so pleased with himself and so certain that after all the pain and discomfort his tail would be curly that he rushed outside to find his brother.

'Take the stick out!' he cried, as soon as he saw his brother. 'I know my tail is curly.'

His brother unfastened the straw and took away the stick.

'Well?' Percy demanded. 'Is it curly?'

'It's not quite so straight,' said his brother cautiously. 'Yes, I think you could say your tail had a curl in it.'

'I'll go down to the duck pond and see for myself!' cried Percy and he trotted off.

Now Percy's tail did have a kink and a curl in it – it wasn't much of a curl and it wasn't much of a kink – but no one could say now that the tail was absolutely straight.

Alas, long before Percy reached the duck pond – down came the rain.

It was such a heavy shower of rain that it soaked Percy's head and back and it soaked his tail. And, oh dear me, the kink and curl in his tail disappeared altogether!

When Percy looked at himself in the duck pond he saw that his tail was as straight as straight can be.

'It didn't work!' he cried in despair. 'All the pain and suffering was for nothing!' And tears rolled down his cheeks.

Just then, as he stood by the duck pond, the picture of misery, along came two of *them* from the big house, and a human voice shouted, 'Look, Ben, one of the old sow's piglets has been born with a straight tail. Well, I never!'

'Let's take him up to the house,' said the second voice. 'He's a bit of a laugh, isn't he?'

As soon as Percy felt himself being picked up he remembered his mother's words, *'They are more likely to turn you into slices of bacon'.*

A shiver of fear and panic ran right through his body with the speed of forked lightning. And, would you believe it, it curled his tail!

'That's odd,' said one of *them*, the one who was carrying him. 'I would have sworn the piglet's tail was straight when I picked him up.'

'So would I,' said the second voice, as the farmhouse came in sight. 'Oh, put him down, Ben – there's no point in showing him off. He's no different from the others.'

Percy trotted away gratefully. Something very nice had happened to him at last. His tail had a curl in it. It must have! Whatever *they* said was always true.

He went back to the duck pond. The rain had stopped, the sun was shining and as he looked at himself in the water he saw that his tail had a curl in it – a beautiful strong curl like a corkscrew – and he knew that it was there for ever and ever!

The Golden Touch

Once upon a time there lived a king called Midas who loved gold better than anything else in the whole world. This king had a pretty little daughter and if you had asked him if he loved his little daughter better than all the bars of gold and the glistening gold coins he kept in his strong box, he would have said, 'Yes, I love my little Marigold best of all.' Then he would have added quickly, 'But I love all the gold I keep in my cellar quite as well – after all, it will belong to her one day.'

As the years passed, King Midas spent more and more time in his cellar with his gold. He was, by now, the richest king in the world. But, somehow or other, he was not satisifed.

Even when his little Marigold persuaded him to walk with her in the palace gardens, his thoughts would turn to ways and means by which he could obtain more precious gold.

The beauty of the roses that grew in the garden gave him no pleasure at all. In fact he usually ended up wishing that he had a gold coin for every rose petal he saw lying there on the ground.

One day King Midas was enjoying himself in his cellar, which he secretly called his treasure-room, when he suddenly saw a shadow fall over the heaps of gold lying on the table. He looked up and there in the room was the figure of a stranger.

Now the king knew that he had carefully turned the key in the lock and that no ordinary man could have broken into his treasure-room.

'This must be a messenger from the gods,' he told himself, not in the least afraid. 'Or some wizard who has come to share my joy in all the gold I have stored here.'

The stranger's face wore a kindly smile as he looked down at the seated king. Then he said, 'You are a very rich man, Midas. You have more gold stored away here than the most high and mighty emperor.'

'Yes, yes, I have done well enough,' Midas answered, somewhat impatiently. 'But it has taken me my whole life to collect it. Now, if only I knew I was going to live to be a thousand – ah, then I would have time to satisfy my heart's desire.'

'And what is your heart's desire, Midas?' asked the stranger, with another smile. 'I would like to know!'

The king hesitated. He had a feeling that this stranger, with his kind smile, was present in the cellar for only one reason. And that reason – why, to grant him a wish!

'I must think carefully before I speak,' he told himself. 'I wonder if I should ask for a great tall mountain of gold, or perhaps several mountains of gold!'

Suddenly a wonderful idea came to him. He knew what he must ask for. It would be something which would put an end to all the trouble he had in collecting the bars of gold, and the chests of golden coins.

'I wish,' he said, speaking slowly, 'I wish that everything I touched changed to gold!'

The stranger's smile grew even broader at these words. And the room

166

seemed to gleam with a dazzling golden light.

'The Golden Touch!' cried he. 'The Golden Touch! Is that really what you wish for, Midas?'

'Yes, yes, that is what I wish,' breathed the king.

'Then your wish is granted,' said the stranger. 'Tomorrow at sunrise you will find you have the gift of "The Golden Touch".'

As he spoke, his face became a shining golden mask, and the king covered his eyes with hands that trembled. When next he dared look up the stranger had gone.

How slowly the rest of that day passed for King Midas! He could scarcely wait for the new day to come. In the night he slept in fits and starts and long before the sun had risen he was wide awake.

Impatient to test his wonderful gift, he stretched out a hand and touched the chair beside his bed. To his disappointment it did not turn to gold but stayed the same plain wood that it was made of.

'I must wait,' he told himself. 'The sun has not yet risen!'

And so he waited. He waited until the sun had risen and, lo and behold, the white sheet which he was clutching was all at once changed to a cloth of purest and brightest gold!

Midas jumped out of bed. He shook all over with excitement. He ran to the window and grasped the tassel to pull back the curtain and the tassel grew heavy in his hand. It had become a solid lump of gold. He ran back to the table and picked up a book. And that too was changed to gold.

'I have The Golden Touch!' he shouted, as he struggled into his clothes, and was overjoyed to find that he was dressed in a suit of gold cloth. Then he picked up his spectacles so that he might see himself all the more clearly in his new magnificent suit. Alas, they were quite useless for the glass was now plates of yellow metal.

'It is no matter,' said the king, addressing himself in the mirror. 'The golden spectacles will be worth a great deal of money.'

Now, King Midas could no longer bear to stay in his room. And though it was still too early to expect to find any of his servants up and about, he rushed out, and ran down the long stairs.

Through the windows he could see the garden with its beautiful roses and the idea came to him that now he had a way of making his roses worth a king's ransom.

So out into the garden he went, and taking the greatest pains, he moved from rose bush to rose bush, touching each delicate flower with careful fingers. Soon all the flowers and buds were changed to gold.

By this time King Midas was beginning to feel hungry, and in the best of spirits he hurried back to the palace. Almost before he sat down, he began to look forward to the ice creams and chocolate cream cakes which he usually ate for breakfast. But before he could take even a sip of his coffee, he heard the sound of bitter sobbing outside the door. And then his little daughter, Marigold, burst into the room.

She was crying as if her tender heart would break in two, and the king begged her to tell him the reason for her grief.

For answer Marigold took out of the deep pocket of her pretty apron one of the roses which Midas had so recently changed to gold.

'Look, father,' she sobbed. 'My beautiful flower, which was so pink and fresh yesterday, has turned into the ugliest flower I've ever seen. And all the other roses are just the same as this one. What can have happened to them? They are all this horrid yellow colour and they don't smell sweetly any more. . . .'

'Don't cry so, my child,' said the king, who did not like to tell his daughter that it was he who had brought about the change. 'Sit down and eat your bread and milk. That golden rose you have there is worth a fortune, and what's more – it will last hundreds of years. . . .'

'I don't care what it is worth!' Marigold cried. 'It has no smell and the hard petals prick my nose. I hate it. I hate all the roses in our garden!'

Midas shook his head as he picked up the coffee pot to pour himself a cup of coffee. He scarcely knew what to say for he truly loved his little daughter and it made him quite sad to see her so upset. Then he noticed that the metal pot had turned to gold, and a slight frown appeared on his face. He had The Golden Touch! He must get used to the fact that everything he touched would turn to gold. But now he must begin to think of new places to store all the treasures that would soon be filling his palace.

Still thinking deeply, he lifted the cup of coffee to his lips, and, sipping it, was astonished to find that the moment his lips touched the coffee it became liquid gold, and then hardened into a lump!

The king let out a gasp, and Marigold asked, 'What is the matter, father?'

'Nothing, nothing at all,' said the king. 'Eat your breakfast, child, and let me enjoy mine!'

Alas for the king's hopes of a good breakfast! The trout, as he began to eat it, turned into a gold fish, the eggs into balls of solid gold, as hard as marbles, and the freshly baked bread into sheets of gold metal.

'Now what am I going to do?' Midas asked himself desperately. 'Here is a delicious breakfast and I cannot eat any of it!'

And for the first time that day the king began to grow worried. He could not hope to live and enjoy his gold if he could not eat.

'Father, is anything wrong?' Marigold asked again, staring at her father's worried face. 'Where is the pretty trout you were about to eat? Why is it all yellow and hard? And why have so many things on the table turned yellow?'

'Hush, child, hush!' Midas exclaimed. Then he groaned, and muttered under his breath, 'What will become of me now?'

The little princess looked at her father with a puzzled frown on her pretty face. Then, longing to comfort him, she got up and went to him, throwing her arms about his knees. Suddenly, Midas knew that his daughter's love was worth a thousand times more to him than a vast treasure-house of gold, and he bent down to kiss her.

But the moment his lips touched her warm cheeks a change took place. His daughter's sweet rosy face became a glittering yellow colour. Her lovely brown hair changed to harsh yellow. Her whole body grew stiff and hard. Marigold was no longer a human child but a golden statue!

When the unhappy king looked down on the statue that now rested against his knee, he was stricken with grief. His merry, lovable little daughter was lost to him, and he could only wring his hands and wish that he was the poorest of men. He would have willingly given away every gold bar, every gold coin, just to see his daughter smile again.

As he sat there, miserably unhappy, the stranger who had come to him in the cellar, appeared suddenly by the door. The stranger was smiling, as he had smiled when Midas had first seen him, and the room seemed to be filled with a dazzling golden light.

'Well, my friend,' said the stranger, 'has my gift of The Golden Touch brought you the happiness your heart desired?'

Midas shook his head.

'I am the most miserable man on earth!' he replied.

'You surprise me,' said the stranger, still smiling.

'Gold is not everything after all!' Midas exclaimed. 'I have lost all that I truly loved. I have lost my dear little Marigold.'

'So you have made a discovery,' said the stranger. 'Yesterday, you thought of nothing but your gold. Today, you can only mourn the loss of your child!'

'That is true', said the king quietly. 'Gold means nothing to me now.'

'Would you choose the gift of the The Golden Touch, or one cup of clear cold water?' asked the stranger, after a pause.

'The water, the water!' cried Midas. 'Alas, I will not be able to drink again. . . .'

'And if you had to choose between the Golden Touch and a crust of bread,' went on the stranger, 'which would it be?'

'The crust of bread, surely!' cried Midas. 'It is worth all the gold in the world.'

'And if you had to choose between The Golden Touch and your own child?' asked the stranger.

'I would willingly give away every gold bar, every gold coin in my treasure-room if I could have my beloved child restored to me!'

'Then you are wiser than you were, King Midas,' said the stranger, no longer smiling. 'Now I will tell you what you must do to rid yourself of my gift. You must plunge into the river that flows past the bottom of your garden. When you go to the river take a pitcher with you and fill it with water.'

'Then all is not lost!' the king gasped, and he sprang to his feet, leaving the golden statue, which had once been his living child, propped against the chair. 'What else must I do?'

'If you are truly sincere and have now no further use for the gold upon which you once set such store,' said the stranger, 'all you have to do is to sprinkle the water over any object you may wish to change back to what it once was.' And with these words he vanished.

The king lost no time in snatching up a great stone pitcher, which of course, turned to gold at once, and carried it to the river. On reaching the river's bank, he plunged headlong in, without waiting to pull off his shoes.

The king choked and spluttered in the cold water but, as it crept up to his chin, he could only feel a deep thankfulness that the river was washing away the curse of The Golden Touch.

When he began dipping his pitcher into the water he saw it change from gold to earthenware and his heart sang with happiness. He scrambled up the bank and hurried back to the palace.

As he passed through the garden he splashed the roses with the river's clear water and saw, to his joy, the golden roses return to their former beauty. Now, he knew for certain that he had been set free from The Golden Touch, and the water in the pitcher was more precious to him than a mountain of solid gold.

The first thing he did on entering the palace was to sprinkle it, in handfuls, over the golden figure of his little daughter. And no sooner did it fall on her than the rosy colour came back to her cheeks. She began to sneeze and splutter, and she cried out in astonishment as she saw her father still throwing water over her.

'Father, father,' she cried, 'You have wet my pretty frock, and I only put it on this morning!'

The king, on hearing this, realised that his child had no memory of what had happened to her and, once again, he breathed a prayer of thankfulness. 'You must forgive your old father for his foolishness!' he cried, laughing merrily. 'Come, let us go out into the garden. Some of your roses are restored to their former beauty. But there are others waiting for a drink.'

Hand in hand, the two went out into the garden, and the king sprinkled all that remained of the water in the pitcher over the roses which were still a hard glittering gold.

Marigold clapped her hands as she saw her beloved roses bloom again, and the king told her that from now on they would spend much more time in the garden.

'I have no further interest in my gold,' he said. 'We shall have all the time in the world now to spend in each other's company.'

From that day onwards King Midas was the happiest of kings – though not the richest, for he gave away all his gold. And when he was quite old and Marigold was married and had children of her own, he would gather his grandchildren around him sometimes in the evenings, and tell them the wonderful story of a foolish king who thought the gift of The Golden Touch would bring him happiness.

The Flying Trunk

Once upon a time, there was a very rich man. He was so rich that he could have filled a whole room with gold and still had enough over to buy a castle.

Now this very rich man had only one son, and when he died he left all his money to him. Jack was sorry when his father died but he was very pleased to have so much money, and he began to spend it. He bought himself wonderful clothes, he ate huge expensive dinners, and he had parties every night of the week for his friends.

For a whole year Jack lived like a king. Every week he bought presents for

173

his friends and he had so many people wanting to shake him by the hand and tell him how clever and handsome he was that he had no time to himself.

Only one old friend, who had known him when he was a little boy, tried to stop him spending so much of his money.

'One day, Jack, you will wake up and find you are a poor man,' said this old friend. 'Then you won't have any friends!'

Well, one day Jack did wake up to find that he was a poor man. He had spent all his father's riches and all he had left was a few shillings, an old green dressing-gown and a pair of slippers.

'I'll borrow from some of my new friends,' Jack told himself cheerfully.

But when he tried to do this his false friends refused to help him. Only one of them sent him a present. This was an old trunk. Jack could not help laughing when he saw the battered old trunk.

'Why, it's big enough to hold me!' he cried aloud, and he climbed into it.

No sooner had he seated himself comfortably than the trunk rose in the air, and flew away with him up the chimney and over the clouds.

'What a wonderful trunk!' Jack told the birds, as he whizzed past them. 'All I did was to press the lock on it and away it went!'

Well, for a time Jack was thrilled with his adventure that he did not think about bringing the trunk down to earth. But by the end of the afternoon he was beginning to feel hungry, so he tried pressing the lock again and the trunk began to drift downwards.

It landed in a wood and Jack climbed out and covered it with dry leaves for he did not want anyone to find it. Then he set off to walk to the nearest town.

Now, it so happened, that Jack's trunk had landed him in a country called Turkey. This was very lucky for Jack, who was still wearing his old dressing-gown and his old slippers.

Can you guess why? Long, long ago the Turkish men wore robes which looked just like Jack's old dressing-gown. And they wore slippers on their bare feet which looked just like Jack's old slippers.

So, when Jack reached the town, no one took the slightest notice of him in his dressing-gown and slippers. In fact the people thought he was just another poor Turk.

As he wandered about the market-place he saw all kinds of stalls with strange, wonderful foods on them, and he thought Turkey must be a splendid country.

'Does your country have a king?' he asked one of the stallholders.

'We have a sultan to rule over us,' said the stallholder, looking surprised at being asked such a foolish question. 'And the sultan has a daughter, a beautiful princess. She is so beautiful that her father has shut her away in a great castle.'

'Why has he done that?' Jack asked.

'The sultan is afraid she will marry someone he does not approve of,' said the stallholder. 'He has forbidden her to receive any young men.'

Jack thanked the friendly stallholder and went back to the wood. He was very curious to see this beautiful princess and he knew just how to manage it. He climbed into his flying trunk and pressed the lock. It rose in the air like a big bird and carried him through the cloudless sky. It flew over the town and then it flew over the great castle and Jack pressed the lock a second time to make it land on the roof.

No sooner was he on the roof than he climbed down and entered the tower's topmost window. And there, fast asleep on the couch, was the most beautiful girl Jack had ever set eyes on. He watched her for a while; then bending over, he woke her up with a gentle kiss.

Goodness me – how frightened she was when she found a stranger in her room! But Jack, who had a merry smile, soon put all her fears at rest. He began telling her stories about the mountains and the caves and the sea and the princess listened eagerly. No other young man had ever told her such wonderful stories.

'Who are you? Where do you come from?' she asked shyly, when Jack could not think of more enchanting tales.

'You could say I came out of the sky,' said Jack.

'Then you must be some kind of angel!' cried the princess. 'Oh, please don't think of going away and leaving me here in this dull castle.'

'I do not want to leave you,' said Jack, who had by now fallen in love with the beautiful princess. 'I should like to marry you.'

'And I should very much like to marry you,' whispered the princess shyly. 'But we cannot be married until my father, the sultan, gives his permission.'

'I am not a rich man,' said Jack. And that was very true. 'But I can tell very wonderful stories. Does you father care for stories?'

'There is nothing he likes better than a good story,' cried the princess. 'And he admires the angels very much too. When he knows that you have come out of the sky and can tell stories he will let me marry you, I am sure.'

Jack hoped very much that the princess would prove to be right, and he

said, 'We must arrange a meeting.'

'He is coming to tea tomorrow,' said the princess. 'Come back tomorrow at four.' And she gave him a little bag with some gold pieces in it.

'I will be here without fail,' said Jack happily, and he bowed low to the beautiful princess before climbing out of the window on to the roof. Once there he climbed into his trunk, and pressed the lock.

The trunk flew away with him to the woods where he hid it once again under the dry leaves. Then he took the gold pieces the princess had given him and walked into the town to spend them.

He bought a new dressing-gown and a new pair of slippers. The dressing-gown was very splendid. It was made of some very rich material and embroidered all over with red and gold dragons. The slippers were sewn with pearls and turned up at the toes.

The next day, just as one of the clocks in the castle was striking four, Jack landed on the roof of the castle and climbed in through the window of the princess's room.

There, seated on a magnificent cushion, was the sultan, and Jack bowed deeply to him.

'High and mighty Sultan,' said he, 'I beg permission to marry your daughter.'

Now Jack looked very grand in his new dressing-gown and slippers and the sultan decided he must be some kind of powerful angel, for no ordinary man could fly through the sky. He thought for a moment, then he said, 'You may marry the princess on one condition. You must keep me amused for the time it takes to drink this Turkish coffee.'

Jack, of course, being invited to tea had expected to drink tea. But in the land of Turkey all the people drank Turkish coffee at teatime. This was a pity because he liked tea better than coffee. But he knew he must not upset the sultan by saying so.

'I will tell my story, oh high and mighty one,' said Jack who had already thought of one. 'If you are seated comfortably I will begin.'

And he began telling the sultan and the princess the story of the matches, who began life in a forest, and the old iron pot who liked talking about the days when she was young. The story was meant to finish when the boastful matches met their end in the hands of a little serving girl. But when Jack saw that the sultan was still sipping his Turkish coffee, he told the proud shopping basket's story – how she was lost in the market-place and found again, but she was so broken and battered when found that her grand days were over for ever, and she was no longer too proud to speak to her friends.

'She ended up in a corner of the kitchen,' said Jack, 'full of vegetables and was never again taken out for a walk.'

The sultan put down his coffee cup. 'I liked that story.' he cried. 'It was excellent. Never before have I heard such a fairy-tale.'

'Then I have your consent to marry the princess?' Jack asked.

'Certainly,' said the sultan. 'You may marry her on Monday.'

As soon as the town learnt about the wedding, all the people shouted 'Hurrah!' And all the lights were lit in the streets. The little boys ran about waving flags, and their mothers went into their kitchens and baked fancy cakes.

Jack flew back to the woods and, as before, buried his trunk under the dry leaves. Then he went back to the town and spent the last of his gold pieces on a box of fireworks – rockets and crackers.

'The fireworks will be my gift to the people of this town,' he told himself.

The night before his wedding with the princess, Jack climbed up the hill behind the castle and let off all his fireworks. The rockets shot up into the dark sky and made a brilliant display and so too did the firecrackers and the wheels.

In the streets below the people stared into the sky and gasped and cheered at the sparkling stars and streaks of dazzling light that appeared high above their heads.

Jack was so pleased with himself that he wondered if he should return to the forest that night. Then he remembered that he would need his trunk in the morning to fly up to the castle, so at last, he made his way slowly back to the spot where his flying trunk was buried under the leaves.

'Alas, what had become of it? It wasn't there – only a heap of ashes! A spark from one of his fireworks had set fire to the dry leaves and the fire had burnt not only the heap of leaves but the trunk as well! He could not fly any more and he could not go to his princess.

On her wedding day, the beautiful princess stood all day on the roof hoping to catch sight of her 'angel-man'. But, of course, he did not come, and the poor princess wept as if her heart would break and vowed she would never marry, but would wait for Jack for ever.

As for Jack – he, too, decided that his heart was broken. He wandered away from the woods and from the town, but the farther he got from them the more cheerful he began to feel!

'After all,' he told himself, 'I still have my new dressing-gown and my new slippers – and I can tell stories that are good enough to amuse a sultan!'

And the very next town he came to Jack set himself up as a Master Storyteller, and told his fairy-tales so well that he soon grew rich and famous. The only story he kept to himself was the story of the flying trunk and the beautiful princess who had given him her heart. And nobody can blame him for that!

The Goosegirl

There was once a queen who had a beautiful daughter who was dearer than all the world to her. The girl had hair of gold and eyes that were as blue as a summer sea.

Everybody liked the princess because she was always happy and cheerful, and always kind to those she met. However, there was someone who did not like the princess, and that was her maid. The maid was terribly jealous of her mistress. She was jealous of the beautiful clothes the princess wore and of the royal horse from the royal stables that she went out riding on. But what she most envied the princess for was that she never had to do anything. Everything was done for the princess – absolutely everything.

When the princess rose in the morning, it was her maid who filled her bath and perfumed the water. It was the maid who laid out the princess's clothes ready for her and sewed on any buttons that had come off. Every morning she combed the princess's tresses of gold, and when her hair shone like the rays of the sun it was the maid who set the coronet on her mistress's head.

'If only I were a princess,' the maid thought, 'then I wouldn't have to go on doing all this work.'

One day the queen decided that it was time to look for a husband for the princess. This was not at all easy, for the queen thought that even the best of young men could not be good enough for her lovely daughter. She sent for princes from all countries, near and far, to come to the court. But one prince would be too old, another too fat, and a third not really handsome enough. But at last she heard of a prince in a far-off land who she thought was a suitable young man for her daughter to marry, and she began to make the arrangements with the prince's father.

The day of the wedding was fixed and then the queen sent for her daugher to tell her the news. The queen could not help feeling rather sad. She would miss her dear daughter greatly when she had gone. Since the old king had died the two of them had become especially dear to each other.

'I have chosen a good husband for you,' the queen told the princess. 'He is the son of a mighty king and he lives a long way from here.'

The princess nodded. She had already guessed what was to happen, because in the last few days dozens of trunks had been packed with her trousseau and all her gold and jewels. She had also had to try on a lot of new dresses, which she found very boring. But now everything was ready. She was going to make a long journey and soon after that she was going to be a bride. That night the princess was so excited she could hardly sleep.

The next day the princess said goodbye to her mother.

'I have had my best horse saddled for you,' said the queen. 'He is called Falada and he will take you to the far country where the prince lives. He is a very special horse. I have also ordered your maid to travel with you for company and there is a horse ready for her too. Finally, I want to give you this handkerchief. You must always keep it on you, for it can help you if you are ever in trouble.'

The evening before, the queen had cut her finger so as to let three drops of her blood fall on to the silk handkerchief. Now, as she gave it to her daughter, she warned her once again, 'Remember, don't lose it!' Then they parted.

The princess set out on the long journey in cheerful spirits. The weather was fine and she was delighted by everything she saw, the flowers, the birds, the butterflies, the rabbits . . . for the princess was very fond of all living creatures.

The maid rode ahead of the princess and every now and then she turned and looked back with a discontented expression on her face.

'If I could wear those beautiful clothes that the princess has, then I would look much prettier than she does,' the girl thought to herself. 'And then there's her horse! I hate to see her riding on such a fine animal while I have to make do with this old nag. But I shall think of something. Just give me the chance and then we shall see . . .'

The princess had no idea that her maid was hatching evil plans. She was hot now from riding and she wanted something to drink. So in a friendly tone of voice she asked the maid, 'Would you please fill my gold cup with water from that stream over there? I'm so thirsty!'

'Fill it yourself,' the maid answered rudely and spitefully. 'I'm not working my fingers to the bone for you any more.'

'Whatever next?' the astonished princess thought to herself. But then she shrugged her shoulders. 'I expect she did not sleep very well last night. I'll get the water myself.'

When she went to mount her horse Falada again, the animal said:

> 'Your good heart is tender and dear,
> But wicked and wily your maid.
> But to me the future is clear –
> They'll all come to nothing,
> The terrible plans she has laid.'

'Have no fear, Falada,' said the princess. 'So long as I have the handkerchief my mother gave me, the maid can do me no harm.'

The princess mounted the horse and rode on, quite carefree again. She soon forgot what had happened with the maid.

About the middle of the day the princess was thirsty again. Without thinking she once again asked the maid, 'Would you please fetch me a cup of water?'

'I've told you once already that I'm not going to go on working my fingers to the bone for the likes of you.'

Without saying a word, the princess got down from her horse and ran to the stream. She bent over the water – and she dropped the handkerchief her mother had given her, and it quickly floated away down the stream! The princess had not noticed her loss, but the maid had.

'Just you wait a minute,' she said when the princess was about to mount her horse again. 'Take those clothes off. I want to wear them.'

Only then did the princess discover that she had lost the handkerchief, and now she was powerless.

'That's better!' said the maid when she had put on the princess's fine clothes. 'Now I'm going to take Falada and you can ride my horse.' But when he heard this, Falada began to buck and rear, kicking out with his hooves, so that the maid had to keep riding her old horse after all.

When they had reached the country where the prince lived, and had arrived at the royal court, the wicked maid acted as if she was the princess. The prince kissed her hand courteously, but he was very disappointed. He had hoped that his bride would be prettier than this girl in front of him. Could this be the lovely princess of whom his father had told him? The prince thought she looked very discontented and disagreeable.

'And tell me, who is that?' he asked, pointing to the real princess.

'Oh, that's my maid,' said the maid. 'I brought her with me to keep me company, but she annoys me now. I don't want her near me any more. Let her go and work in the kitchens or the stables.'

The prince looked at the fine delicate hands of the real princess and said, 'She certainly won't do for that kind of work. She would do better looking after the geese.'

So the princess had to take the geese to the meadow, with a rude boy called Kurt for company.

'I don't understand why you have to come with me,' said the boy. 'I can tend the geese quite all right by myself, and you don't look as if you have ever been a goosegirl before.'

The princess did not answer. She was thinking of how her maid would be sitting next to the prince at the banquet.

The next day, when she was walking with the geese past the royal stables, she heard her maid saying to the prince, 'That horse should be put down.' The maid was pointing to Falada.

'Why?' asked the prince in astonishment.

'Because he is a bad horse, wild and headstrong, and no one can really manage him,' answered the maid.

'Very well, then, he will be sent for slaughter,' the prince said.

Naturally the real princess was filled with sorrow when she heard that Falada was to be killed. 'If only I could go to the prince and tell him that I am the real princess,' she thought. But she dared not do this, for she was afraid he would not believe her; and in any case the maid had already threatened that she would have her put to death if she said anything. No, she could do nothing to save her horse. However, she would go to the slaughterhouse and ask for Falada's head to be put over the palace gates.

That evening, when the princess came home from the meadow, she saw the head of her horse over the gateway. She said, 'Oh, why have they done this to us and what will happen next?'

And the horse's head answered:

'Tender and dear is your good heart, princess,
Wicked and wily, princess, is your maid.
Let's hope that the plans she has cunningly laid,
Will soon be made plain and have no more success.'

Kurt, who was walking behind the princess, listened in astonishment to all this. What a strange girl this was! She talked to a horse's head – and the horse's head answered! It gave him the shivers.

The next morning exactly the same thing happened. The girl spoke to the horse's head and again the horse's head answered.

A little later, when they were in the meadow with the geese, the princess took of her hat to comb her hair.

How Kurt stared and stared! 'That hair looks just like gold,' he thought. He took a step closer. 'But it really is gold! I've never seen anything like this before! How I would like to have some of that hair!' Greedily he stretched out his hands to pull some out. But the princess already knew what the boy was planning to do and she immediately thought of a trick. She said:

'Will you help me, west wind,
Of all the winds the best?
Come and help me, west wind,
And drive away this pest.
Make him pant and make him puff,
Make him clutch the air –
For a little while will be enough
To let me comb my hair.'

When she had finished speaking, a gust of wind blew off Kurt's hat and dropped it down across the meadow. Kurt rushed off after his hat, but just when he was about to grab it, the wind blew it a little further away.

By the time Kurt had managed to get hold of his hat, the princess had finished combing her hair and she had put her hat back on. Kurt was out of breath from so much running. Angrily he glared at the princess.

'I'll get even with you tomorrow,' he growled. 'Just you wait!'

The next day, however, exactly the same thing happened. The princess sat down in the grass to comb her hair. Greedy as ever, Kurt came closer. The princess called to the wind to help her and the next moment Kurt was chasing after his hat again.

The boy decided it was time to go and tell the king about the extraordinary goosegirl who had been taken into his service. With his hat in his hand, he bowed deeply and told the king everything.

The king listened carefully, stroking his moustache.

'What you have just told me is indeed extraordinary,' the king said. 'And now you mention it, I don't think she looks like an ordinary girl either. I shall have to look into the matter.'

So the next day the king stole quietly after the goosegirl to the meadow. He heard how she talked to the horse's head. Then he watched and saw how a sudden gust of wind tore off Kurt's hat, and he saw too that the girl's hair was of purest gold.

'The boy is right,' the king murmured. 'This goosegirl must be someone quite out of the ordinary.'

At the end of the day the king sent for the goosegirl.

'Tell me girl,' said the king in a kindly voice. 'Who are you? Who are your parents and where do you come from?'

The goosegirl curtsied low and said, 'Sire, I would greatly like to answer your questions, but I cannot. It would cost me my life if I did. No living soul must know who I am and where I come from.' There were tears in the princess's eyes.

'I can see that you would dearly like to pour your heart out to someone,' said the king. 'If you cannot tell your story to a living soul, why not tell it to . . . to the fireplace? You could do that, couldn't you?'

So that was what the girl did. She was happy now that she could pour out the whole story, even to the fireplace. She told it that she was the real princess and that the bride who was dancing in the banqueting hall was an impostor. And there was a great deal more she told the fireplace. She did not know that the king had gone up to the roof-garden, where he could put his ear against the chimney and hear everything that the princess was saying down below.

When the king had heard everything he ran quickly downstairs again. He took the real princess by the arm and led her into the banqueting hall.

The maid uttered a cry of terror when she saw the real princess come in with the king. She fled from the palace and no one ever saw her again.

The prince was overjoyed when he saw his true bride. She was even more beautiful than he had imagined. A magnificent feast was held that evening. Huge dishes loaded with delicious food were brought in. And – after sending their happy news to the princess's mother, the bridal pair danced long into the night.

The Wind's Presents

Erik was a boy who liked baking. He made apple pies and jam tarts and sponge cakes and bread, and he was so good at it that his mother stopped baking altogether.

One morning Erik thought it would be nice to bake an apple pie. He got out his big mixing bowl and his rolling pin and then he reached up and lifted down the big flour container. But when he put the flour into his bowl there was a sudden whooshing noise and the North Wind came into the kitchen through the open window.

The North Wind was in a naughty mood that morning. It whooshed round the kitchen and blew all Erik's flour out of the window.

'Bother,' cried Erik. 'Now I'll have to start all over again!'

But no sooner had he put more flour into the bowl than the North Wind returned and did exactly the same thing again. It blew all Erik's flour through the open window.

'That's the second lot of flour you've taken, you wicked old North Wind!' he shouted. 'How do you expect me to get on with my baking if you keep playing games with me!'

For the third time Erik put more flour into his bowl. He stood over the bowl, determined to guard it against the wicked North Wind for there was no more flour left.

But the North Wind was too clever for him. It came back with a whoosh and a swirl and blew the last of Erik's flour out of the window.

'Now you've taken all my flour!' he cried in despair. 'You'll have to give it back to me!'

And he took off his big blue and white striped apron, washed his hands, and set off to catch the North Wind and make it give back the flour. It took Erik a long time to find the North Wind. He had to climb a high mountain and cross a deep valley. Then there was another valley to cross and another mountain to climb. But he came upon the North Wind at last among some craggy rocks.

'I'm pleased to have caught up with you, North Wind,' he said politely.

'What do you want?' asked the North Wind.

'I only want what is mine,' Eric said. 'You took my flour and I would like it back, please. We are poor, and flour costs money.'

'I cannot help you, boy,' said the North Wind. 'I haven't got your flour any more.'

'Then I don't know what my mother will do,' said Erik sadly. 'She won't be able to afford to buy more flour for some time.'

'Are you really so poor?' asked the North Wind, puffing and blowing.

'Oh yes,' said Erik. 'But we eat well because I am such a good baker.'

'I'll give you something instead of the flour,' said the North Wind, after a long silence. 'I'll give you a magic cloth. When you are hungry all you have to do is to spread it out before you and say, "Cloth, I would eat". You will never go hungry again for the cloth will give you all the food you want.'

'That sounds a very fair exchange,' Erik cried. 'I am grateful to you, North Wind. Now give me the cloth and I'll set out for home immediately.'

So the North Wind gave Erik the magic cloth and wished him the best of luck on his journey homewards.

Erik set off, carrying his cloth carefully, and though he hurried as much as he could down the mountainside and across the valley he still had another mountain to climb and another valley to cross before he was home.

'I shall have to stay the night at one of the inns in the valley,' he told himself, as darkness fell. And he made his way to a lonely inn he saw standing there on the edge of a wood.

The innkeeper said he might have a bed for the night and then enquired what he would like for his supper.

'I have only the price of a bed,' Erik told him. 'But I have no doubt I shall eat well, just the same.'

And he spread out his magic cloth on the table and said, 'Cloth, I would eat!'

No sooner had he spoken than plates of chicken and roast beef and a basket of fresh rolls appeared. And when he had eaten the chicken and the roast beef, there were pears and chocolate biscuits to be eaten, and a glass of the finest red wine to be drunk.

When he could eat no more, Erik folded up his magic cloth and took it to the little back room where he was to spend the night.

'Did you see that?' the innkeeper's wife whispered to her husband, when Erik had retired. 'Did you see all that wonderful food?'

'I saw it,' said her husband. 'If we had that magic cloth – think of the trouble and expense it would save us.'

'I must have it,' declared his wife, her eyes shining with greed and envy. 'I will have it. And I know just how to get it.'

And she went to her linen cupboard and looked out a plain white cloth which looked so much like Erik's magic cloth that no one could have told the difference.

'Here, take this cloth,' she said to her husband. 'Wait until the boy is asleep. Then go into his room and help yourself to his magic cloth. Leave this cloth of mine in its place and he will never know that he has been robbed.'

The innkeeper was pleased with his wife's clever plan, and he agreed at once to carry it out. He waited until he was certain Erik was sound asleep. Then he crept into his room and took the magic cloth leaving in its place the ordinary white cloth his wife had given him.

Early the next morning Erik awoke. He saw the white cloth lying on the chair beside his bed and he smiled to himself at the thought of his mother's surprise and pleasure when he told her of its powers.

'I won't even take time to ask it for my breakfast,' he told himself, as he dressed and went downstairs to pay the landlord for his room. 'If I hurry I'll be home in time for dinner.'

The wicked innkeeper rubbed his hands with delight when he saw Erik stride away down the road, and that morning he and his wife made good use of the magic cloth.

Meantime Erik was drawing closer and closer to his little cottage. When he saw his old mother in the garden he began to run and was soon in her arms.

'Don't cry so, mother,' he said. 'I know I've been away for a while, but I have something very wonderful to show you. It's a present from the North Wind. Come, let's go into the kitchen and I'll show you. . . .'

Once in the kitchen, Erik spread out the white cloth on the table and cried, 'Cloth, I would eat!'

Nothing happened. Once again he cried, 'Cloth, I would eat!' and still nothing happened!

'What nonsense is this?' cried his mother. 'Have you gone out of your mind, son?'

'The North Wind has played me false!' Erik exclaimed. 'He told me the cloth would always provide food. But it has only done so once. I will go back to North Wind and tell him the present is no good.'

And without stopping for a bite to eat Erik rushed from the house. At breakneck speed, he climbed the mountains and crossed the valleys and he made such good progress that he met up again with the North Wind before even the moon was out to light the sky.

'It's you again!' said the North Wind. 'What do you want this time?'

'The cloth you gave me in exchange for the flour is no use,' said Erik. 'It worked only once – and that was all. I would rather have my flour.'

'I haven't got the flour,' said the North Wind.

'I cannot go back and tell my poor mother that,' said Erik.

'I will give you something else,' said the North Wind. 'I will give you another present.'

'What will it be this time?' Erik asked.

'I will give you a donkey,' said the North Wind. 'Make no mistake. The donkey is no ordinary animal. Whenever it opens its mouth gold pieces will fall from it. The gold will buy all the food you need.'

190

'That is a fine present!' Erik exclaimed gratefully. 'Thank you, North Wind!'

As he spoke a small grey donkey appeared and Erik went up to it and led it away over the rocks and then down the mountainside. But though he went as fast as he could, he still had another mountain to climb and another valley to cross before he was home.

And once again he made his way to the lonely inn on the edge of the wood where he had stopped on his first visit to the North Wind.

At the sight of him the innkeeper looked frightened. But when Erik asked him for a bed for the night, he guessed that the boy did not suspect him of stealing the magic cloth.

'Can you pay for it?' the innkeeper's wife demanded, coming up.

'Oh yes,' Erik said, and turning to his little grey donkey, he cried, 'Donkey, let me have some gold!'

Immediately the donkey opened its mouth and out of it tumbled three gold pieces.

The innkeeper's eyes opened wide with astonishment at this, and he ushered Erik into the inn and sat him down at the table he kept for his most important guests.

'Order anything you fancy,' he said. 'I will see to that little donkey of yours and put it in our warmest stable.'

Erik ordered himself a splendid supper and after he had eaten went to bed. But, while he slept, the innkeeper crept out to the stables. It just so happened that he was the owner of a little grey donkey exactly like Erik's magic donkey!

It didn't take the innkeeper long to lead the magic donkey into a small shed at the back of the stables and to leave in its place his own ordinary little grey donkey.

'He won't know the difference,' the innkeeper told himself, as he ran back to his wife. 'This has been a good night's work!'

Early the next morning, Erik awoke, had a good breakfast, and was surprised to hear that the innkeeper did not wish him to pay for it.

'Your donkey is waiting for you,' said he. 'I hope you have enjoyed your stay here!'

'Very much indeed,' Erik replied. And he shook the innkeeper by the hand before setting out for home.

As before, his mother was in the garden when he drew near to their cottage, and he called out joyfully, 'Mother, mother, I have brought you something very special this time. We are not going to worry ever again about being poor.'

'All I see is a small grey donkey,' said his mother. 'There is nothing very special about a donkey!'

Erik smiled and cried, 'Donkey, let me have some gold!'

And immediately the donkey opened its mouth, but all that came out of it was a loud Hee-haw!

'What next?' cried Erik's mother. 'What kind of fool do you take me for, son? Did you expect to see gold pieces tumbling out of the donkey's mouth?'

Now that was exactly what Erik had expected to see, and he was so disappointed that he set out at once to visit the North Wind for the third time.

'So it's you again,' said the North Wind, when Erik stood before him, 'What do you want this time?'

'The donkey you gave me in exchange for the flour is no use,' said Erik. 'Its magic worked only once – and that was all. I would rather have my flour.'

'I haven't got the flour,' said the North Wind.

'I cannot go back and tell my poor mother that,' said Erik.

'Then I will give you something else,' said the North Wind. 'I will give you another present – but it will be the last.'

'What will it be this time?' Erik asked.

'Nothing more than an old club,' said the North Wind. 'But make no mistake – it is no ordinary club. If you tell it to strike your enemy it will do so and will not stop until you give the word of command.'

'I will take the club,' Erik said, 'though for the life of me I cannot think of any use I can put it to. But before I set out for home I would like to ask you two questions.'

'You may ask me two questions,' said the North Wind. 'But be quick about it.'

'The first is about the cloth,' Erik said. 'Was it really and truly magic?'

'It was,' said the North Wind.

'And the second is about the donkey,' Erik went on. 'Was it really and truly magic?'

'It was,' said the North Wind.

'I know now why their magic did not work when I got home,' Erik cried. 'Thank you, North Wind! The club will be useful after all!'

And he hurried away down the mountainside. This time he made straight

for the inn, and was once again welcomed by the innkeeper.

'That's a fine stout club you have there,' remarked the innkeeper, as he led the way into the parlour.

'I'm glad you approve of it,' said Erik, 'for you are going to feel the weight of it on your head and shoulders!'

And before the innkeeper could reply he told his magic club to beat the innkeeper and to keep on striking him until told to stop.

The club performed its task so well that soon the greedy innkeeper was shouting for mercy.

'My club will go on beating you until you give me back my magic cloth and my magic donkey!' Erik cried.

'Wife, wife,' shrieked the miserable innkeeper, 'give him his magic cloth and go out and fetch the magic donkey!'

As soon as Erik had his magic cloth and the magic donkey, he told the club to give up beating the innkeeper and it stopped instantly. Then he put the magic club in a sack so that he could carry it more easily, tied the magic cloth on to the donkey's back, and set out for home.

As soon as he was home, he spread out the cloth and invited his mother to sit down and enjoy the meal of her life. And when she had eaten as much as she could, he took her outside, and told the magic donkey to drop a few gold pieces at her feet.

And when the old lady had recovered from her surprise, he showed her the magic club which he said would help to protect them from thieves and robbers.

'If you go again to visit the North Wind,' said his mother at last. 'You could take him a home-made apple pie!'

But, of course, Erik never did go and visit the North Wind again. He had everything he needed to make him happy at home!

Babuska

Once, long ago, there was an old widow woman who lived in a hut in the middle of a forest. When winter came and the snow lay thick on the ground, Babuska, for that was her name, would huddle in front of her fire with only her cat and her dog to keep her company.

Well, one dark night, in the very middle of winter, she was suddenly alarmed by a loud knocking on her door.

'Who can it be?' she asked herself fearfully, as she went to answer the knock. 'What visitors could I possibly have on such a bitter night?'

Just imagine Bubuska's surprise when she saw three tall men standing there on her step. They were dressed in robes that glittered with gold thread and they were so stately and so noble of face that the poor old woman found herself dropping a curtsey as she asked what they wanted.

'Good woman,' said the tallest of the three, 'will you allow us to shelter here for a time? We have come a long way and have still a great distance to travel.'

'You are welcome to warm yourselves by the fire, noble sirs,' said Bubuska. 'And to the bread and meat I have in my larder – though it be but humble fare.'

When the strangers had made themselves at home in her poor hut, Babuska began asking them where they came from and where they were going.

'You speak and look like kings,' she said timidly. 'But kings do not travel as you are travelling. They are attended by many serving men. . . .'

'We are kings,' said one of the men gently. 'We have come from the East, and we are following a star.'

'Such a bright, shining star' said the second of the kings. 'It shines in the heavens and has led us this far. . . .'

'In time it will lead us to the King of Kings,' put in the third. 'To the Holy Babe. We bring him gifts for his birthday.'

'I have not heard about this shining star,' said Babuska. 'And I have not heard of a King of Kings being born or any talk of a Holy Child. But I am an old woman and news travels slowly in this part of the world.'

'You will see the star for yourself – perhaps,' said one of the three kings. 'And when it leads us to the Holy Child you will have the joy of seeing him. That is – if you will come with us. . . .'

'Oh, I should like very much to visit the King of Kings in your company!' cried Babuska, no longer feeling shy and timid. 'Yes, yes, I will come, and what's more, I will take the little king some presents. They won't be as grand as yours,' she added, 'but they will be gifts that will delight the heart of a child.'

'We shall soon be rested,' said the eldest of the kings, smiling down into the eager face of the old woman. 'Will you be ready to come with us almost at once?'

Babuska hesitated. It would not be easy to leave home without first making some preparations. She might be away a long time and there were certain things she must do.

So she said at last, 'The journey may take many weeks. I could not be ready to accommodate you, noble sirs, within the hour.'

'Then we shall go on ahead,' said another of the kings. 'The snow lies deep in the forest – you will be able to see our tracks and follow after us.'

'Yes, yes,' said Babuska, 'It will be no problem. My husband was a forester. I can read the forest signs. . . .'

Soon after this, the three kings took their leave, and Babuska began busying herself about the hut. First she tidied everything away, and washed and dried the spoons and bowls. Then she shook the dust out of her mats, and filled the water barrel. She found a small clean sack and filled it with little presents – some she had made already for her grandchildren in the big city, and some she had made just for fun to speed the long dark winter nights on their way. Finally she put on her warmest clothes and wrapped her big woollen shawl about her thin bent shoulders. Then she tied a long woollen scarf around her head and pulled on her mittens.

When she was satisfied that the little hut was as neat and tidy as she could make it, she went out and shut and locked the door. But she had only plodded a mile or so through the forest when she remembered that she had not left food for the cat and dog. So she turned back. And when her animals were fed and she had warned them that, from now on, they must hunt their own suppers, she thought she must see her faithful little donkey, and visit her bees.

'Yes, yes,' she muttered to herself, 'I certainly must tell the bees about my journey. They will surely want to know!'

When all these chores were completed to her satisfaction, she went to her bees and she told them about the three kings – the Wise Men as she called them now in her heart – and why it was so important that she should join them and take presents to the Holy Baby for his birthday.

Well, by the time Babuska was ready to set out again, it was snowing hard. And by the time she had reached the edge of the forest the tracks the three kings had left were impossible to find.

Of course Babuska did her very best to catch up with the wonderful strangers. But as she travelled from village to village it soon became clear to her that no one had seen them and no one had heard of the shining star or the Holy Child whose birthday was so very important and special!

'It can't be helped,' Babuska told herself at last. 'I'll just have to give my presents to other little children.' And this is what she did. Every poor, fatherless child she came across received a gift from out of her sack which,

mysteriously, never seemed to grow empty.

Well, the three kings did find the Holy Child and present him with their precious gifts. But, Babuska, in her own way, celebrated that first Christmas too, by making little children happy with the presents from her sack!

The Little Jackal

There was once a little jackal who loved to eat crabs for his dinner. Now the little jackal was in the habit of going down to the river to catch his crabs and when he had caught two or three big ones he would carry them back to his house in the jungle and eat them at his leisure.

Well, one morning, the little jackal went as usual to the river. He dipped one paw into the muddy water as he had done a hundred times before. But, when he tried to draw it back – why, it wouldn't come!

The jackal's bright eyes grew even brighter as he peered down through the mud and the reeds. Something had caught hold of his paw and that something, he suddenly realized, was a huge ugly old crocodile! In another minute he would be pulled into the water and inside the scaly monster!

But instead of letting out a squeal of fright, the little jackal began to laugh.

'Ho-ho, ha-ha!' he chortled. 'What a joke!' The old croc thinks he has found something tasty for his supper and all he has fastened on is a nasty tough tree root!'

It was lucky for the jackal that the old crocodile was both stupid and lazy. He should have raised himself out of the water to see what he had caught. Instead he heard the jackal's words and he opened his big jaws just long enough for the jackal to pull his leg free.

'Now that is most obliging of you, Mister Crocodile!' laughed the jackal. 'I am more than delighted to be free. Good hunting!'

And with another loud laugh, he ran off.

The crocodile was furious at the way he had been tricked. He lashed the water with his powerful tail and he vowed, by all the scales on his huge body, that he would catch the little jackal and teach him a lesson he wouldn't forget in a hurry.

Of course the jackal was pleased that he had escaped so easily from his old enemy. But he was also worried. It would be very dangerous to fish for crabs in the river as long as the fierce crocodile was living there.

'I'll just have to manage without my crabs,' he told himself sadly. 'I'll have to eat other things.'

For two or three days the little jackal managed to stop thinking about crabs. But then, towards the end of the week, when he found he was losing his appetite and growing quite thin, he set out for the river once again.

'Perhaps the old croc has moved on,' he told himself hopefully, as he approached the water's edge. 'But I had better make sure that he is nowhere around. . . .'

And in a loud voice he remarked, 'Well, I can't seem to find any crabs close to the bank. What a nuisance! I shall have to wade into the water. . . .'

As he spoke he watched the river carefully, and he was almost certain that he glimpsed an ugly snout among the water lilies.

'Don't bother swimming towards the bank, dear Mister Crocodile!' the jackal shouted. 'I've seen you. You won't catch me today. I'd rather go without my crabs than end up inside you!'

And away he ran.

The little jackal waited another week before he ventured down to the river again. He had been forced to eat all kinds of food which he didn't like, and his longing for a tasty crab was as strong as ever.

Before he dipped his paw into the water, he scanned the reeds and the water lilies. There was no sign of his ancient enemy and yet he still felt nervous and uncertain.

At last he called out, 'Stop playing hide-and-seek, Mister Crocodile. I can see you!'

No ripple disturbed the water, and the jackal begain to believe that the fierce crocodile had gone. But his natural cunning would not let him take any risks.

'I don't see any bubbles on the water,' he said, as if speaking to himself. 'It's no use fishing for crabs until I see the bubbles. They will tell me where to look for the big ones. . . .'

Now the old crocodile had not left this part of the river. He was hiding on the muddy bed, and he was absolutely certain that this would be the day when he would catch the impudent jackal.

When he heard that the jackal was waiting to see bubbles on the surface of the water, he thought, 'All I have to do now is to blow some bubbles. Then he is mine. . . .'

How that little jackal laughed when, all at once, he saw gigantic bubbles appear.

'So you are still there, dear Mister Crocodile!' he cried. 'I can't see you but those huge bubbles tell me you are somewhere on the river bed. Thank you so much for advertising your presence!'

And away he ran.

The crocodile was so furious at being discovered that he hauled himself out of the river and began following the little jackal. But crocodiles are slow and clumsy on land, and the sun was very hot as it beat down on his great scaly body. He was not used to taking long walks in the jungle, and soon he began to grow very tired and cross.

For a time he managed to keep the little jackal in sight, and then a long, long way ahead, he saw the jackal disappear into a garden where wild fig trees were growing.

'I wonder why he is not going straight home?' the crocodile asked himself. 'What's he doing in that garden?'

Well, the little jackal had not meant to go straight home. He had suddenly remembered the garden of wild fig trees. Next to crabs, the jackal enjoyed wild figs and he was by now so hungry that he determined to fill himself up with figs.

The crocodile moved slowly along towards the garden. He arrived just in time to see the jackal leaving, and he thought that most likely the jackal was now going to feed on figs instead of crabs.

'He'll be back tonight for his supper,' the crocodile told himself, and he grinned a huge toothy grin. 'He won't expect to find me waiting for him!'

And he went to the largest of the fig trees and covered himself all over with the purple figs. This was hard work and by the time he was satisfied that not a single one of his scales was showing the crocodile was very weary. Soon he fell asleep.

When he awoke it was nearly dark and there was the little jackal coming towards the fig tree! The crocodile lay very still, scarcely daring to breathe, and the jackal came closer and closer.

But when he was almost up to the fig tree, he stopped. The huge pile of figs under the tree had not been there in the morning. Somehow its shape reminded him of his old enemy!

'Well, now,' said he, in a loud voice, 'I must remember to choose only the fat ripe figs. I'll choose the ones which are blown about by the wind. . . .'

'And so you shall!' thought the old crocodile. 'I can match my cunning with yours. . . .'

And he humped himself up so that the biggest and fattest of the figs rolled off his back and flew in all directions. But in doing this some of his scales became visible.

Quick as a flash the little jackal sprang away from the tree.

'How kind of you to show yourself, dear Mister Crocodile,' he said quietly, and from a safe distance from the fierce jaws. 'I hope you find it comfortable under that tree!'

And away he ran.

Beside himself with rage, the crocodile shook himself free of the rest of the figs and went off in hot pursuit of the jackal. The jackal ran like the wind. He did not make for his house but went on to visit some of his friends so that he could boast to them about getting the better of the old crocodile.

When the crocodile saw him run past his little house he had another brilliant idea. He would go into the house and wait for the jackal. This time his plan would work!

'Yes, yes, I'll have him for my supper after all,' he told himself, as he dragged his heavy body up the garden path.

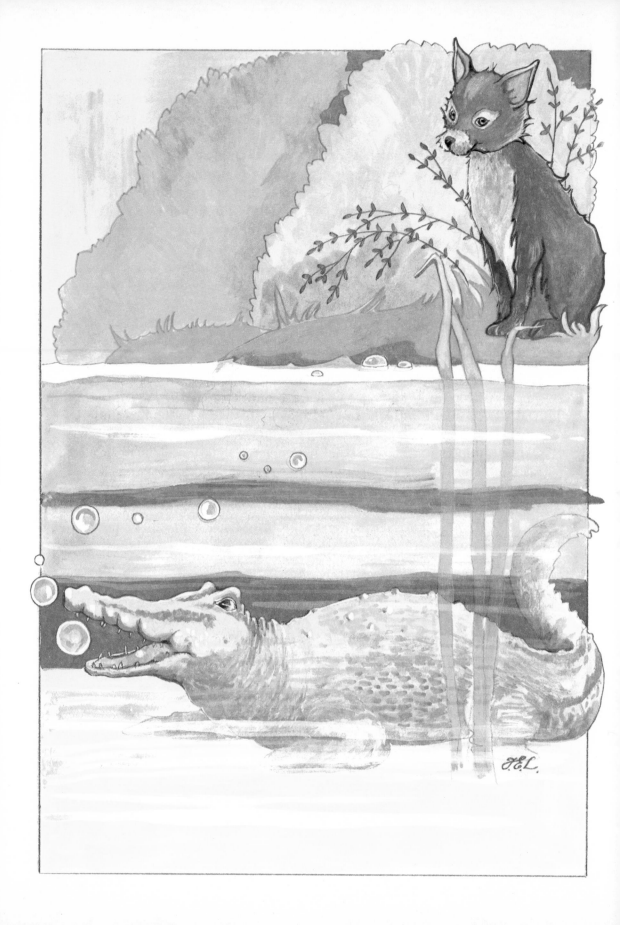

To his relief, the door was standing open. The only problem was getting through the narrow opening. The crocodile made himself as small as possible and just managed to squeeze through, but in doing so he broke down part of the door.

Some time later, the little jackal came dancing home. He was in high spirits. His friends had listened to him most respectfully, and he had enjoyed boasting about his cunning. Now he was ready for bed.

But as he ran up the garden path he saw how disturbed the ground was – as if a great heavy body had been dragging itself over the soft brown earth! Then he saw that the door of his little house was all crushed and broken.

'That's strange,' he thought. 'I wonder who my visitor could have been? I wonder if he is still there – waiting for me inside?'

And he called out, 'Little house, little house, why don't you speak to me? You always greet me when I come home. Why don't you say hello?'

Inside the little house, the crocodile thought, 'He won't come in unless the house speaks to him. I'd better say something.' And in a voice which he made as small and squeaky as possible, he said, 'Hello, little jackal. Hello!'

Now the sound of the crocodile's voice coming from inside his own dear house really did scare the little jackal.

'If I don't make an end of him he will catch me one of these days,' he decided. 'I'll have to finish him off.'

But aloud he said, 'Thank you for speaking to me, little house. I will be with your in a moment. I'm just going to get some logs for the fire. . . .'

Then he went round the garden and he began gathering firewood. He worked hard until he had a heap as high as a fig tree and when he was satisfied that he had enough, he piled it all around the house. Then he set fire to it!

The fire burnt merrily and the smoke blew up into the sky in thick clouds, and inside the house the crocodile was well and truly roasted.

'Well, if he isn't smoked by now he is certain to be roasted,' said the little jackal. And though he was sad that he had lost his little house, he was thankful that he had managed to put an end to the wicked old crocodile once and for all!

The Impossible Tasks

King Pompone the Second of Sardonia ruled his country wisely and well. He lived happy and contented in his castle. What was more, his daughter was the most beautiful princess in the world. She was not only beautiful, but a sensible girl too. That was why she did not feel much like leaving the castle to marry any of the foolish, conceited young knights who were always coming to ask for her hand.

The princess and her father always did their best to refuse these knights as pleasantly and politely as they could, which they managed to do quite well. But lately there had been so many of these offers of marriage that the king and the princess had to spend nearly the whole of every day graciously welcoming suitors – and just as graciously sending the young men away empty-handed.

So the king and the princess decided that they would have to think of something to do about it. 'I've got an idea!' said the king to the princess one evening when they were walking in the castle gardens. 'What would you say if we set a few tasks that these young men would have to perform before they could ask to marry you. But these tasks would be so difficult no one would complete them!'

'Oh yes, father dear, that's a marvellous idea!' said the princess. 'You really are wonderfully clever. You always know just what to do. Let's think up some very, very difficult things for them.'

By the end of the evening they had planned so many funny and impossible things for the young men to do that when the princess thought about them she was overcome with mirth and just laughed and laughed. The king also laughed – so much that he had to hold on to his crown to stop it rolling off his head.

'Daughter', he said at last, 'it's time to go to bed. I will have a proclamation made throughout the land, telling everyone of the conditions the young knights must fulfil before they can ask your hand in marriage. However, I think the man who can succeed in these tasks hasn't been born yet.'

Now that he had made up his mind what to do, the king wasted no time. The very next morning the royal heralds rode out of the castle to tell all the people what the king had decided. In every corner of the kingdom they proclaimed:

> In the name of King Pompone the Second, by the grace of God King of Sardonia, Marquis of Umbria, Duke of Lambadia, Count of Belmondo. Let it be known that any young man who wishes to ask for the hand of the princess in marriage must first perform certain tasks set by our Gracious Sovereign.

A number of young knights decided to go and try their luck. They put on their best armour, and splendid harnesses on their horses. They were careful to take their squires and their knightly banners too, for they wanted to make a good impression on the king and his daughter.

Now there was a young goatherd, called Aurelio, who had also heard the proclamation. He told his friends that he too wanted to try his luck.

'Ha! Ha!' they laughed. 'A goatherd who wants to marry a princess! They won't even let you in! And if they do, watch out that they don't throw you in a dungeon!'

But Aurelio took no notice of his teasing friends. He went home, put some food into a big blue handkerchief and tied it to a stick. Then he said good-bye to his mother and father. When he had closed the door behind him he stood still for a moment, sighed deeply, and began to walk away. Just once he turned to look back at the narrow winding street where he lived. Then he marched out of the village.

The goatherd walked and walked and walked until at last he came to the royal castle. There he was stopped by two guards at the gate, who barred his way with their long halberds. Aurelio, however, was not going to let himself be sent away as easily as that, and after a lot of argument the soldiers let him pass into the castle. A footman led him into a big hall. There stood twenty young knights, each one eyeing his rivals rather nervously. In the middle of the hall sat the king on his throne. His daughter, the beautiful princess, stood beside him.

'What on earth is that village boy doing here?' asked the princess, turning to her father. 'Surely he doesn't think I would ever marry a poor country bumpkin like him?'

'Now, my dear,' whispered the king, 'don't upset yourself so.' Then to the young men he said, 'The princess and I would like you to take part in a rather – er – unusual trial contest. Whoever is successful can go on to the special tasks we have set for you.' And the king suddenly burst into a strange little rhyme, which he had made up the day before:

> We're sure you'll do your valiant best,
> Young sirs, to pass this simple test.
> It's not a joust with lance and shield,
> It's just a game out in the field,
> To prove your speed of hand and eye.
> Now, sirs, are you ready to try?

'Yes!' replied all the young men together. 'We are ready!' The whole company then went outside. The king walked in front. When they reached a small meadow, the king called out:

'This is the test. My daughter, the princess, is going to throw an apple in the air. You must try to catch it. Whoever catches the apple more than ten times can go on to try his luck at the special tasks.'

The king gave a sign and the princess threw an apple in the air. But she threw it up in such a way that no one could catch it. No one, that is, except Aurelio, for he could run better than the best of them. Besides, he was not hampered by a suit of armour or big heavy boots. Every time the princess threw the apple in the air, no matter in what direction, Aurelio caught it so deftly that it looked as if he had done nothing else all his life except dart about after apples.

As the contest went on the knights became more and more tired, until in the end they were all sprawled exhausted and out of breath in the grass. When the goatherd had caught the apple for the eleventh time the king solemnly announced that only the young man called Aurelio had been successful.

When the young knights, all looking sheepish and rather ashamed of themselves, had left, the king said to Aurelio, 'I will now tell you what your first task is to be. Tomorrow morning you will take my hares, all one hundred of them, to the meadow to graze on the grass. You must watch them the whole day and then bring them all back in the evening. But when evening comes not one of the hares must be missing!'

Aurelio looked at the king in shock and amazement. He knew what giddy creatures hares were. This was an impossible task and he would never succeed! Dejected, he walked out of the castle and into the hills. When he felt hungry he sat down and ate a piece of his bread. He sat there deep in thought, staring straight in front of him. That was why he did not notice that a little old woman had come and sat down beside him.

'Have pity on a poor old woman and give me a piece of your bread,' she said.

'Good lady,' Aurelio answered. 'I am perhaps even poorer than you are, but I can always spare a piece of bread.'

'Thank you very much. You are a good boy. But why do you look so sad and gloomy?'

'Oh,' said Aurelio, 'nobody can help me.'

'Don't you be too quick to say that sort of thing,' replied the little old woman. 'Tell me first what the trouble is.' Aurelio told her about the difficult task the king had set him to perform. The little old woman listened attentively. Then she took out a flute.

'Be careful with it now,' she said as she put the flute in Aurelio's hand. 'You'll find it comes in handy.'

Before Aurelio knew what was happening, the old woman had disappeared. He went and lay down on a mossy bank under a big tree and soon he was fast asleep. He did not wake up till the next day, when the first rays of the morning sun touched his face. He washed himself in a clear stream and hurried to the castle.

'Your majesty, where are the hares?' Aurelio demanded when he stood before the king. 'I will take them to the meadow!'

'Carry on,' the king said. 'Remember, though, that you must bring them all back. If even one is lost, then you have failed!'

The king gave the order and the doors of the barn were opened. In a flash all the hares ran out and dashed and darted about in all directions. With a sigh, Aurelio walked to the little meadow that lay behind the castle. By this time there was not one of the hares to be seen anywhere.

Suddenly he remembered the flute the little old woman had given him the day before. He took it out and began to play on it. In a moment all the hares re-appeared and came scampering towards him. They gathered round him and contentedly began to eat the grass. Aurelio was amazed!

By chance, one of the king's councillors passed by. He went straight to the king and told him that all the hares were still there, and the king told the princess. She thought this was dreadful news and with her father she worked out a plan. She disguised herself as a farm girl, picked up a basket and walked to the meadow.

'Just look, a hare-herd!' the princess said when she saw Aurelio sitting there.

'Just look, a pretty farm girl!' Aurelio said. He had recognized the princess straight away, but he pretended not to know who she was.

'Can I buy one of your hares?' the princess asked.

'Oh no, that's impossible!' said Aurelio. 'But you can earn one.'

'How can I do that?'

'Oh, that's easy. All you have to do is give me a kiss.'

'How dare you!' said the princess indignantly, and walked away. But in a little while she came back to the meadow, because she did not want the goatherd to complete his task. She gave Aurelio a kiss and he gave her a hare. The princess had hardly had time to put the hare in her basket when Aurelio began to play on his flute. At once the hare jumped out of the basket and scampered back to the others. Angrily the princess walked back to the castle.

When she told her father that she had not been able to make Aurelio fail in his task, the king said, 'Never mind. This time we're going to do better.'

The king dressed up as a farmer. He got on to a donkey and rode out to the meadow.

'What have we here? A hare-herd! Good day to you!' he called out in a jolly sort of way.

'What have we here? A farmer who doesn't know how to ride a donkey properly!' laughed Aurelio, who had seen straight away that it was King Pompone.

The king got down from the donkey and said to Aurelio, 'I would like to buy one of those hares.'

'These hares are not for sale, but you can earn one of them.'

'How can I do that?'

'Oh, that's easy. All you have to do is kiss your donkey's nose.'

'Kiss my donkey's nose? You must be mad!'

The king tried to persuade Aurelio to sell him a hare for money, but the goatherd would have none of it. At last, with a shudder, the king bent over and kissed the donkey's rough, hairy muzzle. Ugh! How disgusting it was to have to do such a thing! But it was worth it, for the goatherd picked up one of the hares and put it in the king's hands.

The king climbed on to the donkey again, clutching the hare firmly in his hands. However, riding a donkey without using his hands was harder than the king expected. He had hardly had time to settle himself on the donkey when Aurelio began to play on his flute. There was no holding the hare then. The little creature struggled with all its might to get free. The king swayed and wobbled about on the donkey and almost fell off. Then with one bound the hare jumped free and landed on the donkey's head. This so alarmed the donkey that he gave a sudden start; the king lost his balance and tumbled to the ground with a thud.

'Good gracious!' he thought to himself. 'Nothing like this has ever happened to me before in all my life!'

The king scrambled to his feet. He rubbed himself in all the places where it hurt and decided he had better walk the rest of the way.

When the king was back in the castle and had taken off his farmer's clothes he said to the princess: 'That goatherd is a very clever young fellow, you know. Even I was not able to make him fail in the first task.' But the king did not tell the princess that he had fallen off his donkey.

When it was evening Aurelio blew on his flute once more. The hares came and crouched around him and when he began to walk towards the castle they all followed him. When Aurelio shut them in for the night not a single hare was missing!

'You have carried out the first task very well, goatherd,' said the king. 'The second task will give you more trouble. In the big barn where grain is stored I have one hundred sacks of lentils and one hundred sacks of peas, and I have had them tipped into one big heap. If you can sort the lentils and the peas into separate heaps in the dark, then you will have succeeded in the second task.'

'I accept the task!' said Aurelio, speaking as if it were quite an ordinary thing to have to do.

When it was dark two guards led him to the barn and bolted the door behind him. Aurelio took out the flute and began to play a tune. From every crack and corner, from every nook and cranny, thousands and thousands of ants came creeping out. They scurried to the pile of lentils and peas and began to take out the peas and build a separate heap of them. The ants worked all the night through and, when the sun rose in the morning, Aurelio saw that there were two neat heaps, one of lentils and the other of peas.

The guards who came to see how the goatherd had been getting on could not believe their eyes. 'They ran to the king and cried, 'Your majesty! Your majesty! The goatherd has done it!'

'Impossible!' said the king, 'This I must see for myself!' He hurried to the barn and was astonished when he saw the lentils and the peas in their separate heaps.

'How have you managed this?' he asked Aurelio.

'Sire, that is my secret,' was the goatherd's reply.

'Very well then,' said the king. 'We will go on to the third task, if you have no objections.'

'Not at all, sire. I'm looking forward to it.'

'Listen carefully. This evening I'm going to have a great room filled right up to the ceiling with bread. We have an excellent baker here at court, so you will have no reason to complain about the quality. In the morning, when I come to see you, not a single crumb must be left. Every piece must be eaten up. Understand? How you do it is up to you, but let me warn you that the door will be locked and the guards will not stand for any tricks. If you succeed in this task then you can marry my daughter. If you do not, then there will be nothing for you to do but go back home and look after your goats.'

That day, strange to tell, Aurelio was surrounded by servants who waited on him most attentively. 'What would you like for your lunch, sir?' the head chef came in person to ask him.

'Oh, anything nice will do,' said Aurelio.

The lunch was so good that he felt as if he were the king. First he had soup, then fish and then meat with the finest of vegetables, all beautifully cooked. Then there was blancmange and fruit tart for dessert. Aurelio had never eaten so well in all his life.

After lunch, which Aurelio had taken at least three hours to eat, he felt rather sleepy. 'Would you like to take an afternoon nap, sir?' one of the footmen asked him. When Aurelio nodded, he was led to a beautiful guest room. There he lay back on the soft bed and was soon pleasantly asleep.

He dreamed that he had performed the last task and was marrying the princess. The king made such a moving speech at the wedding that it brought tears to the eyes of every guest. All the knights who had tried so hard to catch the apple were at the splendid banquet. They treated him with great respect and every time they drank their wine they raised their glasses and called out in chorus, 'To Aurelio and his beautiful bride!'

When the goatherd woke up it was a long time before he understood that it had all been just a wonderful dream. He got up and looked out of the window. He saw servants walking by carrying baskets and baskets of bread. He had never seen so much bread at one time before. There must have been hundreds of loaves.

Towards the evening Aurelio was taken to a room where there was so much bread piled up that there was hardly enough room for him to squeeze in. He felt stifled and hemmed in, especially when he heard the door being locked and bolted behind him.

It was quiet and still inside the room. From time to time he could hear the sound of the heavy footsteps of the guards out in the corridor. Aurelio sat down on a pile of loaves and took out his flute and began to play. Suddenly he heard a rustling sound. He turned in the direction of the sound and then he heard *squeak! squeak!* It was a mouse, a very little mouse. *Squeak! squeak! squeak!* He heard another mouse scampering on the floor, then another and another. In no time at all there were a thousand mice nibbling and gnawing away at the piles of loaves. By the morning they had eaten up all the bread. Once again, the flute had worked a miracle.

Aurelio banged on the door and shouted, 'Guards! Bring me something to eat. I'm famished!'

The guards opened the door and could not believe their eyes. There was not a single crumb of bread left! They were so frightened they dropped their pikes and rushes as fast as they could to the king:

'Sire, the bread has all been eaten!
White and brown, and rye and wheaten,
Not a morsel now is left –
Leaving us with the suspicion
That the lad's a real magician.
And what's even more astounding
On the door he keeps on pounding,
And, unless we're much mistaken,
Shouting for his eggs and bacon.'

When King Pompone had seen for himself that all the bread had really been consumed, he thought of one more little plan. He sent for Aurelio and said, 'Any performer is always ready to do an encore, and I expect one from you too. So, if you can fill this sack with lies, there will be nothing more to stop you marrying the princess my daughter.'

Aurelio told one lie after another and stuffed them all into the sack. But when he looked at the sack he could see that it was not full yet. So he went on, 'There was once a princess who kissed a common goatherd just for a hare that she wanted to take away from him. Then she. . . .'

All the king's ministers and the ladies of the court laughed so loudly when they heard this that Aurelio could not go on with the story. The princess went red and stalked angrily away. The king was alarmed but he did not let anyone see it. 'Do go on,' he said. 'As you see, the sack is not full yet.'

So Aurelio continued: 'There was once a king who was so stupid he even fell off a donkey. . . .'

'Stop! Stop!' shouted the king in horror. 'The sack is full enough now!' He did not want anyone at court to find out how he had fallen off the donkey.

The princess and Aurelio were married. Whenever anyone asked the king why he had let his daughter marry a common goatherd he always answered: 'A young man who could do so much when he was only a goatherd will be able to do great things one day when he is a king!'

Hansel and Gretel

Once upon a time, a very long time ago, there were two happy little children, a boy and a girl.

Their names were Hansel and Gretel, and they lived in a cottage on the edge of a big dark wood.

Hansel and Gretel often played in the woods because their father was a woodcutter and sometimes, but not very often, he took his children with him when he set off for work. Mostly, however, Hansel and Gretel were content to play on the edge of the wood where it was light and sunny.

Hansel knew the names of most of the pretty birds that sang in the trees, and Gretel had her own special friends among the busy little squirrels and the shy little rabbits.

'I wish – oh, how I wish that everything could stay the same for ever and ever,' Gretel would sometimes say.

And Hansel would answer, 'That's a silly kind of wish, little sister. Nothing stays exactly the same.'

Well, Hansel was right. One sad, sad day their mother became ill and, very shortly afterwards, she died.

For a time their father was too upset even to work. Then he met and married another woman, and put all his sadness behind him.

'Children,' said he, very gaily. 'Now you have a new mother who will love you and take care of you just as if she was your proper mother.'

The wood-cutter was wrong in thinking that he had chosen a kind, motherly woman as his new wife. She was not kind and she was not motherly and it became clear to the wood-cutter that he had made a mistake in asking her to be his wife.

Hansel and Gretel did their best to make their stepmother love them. But nothing they ever said or did seemed to please her.

To make matters worse the wood-cutter suddenly found that he was using up all his savings to keep his family in food. He could no longer count on selling his logs for a good price. The people in the surrounding villages were going through a hard time and could not afford to buy his firewood.

When the wood-cutter's wife saw how poor they were becoming, she began to grudge spending what money they had left on food for the children.

She scolded them if they asked for a second slice of bread.

The wood-cutter loved his children and he was often very sad when he saw how hungry they were. But he was afraid of his wife and dared not say anything.

Soon his wife began to give Hansel and Gretel black looks whenever they sat down to eat, and one dreadful night she said to her husband:

'We must rid ourselves of these two children of yours. They have such huge appetites that soon there will be nothing left for us to eat.'

The wood-cutter buried his face in his hands when he heard his wife's cruel suggestion. And his wife, enraged, began to shout and scream at him.

Her shouts roused the children and they crept downstairs to listen.

'Be as quite as a mouse,' Hansel whispered to his sister. 'We mustn't let them know we are listening.'

They heard their father plead with his wife over and over again, but this only made her shout even more loudly.

At last she cried, 'We shall take them into the forest tomorrow and leave them there. They will never find their way home if we take them to a part where there are no familiar paths.'

When Hansel saw his poor father nod his head in agreement, he took his little sister's hand and together they crept back to bed.

'Don't worry,' he whispered, 'I have already thought of a plan.'

Long before his father and stepmother were awake. Hansel crept down the stairs and out into the garden.

He filled his pockets with round, shiny pebbles, as many as they would hold, and then, very quietly, he went back into the house and up the stairs to bed.

Before the sun had properly risen he heard his stepmother call:

'Hansel, Gretel, get dressed at once and come downstairs! We are going to take you into the forest for a picnic.'

'Don't worry, little sister,' Hansel said, as Gretel began to cry. 'I have a plan and I know it will work.'

Their stepmother greeted them with a sour smile when they appeared in the kitchen.

'Hurry,' she said. 'Eat this slice of bread now, and take another piece for your picnic.'

The children ate their bread quickly whilst their father got out his big axe. Soon they were ready to set out, the wood-cutter leading the way into the dark, deep forest.

When they had walked for some time, Hansel stopped and looked back.

'Hurry, you lazy boy,' said his stepmother over her shoulder.

'I just wanted to see if our cat was on the cottage roof,' said Hansel.

As he spoke he dropped one of his shiny white pebbles on the grass. His plan was working. So long as he could linger behind his stepmother he could go on dropping his pebbles.

Hansel had no idea how far they walked that day. When his father stopped at last they were in a strange part of the forest and miles and miles from home.

'We have gone far enough,' said the wood-cutter with a sad, bitter smile.

'Rest here, children, whilst your mother and I go farther into the forest to gather wood.'

'They will not come back for us,' Gretel whispered fearfully.

'Don't worry, little sister,' Hansel said, taking her hand. 'I have laid a trail of shiny white pebbles. The pebbles will show us the way home.'

Then the children ate their bread and shared some of it with two friendly squirrels.

'We must wait for a time,' Hansel said, when they had eaten. 'We must not arrive at our cottage before they do!' And he laughed so cheerfully that Gretel laughed too.

'How clever you are, Hansel,' she smiled. 'Now I'm sure we shall get home safely and I'm no longer afraid.'

When it was beginning to grow dark Hansel took his sister's hand and led her through the trees.

'Look! Can you see?' he cried. 'How brightly the pebbles shine even in the dark! Soon the moon will be riding high in the sky and then my pebbles will look like gleaming silver pennies.'

When the moon came out at last it was easier than ever to find the pebbles and in no time at all, it seemed to Hansel, their cottage was in sight and they were home. How wonderful to be home!

What a warm, welcoming hug their father gave them, and how darkly did their stepmother scowl as she stared at them. But Hansel and Gretel cared nothing for her black looks. They were safely home and that was all that mattered!

All was peaceful in the little house for some weeks and then one night, just as the children were going to sleep, they heard the harsh voice of their stepmother raging again at their father.

'We must find out if she is trying to persuade him to lose us again in the forest,' Hansel whispered to Gretel. 'Come on, let's listen to what they are saying . . .'

So they crept to the top of the stairs and they listened and they listened. And, sad to say, they heard their father murmur, 'Oh, very well, wife. We shall take them into the forest early in the morning. And this time, I promise you, they shall not find their way home.'

Hansel waited until his parents had gone to bed. Then he crept downstairs expecting to find the back door unlocked. But this time the door was locked and barred and, no matter how hard he tried, he could not turn the big heavy key.

'You must save your bread,' he told Gretel in the morning, as they were setting out. 'I will lay a trail of breadcrumbs. The crumbs will show up just as well as the pebbles did.'

Gretel nodded her little head and promised that she would not eat her share of the bread but give it to Hansel before they set out.

How quickly their stepmother walked as she and the wood-cutter pushed the children in front of them through the woods.

But soon Hansel and Gretel were able to run ahead, and then Hansel was able to drop his breadcrumbs in secret places.

This time the wood-cutter took his children a great long way into the forest to a quiet, dark, deserted place.

'Rest here,' he told them at last. 'Your mother and I'll go a little farther on, and then we shall come back 'for you.' And he kissed them tenderly.

'He won't come back. I know he won't! Gretel cried.

'It doesn't matter,' Hansel said cheerfully. 'I've laid a splendid trail of breadcrumbs. As soon as the moon appears in the sky, we shall set out for home. Let's try to sleep.'

When the children awoke, it was dark. Presently the moon came out but, oh dear, search as he might, Hansel could not find a single breadcrumb. The little birds had found the bread first and eaten up every bit of it.

How dark and scary it was in that thick gloomy wood, and how wildly did the children run, this way and that – and all the time, had they but known it, they were going farther and farther away from their own little cottage!

At last they were so tired that even Hansel was ready to give up. They had walked most of the night and now it was morning again, and they were so weary and so hungry they thought they would surely die. And then, just when Gretel was ready to burst into tears, she saw a beautiful snow-white bird sitting in a tree.

'Look, Hansel,' she whispered, 'that pretty white bird seems to be trying to tell us something. How sweetly it sings. I think it wants us to follow it.'

As she spoke, the white bird spread its wings and flew just a little way, and Hansel and Gretel followed it. It led them to the most wonderful little house they had ever seen.

'Goodness!' shouted Hansel. 'It's a house made of bread and covered with cake and icing and sugary biscuits!'

Gretel clapped her hands and shrieked with delight, all her tiredness forgotten.

'Clever bird!' she cried. 'It has led us to this wonderful cake house. Ooh, I'm so hungry! Look, Hansel, the porch has pillars of gorgeous sticky rock. Isn't it tempting! Let's try the sugary cake walls first . . .'

As they began to help themselves to the cake house the door opened suddenly, and out came a motherly old woman. She had a soft, purring voice and bright red eyes and she walked with a stick.

'Come in, dear children,' she said softly. 'You like nibbling at my house, but wait until you see what I have for you inside. You can feast on sugared buns and apples and pears and delicious cakes all day long if you wish.'

'We're lost, and we'd love to come inside,' said Hansel, his mouth full of cake. 'Thank you very much.'

So the children went into the cake house and soon they were seated at the table and eating all the nicest things imaginable. The old lady watched them with a kindly expression on her gnarled and wrinkled face.

'Eat up, my dears,' she would say, whenever Hansel or Gretel vowed they couldn't eat or drink anything more. 'I like my children to be round and plump.' And she would give the oddest little chuckle, as if she were sharing a secret joke with herself.

'How lucky we are to have you,' said Hansel at last. 'May we stay here just for one night? Then tomorrow you will perhaps guide us to the path that will lead us out of this deep forest.'

The old woman made no answer, but presently she showed Hansel and Gretel where they would sleep.

And when they were safely tucked up in their beds, she watched over them until they had fallen sound asleep.

Then, and only then, did she allow herself to cackle loudly and, as she hobbled about the room, chuckling and talking to herself, her red eyes blazed with greed and spite.

The old woman, you see, was none other than the most wicked witch you can imagine, and her wonderful cake house was simply there to trap little children. Whenever she was hungry she sent out her pet white bird to look for little boys and girls, just like Hansel and Gretel. How fortunate it was that her bird had performed so well, for it was a long time now since she had managed to catch two such pleasant children. No wonder she smiled and chuckled as she prepared the cage into which she would put young Hansel in the morning.

Poor Hansel! He could scarcely believe what was happening to him when the wicked witch carried him away early the next morning and thrust him into the small wooden cage. This horrid cage was anchored to the floor of the witch's tower with strong chains.

'Let me out! Let me out!' Hansel screamed, when he saw his sister.

'I can't help you, brother,' she replied. 'We are in the power of a witch who eats little children. Now she has forced me to be her servant.'

Hansel shook the bars of his prison, but they were so thick and set so closely together that he soon gave up. He would never move them.

'We must think of another way to save ourselves,' he told Gretel. 'Do whatever the old witch asks of you, and don't despair.'

It was hard to do everything the witch asked because now she expected Gretel to do all the fetching and carrying, all the washing and sweeping of floors.

'I'm far too busy cooking for that brother of yours,' the witch would cackle. 'He must have the best of everything and all of it must be cooked with butter and cream. Oh, ho, it won't be long before he is fat enough to roast and eat.'

Gretel had nothing but crab-shells and stale crusts to eat, for the witch had decided she would never make a tasty meal to enjoy.

Every day for a week the witch paid a visit to Hansel.

Now, you may not know, but witches with very red eyes do not see very clearly. The wicked witch of the cake house had red, red eyes and she did not see at all well, which was very lucky for Hansel.

Each time the old woman went to the cage and said, 'Hansel, let me feel if your finger grows fatter,' Hansel thrust out a little chicken bone for her to feel.

After three weeks, the wicked witch could not hide her disappointment from little Gretel.

'That brother of yours eats like a lord,' she said angrily, 'and yet he grows no fatter. Ah well, I shall eat him tomorrow. I cannot wait any longer for my feast.'

Then she sent Gretel into the yard to fetch water and, when she returned, told her to get out the largest dishes and biggest bowls, because she had a mind to make a tasty sauce and wished to have all the various ingredients ready mixed for tomorrow's dinner.

How Gretel wept as she was forced to obey the wicked witch. How she pleaded and begged for mercy for her brother! But the witch only laughed and seemed very pleased at the sight of her tears.

Early the next morning the witch set about preparing for her feast.

'I have a mind to bake first,' she said to Gretel. 'Light the fire and I will heat up the oven.'

The witch began to bake and, as she kneaded the dough, she called out to Gretel to go to the oven, open the door and see if it was heating up nicely.

'The door is too big and heavy for me to open,' said Gretel. 'And I'm too small to look inside.'

'Stupid child!' muttered the old witch. 'I will look for myself!' And she went over to the big oven in the wall and thrust her head inside.

Silent as a mouse, Gretel crept up behind and, with all her strength, pushed the old witch deep inside her own oven. Then she shut and bolted the great iron door in the wall.

So that was the end of the wicked red-eyed witch. Gretel quickly found the key to Hansel's prison and set him free.

'The witch is dead,' she told him excitedly. 'And I know where she keeps all her treasure.'

Soon Hansel was filling his pockets with gold and precious stones taken from the witch's treasure chests, while Gretel waited by the door.

Then they left that dreadful house and set out for home. They had walked for two hours or more when they came, at last, to a great wide lake. And at the sight of so much water, Gretel cried out in despair, 'Oh, Hansel, what shall we do? We can't swim and there isn't a bridge or a boat anywhere in sight.'

As she spoke, a lovely white swan came swimming straight towards them.

'Please take us across this wide, wide lake,' Gretel said to the graceful white bird. And Hansel waded out into the water and climbed on its back. The swan opened its wings so that Hansel could sit safely, then took him across the lake before returning to ferry Gretel across.

So, thanks to the bird, Hansel and Gretel were carried across the water and, to their surprise and delight, very soon spied their own little cottage through a gap in the trees.

'Look, there's Father!' Gretel shouted in delight as the wood-cutter appeared on the doorstep of the old cottage.

With cries of joy both children ran into his outstretched arms.

Oh, what happiness, to be hugged and kissed and drawn into the cosy kitchen where Hansel told his amazing story!

When the wood-cutter had heard it at least three times over and seen all the witch's treasure, he said:

'Your stepmother left me. She did not love me after all.'

'We love you, father,' said Gretel, her eyes shining like stars.

'And you love us,' said Hansel. 'You didn't want to leave us all alone in the dark forest, did you?'

'Indeed not,' said the wood-cutter.

'Then let us all be happy together,' said Hansel, holding up a gleaming necklace of diamonds. 'The witch's treasure will take care of all our wants for ever and ever, and we will be able to help all our poor friends in the village whenever they need it.'

And so it proved!

Snow-White and Rose-Red

There was once a poor widow who lived with her two daughters in a lonely little cottage. In her tiny cottage garden two rose trees bloomed all the year round – one white and the other red.

The widow called her daughters Snow-White and Rose-Red after the pretty rose trees, and there were no kinder more loving children than her two beautiful girls.

Snow-White was more gentle, more thoughtful than Rose-Red, but Rose-Red was always full of fun, always willing to take on the most disagreeable tasks around the cottage.

The sisters were the best of friends, and their mother was very happy that this should be so.

'What one has she must share with the other,' their mother told them over and over again.

And Rose-Red would smile and say, 'You're right, mother, and what's more we have promised that we will do everything together.'

In the summer they would go into the forest to gather berries, and no harm ever came to them. The rabbits ran to them trustfully, the birds sang to them from the trees, and even the wild, fierce animals, that had their homes in the lonelier parts of the forest, did not attempt to harm or scare the two sisters.

Their mother knew that her two precious children had their own guardian angel to take care of them whenever they went into the forest, and so she did not worry – even when they came home after darkness had fallen.

Snow-White and Rose-Red spent a lot of time in the forest, which they loved, but they did not neglect their many duties at home.

They kept the cottage as neat and shining as a new pin. Rose-Red dusted and swept and polished the old brass kettle until it shone like gold.

Snow-White did the washing and took care of the garden; and every morning, before her mother was awake, she picked two roses, one from the white rose tree and one from the red, and placed them beside her mother's bed. When the widow awoke, the first thing she saw were the beautiful flowers and she always smiled happily, because they reminded her how lucky she was to have two such loving children.

Rose-Red loved the long summer days best of all. 'I wish we had summer all the year round,' she would sometimes say to her sister, with a little nod and a smile.

'I don't!' Snow-White would reply. 'I like everything just as it is. Have you forgotten what fun it is to draw the curtains on a winter's night and sit round a log fire?'

One year the winter came suddenly with a flurry of snow, and Snow-White bustled about the cottage making certain that all was snug and cosy.

Long before her mother came down in the morning, the stove was lit and the water boiling.

Rose-Red had gathered sticks for the fire, and filled the lamps, for in winter the days were short and the evenings long.

Their cottage was small and humble but the girls knew how to make it as warm and inviting as if it had been the home of a rich landowner.

The snow fell steadily all that day, and as soon as darkness came their mother brought out her sewing; Snow-White read her favourite book, while Rose-Red busied herself in the kitchen.

'This will be a hard winter,' the widow said, as she went on with her embroidery. 'We must be sure we have a good supply of logs for our fire, and that there is plenty of oil for the lamps.'

'Don't worry, Mother,' said Snow-White, looking up from her book. 'You can trust us. We shall take care of everything for you. But if the snow continues to fall, the forest animals will suffer and that makes me sad.'

Snow-White's tender heart could not bear to think of her little friends of the forest going hungry, and she resolved to put food out for them in the morning.

But the next morning, as it happened, the sun was shining and Rose-Red ran into the garden and picked the roses for her mother.

'I don't believe the winter has come after all!' she laughed, when she returned to the cottage. 'Our rose trees are blooming just as if it was the height of summer.'

Snow-White shook her head. She knew better and, as the day wore on, cold winds from the north and dark clouds in the sky told them that winter had really come, and that they could expect more drifting snow.

That night their mother got down her big red book of legends and, putting on her glasses, read to her daughters as the wind howled round their cottage, rattling the windows.

Snow-White and Rose-Red drew their shawls more tightly about their shoulders, and Snow-White could not stop herself from shivering every now and then – although not for the world would she admit that she was cold or that the howling, boisterous wind frightened her.

Suddenly, above the noise of the storm, they heard the sound of knocking on the back door.

'Who can that possibly be?' Snow-White asked fearfully.

'Only some poor traveller who has lost his way in the storm,' said her mother. 'Go quickly, Rose-Red, and open the door. We mustn't leave him outside on such a night.'

Rose-Red ran to the door and pushed back the bolt, expecting to see some poor man soaked to the skin and in need of food and shelter. But it was not so; and she got such a surprise, such a great shock that she could not stop herself from screaming. There, before her, stood a huge brown bear covered in snow!

At the sound of her daughter's scream the widow rushed to the door and was just in time to face the huge bear, whilst her two daughters, losing all their courage cowered behind her.

'Don't be afraid,' said the bear, 'I will not harm you. I only want to warm myself by your fire.'

'Poor bear,' said the widow, 'I believe you don't intend to harm us, and I make you welcome. Come and lie down by the fire.' And turning to her two frightened daughters, she continued, 'Come, children, you can see the bear is harmless. Brush the snow from his coat, and make him feel at home.'

First Rose-Red and then Snow-White came out from behind their mother's skirts and the bear greeted them with such gentle courtesy that almost at once they lost their fear of him.

'You must stand still, Sir Bear,' laughed Rose-Red, 'and refrain from shaking that shaggy coat of yours if we are to brush you.'

'We'll use our kitchen brooms,' said Snow-White, and she stroked the bear just to show him that she trusted him and was not afraid.

Soon, thanks to the brooms, the bear was brushed clean, and when he was warm and dry, Snow-White brought him warm creamy porridge to eat.

The great bear was so gentle, so anxious to please, that Snow-White and Rose-Red invited him to play some of their games.

'I'll teach you,' said Snow-White, when the bear protested that he did not know how to play hide-and-seek.

What fun they had, and as they grew bolder, the sisters tugged his hair, rode on his big broad back and rolled him over. And the bear took everything in good humour and seemed to enjoy the fun as much as they did.

The widow sat in her corner chair and watched over the happy group with kindly, amused eyes. Never before had they received such a strange guest into their midst – and never before had the cottage run with such happy laughter.

At last, when it was bed-time, Snow-White and Rose-Red kissed their mother and hugged the bear and went upstairs to bed, leaving her alone with their strange guest.

'You are welcome, if you choose, to stay the night here by the fire,' said the widow.

'I should like that,' said the bear. 'I should like to think that I am among friends and that I may come to this cottage whenever I wish.'

Then he stretched out before the fire and was soon fast asleep.

After that first evening, the bear came to the cottage most nights. And Snow-White and Rose-Red came to look forward to his visits.

They ran out into the snow to greet him, and sometimes he would allow one or other of them to ride on his broad back.

Then he would settle down by the hearth, and the girls would tumble around him and tease him and tell him stories of their childhood days.

'Will you still come and see us when the winter is over?' Snow-White asked him one day.

The bear did not answer, and for a moment she was sad, thinking how lonely it would be without their shaggy friend to play with. But then the bear suddenly performed a trick which made her smile and look happy again.

That winter was a long one, but one day the snow disappeared and once again everything was green. It was spring at last, and Rose-Red was full of joy at the thought of being able to go into the forest again.

Soon afterwards the bear came to see them at the cottage.

'I can't come and visit you any more,' he told Snow-White and her sister. 'I must go into the forest and guard my treasure. . . .'

'Oh, don't leave us,' Snow-White cried, her pretty face turning quite sad.

'I must,' said the bear. 'If I don't stay in the forest all the time the wicked dwarfs will steal my treasure.'

'But why do they leave it alone in the winter?' asked Rose-Red.

'In the winter,' the bear said, 'the earth is frozen hard, and they must stay underground and cannot break through. In the summer, the earth is warmed by the sun and they are able to break free.'

'You mean there are wicked dwarfs in our forest!' Rose-Red exclaimed.

'I tell you there are such dwarfs,' said the bear, and for the first time the sisters saw a fierce look in his eyes. 'And if they're not watched, they steal everything they can lay their hands on and take the treasure to their caves.'

Snow-White and Rose-Red listened spellbound to this, but even the bear's surprising talk of dwarfs and treasure could not banish their feeling of sadness when the time came to say good-bye to their old friend.

'Come and see us when winter comes again,' Snow-White called as the bear ambled slowly away. 'Don't ever forget us, because we'll never forget you.'

A short time after the bear's final departure, Snow-White and Rose-Red went into the forest to gather firewood. It was a beautiful day, and the girls were delighted to be out in the forest again.

As they ran through the trees, hand in hand, they stopped every now and then to admire the wild flowers or listen to the welcoming song from their little friends, the birds.

Presently they found the broken branch of a tree and Rose-Red cried, 'This will do. We'll get all the firewood we need from this old branch.'

The two sisters set to work and for a time they were so busy that they noticed nothing unusual. It was Snow-White who suddenly saw something jumping up and down in the long grass.

'Whatever can it be?' she whispered to Rose-Red. 'There's some queer animal jumping up and down close to that big tree over there that must have been felled in the winter.'

Feeling strangely frightened, Rose-Red and Snow-White went up closer to the tree and saw a little man, a dwarf, with an old wrinkled face and a long white beard.

His long beard had been caught in a split in the tree and he was hopping up and down, trying to pull it free.

When he saw the two girls he stared at them fiercely. 'Don't just stand there,' he shrieked. 'Do something! Help me to free myself.'

'How can we help you?' Snow-White asked. 'You're caught fast and we can't lift the tree.'

'Idiots!' snapped the dwarf. 'Take hold of my beard and pull!'

Snow-White bent down and took hold of the dwarf's beard, and her sister grabbed her by the waist and together they tugged and tugged and tugged. But no matter how hard they tried they could not free the little man.

'It's no use!' Snow-White gasped. 'We can't pull you free.'

'You must! You must!' cried the dwarf, his eyes blazing with fury. 'Think of something else to do!'

The sisters looked at each other in dismay. Then Rose-Red whispered, 'There is something we could do. I could cut him free. I have a pair of small scissors with me.'

'Let's do that!' Snow-White replied. 'We can't leave him here. If we do, he'll die of starvation.'

So Rose-Red took out her scissors and, bending over, she went snip, snip with her scissors and cut the long white beard.

The dwarf was now at liberty, but oh, how angry he was!

'Stupid, senseless goose!' he stormed. 'You've cut off a piece of my fine white beard. What idiots you girls are! I'll not forget you in a hurry!' And he took hold of a little bag which was lying among the tree roots and dragged it away.

'What a horrid, ungrateful dwarf that was!' said Rose-Red as they made their way home. 'And did you see what was in the bag? It was filled with gold.'

Not very long after this, the widow asked her daughters to go down to the stream and try and catch a fish for supper.

Rose-Red and Snow-White set off in good spirits, because they loved fishing, but when they got to the river, they were astonished to see something that looked like a huge grasshopper jumping up and down and being dragged closer and closer to the river's edge.

'It – it couldn't be our horrid little dwarf!' Rose-Red exclaimed, as she ran forward. 'I do believe it is!'

'Ask him what he's doing,' said Snow-White, for she was afraid of the little man's temper and did not wish to speak to him.

'What are you doing?' Rose-Red asked the dwarf.

'Use your eyes, you fool!' the dwarf screamed at her. 'Can't you see what's happening to me? I'm being pulled into the water by that monster fish!'

'His long white beard is twisted round and round his fishing rod,' said Snow-White, as she peered at the dwarf from behind some tall rushes. 'I can see what will happen if we don't go to his aid. Shall we help him, Rose-Red?'

'I suppose we'll have to,' said Rose-Red. 'It's lucky I still have my scissors with me.'

And she ran down to the water's edge and cut the little man's beard, snip, snip, with her scissors.

The dwarf, though he had been so close to drowning, showed no gratitude at being saved. Instead he shouted angrily, 'You stupid girl! Now I've lost another part of my fine white beard! What an idiot you are! Don't you know my beard is my pride and joy. May bad luck dog your footsteps for the rest of your days!' And with that he picked up a bag of pearls, which lay half hidden among the rushes, and stormed off.

'Oh, I do hope and pray we shall never see him again!' Snow-White murmured as she joined her sister. 'I'm sure he means to do us harm if he can.'

'Maybe we've seen the last of him,' said Rose-Red, and she began to fish.

But oh, how wrong she was! The very next day, as they were walking through the forest on their way to the village, they saw a huge bird hovering in the sky above some big boulders.

'Perhaps there's some poor little rabbit trapped under the rocks!' Snow-White exclaimed, 'and that ugly bird of prey is getting ready to swoop down on it.'

'It's certainly not a rabbit!' cried Rose-Red, staring hard at the boulders. 'Look! It's our nasty little friend with the white beard. . . .'

'He's seen the bird and he's trying to escape from it,' whispered Snow-White clutching her sister's arm. 'Oh, why doesn't he put down his sack. Then he would be able to run all the faster.'

'He would never be able to escape from that big bird – no matter how fast he ran,' Rose-Red declared.

As she spoke, the dwarf let out a shrill cry for help and dropped the sack.

Then he ran, as fast as he could towards one of the big boulders and crouched low behind it as if to make himself invisible from his enemy in the air. But the big, ugly bird with its cruel hooked beak was not deceived. It came down and down, ever closer to its prey.

The dwarf gave a wild scream of dismay as, suddenly, the bird swooped down on him. He had no chance because he had chosen a hiding-place from which there was simply no escape.

'Can't we save him!' Snow-White asked, as she watched, horrified. 'I know he's horrid and rude and ungrateful, but in another second he will be taken up into the sky and lost forever.'

As she spoke the bird pounced on the dwarf and began flying upwards. But its victim was unexpectedly heavy and so it did not fly away immediately.

'Quick, we can still save him!' Rose-Red exclaimed, as the little man began to let out the most hideous screams. 'You grab one of his legs and I'll grab the other.' And, followed by her sister, she ran forward towards the bird.

What a tug-of-war followed! The bird had no intention of letting its prey escape, and the two sisters had no intention of letting the bird fly away with the little man. So the bird pulled against them, and they pulled against the bird. And in the battle, the dwarf's clothes were torn and the front of his jacket ripped to shreds.

At last the big bird suddenly seemed to grow weary of the tug-of-war. It let its victim go and the dwarf fell to the ground with a thud.

'Stupid, stupid girls!' he cried, picking himself up. 'You've torn my jacket and spoilt it for good. What clumsy fools you both are to be sure! First you ruin my beard and now my clothes!'

He glared fiercely at them for a moment, then ran to the sack which had burst open and began putting back into it the diamonds and rubies that lay in the grass. Then he stamped away towards a hole in the ground.

On their way back from the village, Snow-White and Rose-Red were surprised to come upon the dwarf again. As they tried to run away from him without being seen, the dwarf looked up from counting his treasure.

'Caught you!' he yelled. 'So now you're spying on me!' And he began to threaten and curse them.

Suddenly a huge brown bear came out of the bushes. The dwarf, catching sight of him, turned to flee, but he was too late. With a mighty swipe of his huge paw the bear felled the wicked dwarf to the ground and killed him.

No sooner did this happen than the bearskin fell away and a handsome young man stood before the astonished sisters, dressed all in gold.

'I am a king's son,' he said. 'I was under the spell of the wicked little creature who lies there. He stole my treasure and changed me into a savage bear. Only his death could release me from his power.'

Then the handsome prince knelt before Snow-White and begged her to marry him. She consented gladly and, in no time at all, the wedding took place.

Rose-Red and the widow-mother also went to live in the grand palace, and with them went the two rose-trees, one white and the other red, which every year bore the loveliest roses.

The Little Shepherd

Long, long ago, on the night the Baby Jesus was born in a stable in
Bethlehem, there were some shepherds guarding their sheep on the hills
outside the city.

In those far-off times, it was not uncommon for people to sleep on
feather-beds which were, as often as not, just big sacks stuffed with feathers.

Well, on this particular night one of the shepherds had taken his
feather-bed to the hillside.

'It is such a bitter cold night,' he told himself, as he unrolled his bed. 'I'll be able to keep warm by sleeping on it when it is my turn to rest.'

The shepherd was one of the first to take his turn at watching over the sheep, and after his spell of duty, he found a sheltered spot, put down his bed, and stretched out on it.

Sleep comes quickly to those who are weary and who are getting on in years, and it wasn't long before the shepherd was fast asleep and dreaming. And what a strange dream it was! First he dreamt about the wonderful angels who had come down from heaven to tell his friends about the birth of the little Lord Jesus. Then he began dreaming about the baby himself. In his dream he saw that the child was lying in a poor manger on a bed of hay.

'No, no, the Holy Child should have a much better bed!' the shepherd cried out. And then he awoke. He could not decide what had roused him from his deep sleep or spoilt his dream. But it had been such a vivid dream he could remember it all.

'Here am I, lying snug and warm on my feather-bed,' he told himself. 'And there is the little Lord Jesus with nothing better to sleep on than a bed of hay. How cold it must be in that stable!'

He lay there for a moment picturing the poor stable and the animals which, no doubt, were sharing their shelter with the child. Then he sprang to his feet. At first he had only wished that he might do something for the baby. Now, quite suddenly, he knew what he could do. He could take his beautiful, cosy feather-bed to the stable and give it to the child!

The shepherd did not tell his friends what he meant to do. They would not miss him for he had plenty of time to go down to Bethlehem and be back before it was his turn again to guard the sheep. He slung his feather-bed over his shoulder and set off down the hill, following the track which he knew would take him within sight of the city walls.

When he came to the city gates, the watchman called out, 'Who goes there? State your business!'

'I am a poor shepherd from the hills,' said the shepherd. 'I have a present for a certain child?'

'What is it?' asked the watchman.

'Just a feather-bed,' said the shepherd. 'You can see it for yourself. I am taking it to him because I know it will keep him warm.'

'That's a kind thought,' said the watchman, beginning to smile. 'It is a cold night, no doubt!'

And he blew on his hands and then told the shepherd to pass through the gates and be on his way.

Thankful that there had been no trouble at the gates, the shepherd hurried on. Then he began to wonder what he would say when he found himself in the stable. Perhaps the best thing to do would be to leave his feather-bed beside the manger, and steal quietly away without saying anything. After all, there wouldn't be any real need for him to explain his gift. And he was a man of few words.

As he turned a corner of the road the shepherd suddenly found himself confronted by a shining angel. The sight so astonished him that he let out a gasp, and almost dropped his feather-bed.

'I know where you are going and why you are carrying that feather-bed,' said the angel to the astonished man. 'I come to tell you that the Lord Jesus has no need of your bed to keep him warm.'

'But – but I have walked a long way . . .' the shepherd began, scarcely daring to raise his voice above a whisper. 'And the stable will be so cold on a night such as this!'

'I tell you again,' said the angel, 'the child has no need of the bed. It is your love he needs. And you have shown that by your presence in the city.'

'I – I don't understand,' the shepherd said humbly. 'The baby is lying in a crib of hay. Surely, my feather-bed would be welcome!'

'No, it is your love which is welcome,' answered the angel gently. 'And I promise you that your gift will not be overlooked or forgotten.'

'But you are sending me back to the hills,' protested the old man, tears of disappointment springing to his eyes.

'Listen,' said the angel, 'when your time comes to go to heaven, you may scatter the feathers from your bed all over the earth. . . .'

'When – at what time of the year?' asked the shepherd, beginning to smile at the very idea of a poor shepherd being granted such a favour.

'Why, on Christmas Eve,' said the angel. 'Your feathers will delight the children's hearts.'

'I should enjoy that!' exclaimed the shepherd. 'To think of doing such a thing makes me happy. Yes, yes, I am greatly favoured . . . forgive me for doubting for a moment that everything you said was not right and proper. Why, I am already beginning to look forward to the end. The children will take my feathers for snowflakes, you see if they don't!'

He would have said much more to the shining angel if given the chance, for now that he was growing more confident and more sure of himself, there were certain questions he longed to ask him. But the angel was suddenly no longer there. The street was empty, and the old shepherd turned his face

towards the city gates, and set out for the hills again.

Well, not very long after his meeting with the angel, the shepherd died and went to heaven. And that very next Christmas Eve, he had the great pleasure and honour of scattering the soft white feathers from his bed on the earth beneath.

Of course, there were children who said that it was truly wonderful that the snow had come, and who made plans to have snowball fights and build snowmen.

But there were some children – especially those who had known the old shepherd and heard his story, and they said happily to each other, 'Look, look, the shepherd has been as good as his promise. He is showering us with lovely soft white feathers from his feather-bed!'

Chicken Little

One day Chicken-Little was out for a walk in the forest when – plonk – an acorn fell on his head.

'Goodness, gracious me!' cried Chicken-Little. 'The sky is falling down. I must go and tell the king.'

So he ran and he ran and he ran until he met Henny-Penny.

'Henny-Penny, Henny-Penny!' cried Chicken-Little. 'The sky is falling down.'

'Who told you that?' asked Henny-Penny.

'I heard it and I felt it,' said Chicken-Little. 'There is no time to waste. We must go and tell the king.'

So Henny-Penny and Chicken-Little ran and they ran and they ran until they met Ducky-Lucky.

'Ducky-Lucky, Ducky-Lucky, the sky is falling down!' cried Chicken-Little and Henny-Penny together.

'Who told you that?' asked Ducky-Lucky.

'I heard it and I felt it,' said Chicken-Little.

'That's true,' said Henny-Penny. 'We are going to tell the king.'

So Ducky-Lucky, Henny-Penny and Chicken-Little ran and they ran and they ran until they met Goosey-Poosey.

'Goosey-Poosey, Goosey-Poosey, the sky is falling down!' cried Ducky-Lucky and Henny-Penny and Chicken-Little.

'Who told you that?' asked Goosey-Poosey.

'I heard it and I felt it,' said Chicken-Little. 'We are going to tell the king.'

So Goosey-Poosey and Ducky-Lucky and Henny-Penny and Chicken-Little ran and they ran and they ran until they met Turkey-Lurkey.

'Turkey-Lurkey, Turkey-Lurkey, the sky is falling down!' cried Goosey-Poosey and Ducky-Lucky and Henny-Penny and Chicken-Little.

'Who told you that?' asked Turkey-Lurkey.

'I heard it and I felt it,' said Chicken-Little. 'We are going to tell the king.'

So Turkey-Lurkey and Goosey-Poosey and Ducky-Lucky and Henny-Penny and Chicken-Little ran and they ran and they ran until they met Foxy-Woxy.

'Foxy-Woxy, Foxy-Woxy, the sky is falling down!' cried Turkey-Lurkey and Goosey-Poosey and Ducky-Lucky and Henny-Penny and Chicken-Little.

'Who told you that?' asked Foxy-Woxy.

'I heard it and I felt it,' said Chicken-Little. 'We are going to tell the king.'

'But you are all going the wrong way to find the king,' said Foxy-Woxy. 'I will show you the way to the king.'

So Turkey-Lurkey and Goosey-Poosey and Ducky-Lucky and Henny-Penny and Chicken-Little began following Foxy-Woxy. And he led them straight to his den.

'This is a quick way to the king's palace,' said Foxy-Woxy. 'I'll go in first

and then Turkey-Lurkey can follow me inside and then Goosey-Poosey and then Ducky-Lucky and last of all Henny-Penny and Chicken-Little.'

So Foxy-Woxy went into his den. And after him came Goosey-Poosey and Ducky-Lucky and Henny-Penny and Chicken-little, and Foxy-Woxy was waiting for them in the dark, and they were never seen again.

So, after all, the king was never told about the sky falling down!

The Great Race

One day an old tortoise, who went by the name of Tatty, met a sprightly young hare called Harry and fell into conversation with him.

'I hear you are a very swift runner,' said old Tatty. 'Is that true?'

'I'll say it is!' cried Harry. 'I'm the fastest! You should see me when I really get going!'

Before the old tortoise could make any reply, the hare ran up and down the field once or twice just to show her what he could do. When he stopped before her again, he laughed and then asked if she would like to do the same.

'I'm too old for chasing up and down a field,' Tatty replied, with dignity. 'But I tell you what – I'll challenge you to a race.'

'That's the funniest thing I've heard for months,' gasped Harry. 'You'll challenge me to a race! Why, you're an old slow-coach. You – you couldn't beat anything that runs on four legs. And you certainly couldn't beat me!'

'I'm serious,' the tortoise said. 'We'll do it properly. We'll have a judge and a starter. . . .'

'You must be joking,' Harry cried. 'You must be!'

'Of course if you refuse the challenge,' Tatty said, 'everybody will think you are afraid of losing.'

'I'm not afraid of anything,' Harry said boastfully. 'And I'm certainly not afraid of losing a race. Oh very well then – we'll arrange it for this afternoon. Who do you want for judge?'

Tatty thought for a moment. Then she said, 'I'll ask Willy Weasel. He has sharp eyes and if I should just inch in ahead, he'll notice that I've beaten you.'

This remark caused Harry Hare such acute amusement that he rolled over on his back and nearly choked himself with laughing. Then, when he had recovered somewhat, he spluttered, 'You can have Willy Weasel for judge. I'll have Berty Badger for starter.'

'I agree that Berty will make a reliable starter,' said Tatty. 'You can tell your friends to come and cheer you on and I'll tell some of mine. Whoever loses must pay for the party.'

'What party?' asked Harry.

'The party for the winner,' Tatty said. 'We'll have it in the woods after the race.'

Now it simply did not enter Harry's head that he could possibly lose the great race so he agreed at once to Tatty's idea of the party. Then he rushed off to tell his friends about the great race.

'Be sure and line the route,' he said, as soon as he came upon a number of his cronies. 'And then come to the party. I won't be paying for it – that stupid old Tatty has actually challenged me, Harry Hare, to a race!' And he laughed.

His friends joined in his laughter and Harry Hare enjoyed himself hugely as he listened to their unkind remarks about silly old tortoises who thought they were speed merchants.

Meanwhile Tatty had sought out some of her friends so that she could be certain of some support as she ran the race.

'I don't see how you can possibly win,' said one little rabbit, who was fond of the old lady. 'I mean – *we* can't beat that hare, and yet we can all run pretty fast, as you know.'

'Don't worry about me,' said the old tortoise. 'Just make sure you are all at the finishing post to give me a cheer when I come in.'

When they heard about the party, both Willy Weasel and Berty Badger declared themselves willing to act as judge and starter, and Berty Badger said he would line up the two contestants at two o'clock sharp in the afternoon.

'That's a bit early, isn't it?' Harry Hare protested. 'I always enjoy a nap after my dinner.'

'I agree to the time,' Tatty said quickly. 'We must fall in with the starter's wishes.'

Long before two o'clock Tatty Tortoise made her way to the starting point, and was waiting quietly when Harry Hare dashed up with scarcely a minute to spare.

'What idiots we are!' he cried. 'We don't know where we are racing to!'

'Oh yes, we do!' Tatty said. 'I've seen Willy Weasel and told him we'll race to the windmill.'

'That's all right by me,' Harry declared. 'I suppose he's gone there to wait? My, you're more likely to arrive tomorrow afternoon than today!'

'We'll see about that,' Tatty answered, not in the least put out by Harry's remark. 'We'll see. . . .'

As the spectators began to arrive, Berty Badger lined up the two challengers.

'Are you ready?' he shouted. 'Get set!' And he gave a short blast on his whistle.

The crowd cheered as Harry Hare went off at lightning speed, and Tatty began plodding slowly forward.

'I don't know why Tatty Tortoise agreed to race to the windmill,' said the same little rabbit who had first warned the old tortoise about trying to beat the hare. 'It's such a long way off and some of the road is uphill. . . .'

'Don't worry,' said one of the smart young hares, who had come to cheer Harry on. 'We'll have our party all the sooner. Harry won't take long to reach the windmill, I assure you.'

Meanwhile Harry was loping along at top speed. Soon he had left both Tatty and the crowd far behind. He was so confident that he would win the great race with hours to spare that he began to think he needn't run so fast.

So he slowed down. Then he began to think how pleasant it would be to sit down and enjoy the sunshine.

'After all,' he told himself, 'I haven't yet had my afternoon nap.'

So he sat down and presently he closed his eyes. Soon Harry Hare was fast asleep. He was roused by the twittering of the birds in the tree above his head and he opened his eyes and sat up with a start. How long had he slept? Was the whole afternoon gone? Had the stupid old slowcoach passed him?

To his immense relief Harry saw that Tatty had indeed passed him. But she was only a short distance ahead, and he sprang to his feet and chased after her. He gained on the slow-moving tortoise in no time at all and, as he flashed past, he shouted triumphantly, 'See you at the windmill – this time tomorrow!'

Tatty made no reply. There was still a very long way to go and she knew she would need all her strength, so why waste it on idle remarks! She watched the hare race up the road and turn a corner into some shady woods, but not for a moment did she think of giving up.

Much refreshed by his sleep, Harry Hare ran on through the woods. There was still a field to cross and then a stretch of road with grassy banks on either side to climb before the windmill came in sight. He was making such good progress that it seemed to him he could afford to linger – not in the woods but in the field which had tasty green stuff growing in it.

When he reached the field Harry felt so hungry that he began to nibble as he went along. Then he ran off to the right to the place where his old form had been and finding the nest made him think how pleasant it would be to lie there for a minute or two now that his hunger was satisfied. So once again he settled down, telling himself that even if Tatty passed him it wouldn't do her any good – for he would be able to catch up on her in a matter of seconds.

Well, the afternoon sun was warm and soothing and Harry Hare had eaten rather too much for comfort. Soon, to ease the nagging little pain in his tummy, he had stretched out and closed his eyes.

A long, long time after this Tatty Tortoise plodded into the field. She did not go anywhere near the hare's resting place, but took the shortest way through the field. She moved steadily forward and presently came to the road which led up to the windmill.

Tatty did not look backwards or to the left or right. She kept plodding on and on and on. And the finishing post was there beckoning her. So too were all her friends.

'What have you done with Harry?' called the little rabbits, as Tatty drew nearer and nearer to the windmill.

And some of Harry's cronies, dismay written all over their faces, cried, 'Something must have happened to him! He's had an accident!'

Then a great shout went up as, suddenly, Harry himself appeared. He was running like the wind – up the road, towards the windmill. But, alas for him, his efforts were all in vain. When he was only half way up, Tatty Tortoise plodded past the winning post.

'Well, you've won the great race,' said Willy Weasel. 'You kept going all the way and so you won!'

Harry Hare arrived just in time to hear this. He felt like running away – so furious was he with himself. Instead – he smiled and said grandly, 'Oh well – it's about time I had a party anyway. Come on, folks! The party is on me! I'll pay for it.'

And of course he did pay – not only for the party but for his foolishness in thinking he could win a race without even trying!

Mr Periwinkle

There was once a little old man called Mr Periwinkle. When his wife died and his children had grown up and left home, Mr Periwinkle was very lonely. He was so lonely that he often went to the zoo.

One day Mr Periwinkle read in his newspaper that the zoo had not enough money to feed all the animals.

'Well, that is sad,' said Mr Periwinkle to himself. 'I wonder if I could help?'

And he put on his hat and coat and went off to see the zoo keeper.

'I have a small house and a very large green field,' said Mr Periwinkle, as soon as he was invited into the zoo keeper's office. 'I would like to take one of your animals and keep it in my field.'

'That is very kind of you, sir,' said the zoo keeper. 'But I'm afraid we are not allowed to give away any of our animals.'

'I have been thinking a great deal about the creatures you keep here,' Mr Periwinkle went on, just as if the zoo keeper had not spoken. 'Of course I like most of them – except perhaps some of the birds of prey, the vultures and the eagles. . . .'

'I'm sorry,' the keeper began again. But Mr Periwinkle waved the apology aside as if it was of no importance.

'I have considered taking one of your smaller antelopes – but some of them have antlers which I find quite terrifying. And I could not, of course, take anything that might consider me a tasty bite – like a lion or a tiger!' And he gave a merry little laugh, his blue eyes twinkling.

'Of course not!' said the keeper, laughing in his turn. There was really something very attractive about the old gentleman!

'So . . .' continued Mr Periwinkle, 'I am here to offer a home to one of your kangaroos. I have read in my animal book that kangaroos eat grass. Can that be right?'

'Kangaroos certainly do eat grass,' said the keeper.

'Then the animal will be perfectly happy in my field,' said Mr Periwinkle. 'It is a very fine field and has plenty of good green grass in it.'

'I'm sure the kangaroo would be happy,' said the zoo keeper, who was the kindest and most patient of men. 'But the fact is that our kangaroos are very popular and one of the zoo's great attractions.'

'Oh, I know that!' exclaimed the old gentleman, with another laugh. I enjoy watching the young ones at their boxing games. They are capital fellows. I'm sure I shall make friends with my kangaroo in no time at all.'

'You wouldn't consider keeping a kitten or a puppy, I suppose?' asked the keeper. 'I have never heard of anyone making a pet out of a kangaroo!'

'There is always a first time for everything,' said Mr Periwinkle firmly, and he folded his podgy hands over his podgy stomach as he met the keeper's kindly gaze.

'Now it so happens my wife's cat has just had four very pretty kittens,' the keeper remarked. 'I should be happy to give you one of them for a present when they are old enough to leave their mother – say in eight weeks time. . . .'

'I don't really care for cats,' said Mr Periwinkle, with a sniff. 'They leave so many of their hairs around the house – and kittens grow into cats, you know. Besides, my beautiful green field would be of no great interest to a small kitten.'

'What about a dog?' asked the keeper, who had guessed, by now, that Mr Periwinkle, for all his merry smile, was a very lonely little man.

'Dogs,' said Mr Periwinkle, with another sniff, 'need exercise, and I am not given to taking long walks. No, I think one of your kangaroos would suit me best. What do you say?'

'I'm afraid it is quite out of the question,' replied the zoo keeper. 'Our kangaroos are not – er – for sale or to be given away.'

'I heard you were in need of money,' said Mr Periwinkle loudly, 'and here am I offering to take one of your animals and give it a very superior home. . . .'

'It is most kind – and I appreciate the thought very much,' said the keeper tactfully. 'However, the answer must still be no.'

But once again Mr Periwinkle was not listening. He was busy with his own thoughts.

'If I had a kangaroo,' he said, almost to himself, 'I could watch it jumping and hopping all round my field. My sitting-room looks straight on to the field at the back. It would give me a sense of – well having a friend close by. . . .'

'Out of the question,' said the keeper very, very loudly and sternly.

It was more the tone of the keeper's voice than his words that made Mr Periwinkle suddenly realise that his wish would never be granted. He was not going to get his kangaroo! And the disappointment made his blue eyes dim over, and his lower lip tremble.

'It is not as if . . .' he began. And then stopped, for the zoo keeper's face which, a moment before, had been serious and stern, was now lit up and smiling.

'Don't get upset!' he cried. 'I have just had a first-class idea. Be kind enough to come with me.'

Mr Periwinkle followed the zoo keeper out of his office and down a long walk bordered by bird cages. When they reached more open ground his heart took an unexpected leap of joy. For now they were approaching the enclosure which held the kangaroos. He quickened his step and the keeper, with great understanding, kept silent.

For a few minutes Mr Periwinkle gazed happily at the kangaroos, and

then laughed outright when two of the young ones began to box each other playfully.

'Oh, well done!' he shouted. 'That's capital! Lead with your left!'

The keeper joined in Mr Periwinkle's laughter before taking his arm and leading him away from the enclosure.

'They are very content here,' he said gently, 'and they enjoy each other's company. Shall we go on farther now? I want you to meet a friend of mine. She's a lonely little lady and looks forward to my visits – all too few, I'm afraid,' he added, with a sigh, and a sly, sideways look at Mr Periwinkle.

They walked on until they came to a paddock and there, by the fence, was a small brown donkey.

'There she is – Mr Periwinkle say "hello" to Victoria. . . .'

'Victoria! Did you say Victoria?' asked Mr Periwinkle. 'What a strange coincidence! Our eldest daughter is called Victoria – one of my favourite names. . . .'

'And this Victoria is a very friendly, gentle little lady,' said the keeper. 'And do you know – she just happens to be looking for a kind person to take care of her. You did say you had a fair-sized field?'

'Indeed yes,' said Mr Periwinkle. And he put out his hand and rubbed the donkey's head. 'Yes, yes, it's a beautiful field, and there's a small shed – why, it could quite easily be made suitable – I mean warm and snug in the winter. In fact I'm quite handy with a saw . . .' he broke off again, as Victoria pushed an inquisitive head at him over the fence. 'Yes, yes – why not?'

'You will need a supply of hay, of course,' said the keeper, smiling broadly as he watched Mr Periwinkle stroke the donkey. 'And she's very fond of carrots and apples. But I'll tell you all you need to know to look after her properly – if you really want her.'

Mr Periwinkle scarcely seemed to hear the keeper so taken up was he with Victoria. When he turned, at last, to face him, he drew a deep breath, and the words came out with a rush.

'What's that? What did you say? Yes, yes, I'll be most happy to give the little lady a home. She can come to me just as soon as you can make the arrangements.'

The little brown donkey settled down very happily with her new master, and you may be sure Mr Periwinkle had very little time to feel lonely or even to visit the kangaroos. Victoria saw to that!

252

CAR

CARRUTH, JANE

BEST BEDTIME STORIES